# SO TRUE

## SERENA BELL

JMG
JELSBA
MEDIA
GROUP

## 1

Chiara Campbell had been hoping all day for a customer. So, of course, fate delivered her the one person she'd been avoiding.

"Hey, you!" her sister sang out, to the accompaniment of the dull shop bells.

"Hey, hon!"

Chiara tried to echo the cheerful tone of her sister's greeting—but didn't quite make it.

She came out from behind the shop's front desk and hugged Auburn. Her sister gave great, big, warm hugs, and Chiara relished this one—and the opportunity to hide her face for a moment longer.

On any other day, her sister would be the most welcome sight, but right now? Not so much. Chiara had successfully dodged Auburn for a few days. Which she *never* did. She and Auburn had been close as teenagers—Auburn was less than two years younger than Chiara—and since Auburn's return to Tierney Bay seven months ago, they'd grown even closer.

They hung out in their free time and told each other everything.

Or *almost* everything.

Everything except this: Chiara was interviewing for a job, and if she got it, she'd have to move to Seattle, four hours away. And even though she knew all her siblings, including Auburn, would do their best to be happy for her, it would still be hard to tell them she was leaving. It would be, at best, bittersweet.

Especially since Auburn had just come *back* to Tierney Bay after years away.

Chiara was planning to tell all her siblings her news this coming Tuesday night at family dinner—a more-or-less weekly event. It felt fairest to tell them all at the same time, which was part of why she'd been avoiding Auburn. Because Chiara *sucked* at keeping secrets from her sister.

Auburn released her from the hug, and Chiara snuck her a guilty look, expecting her sister to be wearing a "what's-going-on" expression. But Auburn was surveying the shop critically, and not looking at her at all.

"Wow," Auburn said. "This place really *is* a hot mess."

"This place" was Meeples, a comic book and board game shop owned by Chiara's friend Evan. And Auburn's *hot mess* assessment was generous.

The building itself could have been charming. Nestled on a back street behind the main part of Tierney Bay, it was one of the oldest structures in their Oregon Coast town. It was a beach shack—compact, gray-shingled—with an orange front door. Under one window, a flower box had once bloomed but now bristled with dead stalks.

Inside, the dingy, unwashed windows gave the whole interior a gray aspect that was not helped by the footworn wall-to-wall carpeting. Formerly a used bookstore, the shop still smelled of the must and dust of books. The shelves were too closely spaced for a game-and-comic book store, and all wrong for displaying Evan's merchandise. The game boxes were hard to see, and the comics sagged where they were propped. The old maps and photos had given the used bookstore atmosphere but made Evan's store feel haunted.

Which wasn't far off—the former owner had died recently, and the family had rented Evan the shop with the used books still on the shelves.

Auburn's nostrils flared like she smelled something rotten.

"I told you it was bad."

"Yeah. I was hoping you were exaggerating."

"If only. I tried to tell him he shouldn't open until he renovated, but—" Chiara shrugged. Eighteen-year-old Evan was all heart and no plan, and she loved him for it—even though she worried his venture might be doomed. "He donated the comics from his own collection, paid rent, and spent the rest of the money on game inventory. Nothing left for renovation."

Auburn was shaking her head. "And he thought—he thought that would work? Like, just put up a new sign, and —magic?"

Chiara shrugged. "He thought the place was charming. He thought if he loved it, everyone would love it."

Auburn was shaking her head. "At least, I don't know, wash the windows, paint the walls..."

Chiara sighed. "I've told him. I said he should tear out the carpet and repaint. And get rid of at least half the shelves. There should be racks for the comics, demo tables, display shelves for the games...." She trailed off. "But to be honest, even if he did all that? I don't know if it would work. With his current sales numbers, he won't survive till next spring. I feel like it's cruel to encourage him to put more money into it."

"Do you think sales would improve if he, um, dressed it up a little?" Auburn asked.

"It couldn't hurt, right? But he's got some branding issues, too. He's going after the gamer crowd with this stuff—" Chiara gestured at the window, where he'd displayed Magic the Gathering, Dungeons & Dragons, and a bunch of complicated strategy games—"but he needs to bring in the family tourist crowd if he's going to make it in Tierney Bay."

Auburn gave her sister a one-armed hug. "You're enough of a saint for minding the shop for him, Kee. You don't need to be trying to save him from his half-assed business plan."

Chiara laughed. "I'm hardly a saint. And so far I can't say I've done anything that would save him. Besides, you know I love Evan like a little brother."

Auburn raised her eyebrows sky-high. Chiara looked away. Okay, poor choice of words. That was another topic she didn't want to delve into with Auburn right now. Quickly, she said, "And you know you would have done the same thing in my shoes. You *did* do the same thing in my shoes, when Carl was in the hospital. You ran Beachcrest for him."

"Yeah, but running Beachcrest actually was my job. You already have a job."

"Which, luckily, is extremely flexible, so I can help the people I love when they need it."

Auburn grinned, probably because she knew Chiara was right—she'd totally have done the same thing if their situations were reversed.

"And seriously, there are a lot worse ways for me to spend my time. I've been reading the inventory." Chiara gestured to the stack of comics that had accumulated at the checkout counter. "Shh. Don't tell Evan. I'm being super gentle. And it's not like they have spines to break."

Auburn scrunched her lovely face. Of course she wouldn't tell. "So Evan's surgery went okay? Thanks for the text."

Chiara nodded. "I was there when he woke up. He was pretty out of it, but the nurses said he was doing great, especially given that it was emergency surgery. They were in there a long time." She frowned.

Auburn shook her head. "I'll go see him tomorrow."

When Evan had called, nearly in tears, to ask if Chiara would watch the shop for a couple of weeks, she'd said of course. He was having an emergency small bowel resection. Evan had Crohn's disease, an inflammatory condition that affected his intestines. He'd had it as long as Chiara had known him, which was a little more than ten years.

*Ten years.*

It was crazy that so much time had passed.

"How—how have you been feeling about it? Having Evan back in town?"

Chiara knew Auburn was asking whether having Evan around had brought up old feelings about Evan's brother, Jax. And yeah, maybe a little bit—but she'd been trying her hardest not to go there. "It's been great."

Auburn raised her eyebrows.

"Really. It's been *fine*."

"Come on, Kee, who do you think you're talking to?"

She should have known it was hopeless. "Okay," she admitted. "It's been a little weird. I have thought more about Jax in the last few weeks than in the last five years put together. But it's okay, honestly. Evan is Jax's little brother. He isn't Jax. They're nothing alike. And I don't hold what Jax did against Evan. It had nothing to do with him. I'm just glad to have Evan back. We lost him when Jax left. And Evan lost us. It's been great to reconnect."

Auburn acknowledged that with a nod, but her expression was hard. In light of Jax's disappearing act, Chiara couldn't blame her. Two weeks before Chiara's senior prom, Jax, Evan, and their mom had skipped town without warning and without a backward glance. And Jax had never gotten in touch with her, or anyone, as far as she knew, to explain.

Jax's leaving had broken Chiara's heart. She had loved him so much, and when he'd disappeared, she'd been gutted. And then there was the timing of his leaving, not only right before prom, but right after the night in his truck....

If she was being totally honest with herself—which wasn't always her strong suit—Evan's coming back to town *had* made things harder. Because all of a sudden she remembered both. The glow that had surrounded those days senior year, and the feeling of having her breath yanked out of her chest by pain and heartbreak.

Auburn's eyes were warm and concerned.

"I'm *fine*," Chiara said. "It was ten years ago. I'm way over it. Jax wouldn't even be my type if I met him now."

"Oh, yeah," Auburn said, laughing. "Hard to picture Jax in a shirt and tie or driving a Tesla or mansplaining bitcoin."

It was Chiara's turn to roll her eyes, because yeah, that *so* would never happen. And because Auburn had not been a fan of her last boyfriend. "Okay, yeah, David turned out to be an asshole—"

"Understatement...and I wasn't talking about David. Who was the one before him? Ferris?"

"He drove an Audi. And he was in finance."

"Finance, bitcoin. It's a blur." Auburn wrinkled her nose at Chiara, who grinned.

"Okay, I'm in a bit of a rut. But the point is, things would never have worked out between me and Jax long term."

She thought of Jax—hair always roughed up, flannel shirts and torn jeans. Honest as they came—blunt, even. If Jax were sculpture, he'd be something someone hand-carved for you.

The guys she dated now, they were a lot smoother around the edges. They shared her interests, in business, finance, and accounting. And they wanted the same things she wanted— career advancement, stability, and, ultimately, enough security to think about a family and kids.

Also, they wanted to be with her, which was more than you could say for Jax.

Auburn started to say something, then stopped.

"What?" Chiara demanded.

"That might be true," Auburn said slowly. "But...I'd still love to see you date guys you actually...like."

Chiara scowled. "I like them fine. You're the one who doesn't."

Auburn's gaze held Chiara's for a long moment—too long. Chiara had to look away.

She needed to change the subject. For many reasons. "Hey. I still need something to wear to the reunion."

"I told you, I'm taking you shopping. We're going to spend an afternoon at Bay Boutique, and we're going to find you something that makes you feel so good about yourself that you won't even worry about mean girls."

Chiara laughed. "No one was mean to me in high school." She'd had a pretty good run. Those years had probably been the happiest of her life—well, right up until they hadn't.

"Is he going to be there?" Auburn gave her a wry little twist of a smile.

Damn Auburn and her mind-reading. She'd hate it—if she didn't love it so much. She shook her head. "He didn't respond to the invitation, and no one's heard from him. And I mean, let's face it—what would make him show up now? After all this time?"

Auburn opened her mouth. And then closed it again.

Chiara knew her sister too well. "No. Seriously, Auburn, no. He's never coming back, and we'll never know why he left."

"Have you asked Evan?"

She hadn't. She'd thought about it—but he'd been eight years old when Jax's family had skipped town. And besides, asking the question out loud would mean she still cared—and she didn't want to. She shook her head. "He's *not* coming to reunion. And thank God for that. That's the last thing I need."

"Amen to that," Auburn said quietly. She picked up a puzzle, a cluster of intertwined curved loops, and messed with it for a moment. Then suddenly, eyes wide, she looked up from it. "Oh! Shoot! So. The whole reason I was stopping by—aside from seeing the shop—was to ask if you could do dinner tonight instead of Tuesday. I guess Levi has some *thing* he has to do Tuesday."

"Tonight?" Her heart skipped.

Then she steadied herself. It would be good to just tell her brothers and sisters about Seattle and get it over with. Then they would have some time to get used to the idea. And she would, too. Because as much as she wanted the job, she did *not* want to leave her siblings. She took a deep breath. "Sure," she said. "Tonight works."

"Can you bring dessert?"

"Takeout okay?"

"Hell, yes. Molten chocolate cake from Tierney Bay Diner?"

"Of course." It was the sisters' favorite; it had gotten them through Auburn's rocky 4th of July and the turmoil of almost losing Beachcrest. Those events had turned out well in the end—happily-ever-after well—but they had definitely required lots of molten chocolate cake.

Chiara would eat a lot less cake with Auburn if she moved to Seattle.

Her heart ached at the thought.

"You okay?" Auburn asked. Her gaze searched Chiara's face.

For a second Chiara thought she was going to have to fess up prematurely.

Then Auburn sighed. "I'm sorry. I shouldn't have brought up Jax."

Jax. She was still talking about Jax. Whew. Chiara's secret was safe until...tonight.

Sigh.

"It's okay. I'm fine. Really." Chiara took a breath, gave her sister a brave face. "At least he's not coming to reunion, right?"

Auburn winced. "You might not want to tempt fate like that."

## 2

Jax Walker took the Tierney Bay exit off U.S. 101 a little too sharply, testament to how damn long it had been since he'd been here. The ramp curled around and deposited him at the head of town. He passed several hotels and a few restaurants that had definitely not been here ten years ago. There were plenty of new shop fronts, and many of the old ones had been spruced up. It looked like Tierney Bay had come into some good luck recently.

Which was more than he could say for himself.

If he did this right, he could be in and out of town in a few hours and there was zero chance he would run into anyone he didn't want to see. Which included any member of the Campbell family.

He shouldn't be here at all—his plans had not called for ever coming back, or not, at least, as long as he knew Chiara Campbell was still here. But his plans had been upended.

Two days ago, he'd driven up the west coast to visit his little brother Evan at his Portland-based community college.

Only, *surprise!* Evan was *not actually enrolled.*

At first Jax thought he'd made a dumbass mistake, and texted Evan to confirm. *Not sure why I don't know this for sure, but it's Portland Community College Yamhill*, right?

*Yup!* Evan replied.

Jax had turned back to the young woman perched behind the reception desk and asked her to check one more time that there was no Evan Walker enrolled. And there wasn't.

That was when Jax finally got it. He'd been *had*. Lied to.

The woman gave him a long look, equal parts pity and curiosity, with some *I'll soothe your sorrows* thrown in for good measure.

Well, fuck. His brother had taken the tuition money Jax had given him and done a runner.

Regretfully, he ignored the woman's interest. She definitely wasn't more than a year out of college herself, and smoking hot, but he had an asshole brother to chase down.

He could have had it out with his brother by text or phone, but now he was pissed. His brother had taken thousands of dollars of his hard-earned money and done what-the-fuck with it, and Jax wanted to ream him out in person. So he holed up in his truck and made a bunch of phone calls, sent a bunch of texts. He finally tracked down a friend of Evan's who was willing to spill the beans. And it turned out that Evan was in, of all places, Tierney Fucking Bay.

Of course. Because it wasn't enough that Evan had stolen Jax's money and ditched his own education—no, he'd gone back to the one place that you couldn't have paid Jax to set foot in.

Maybe it was punishment. Because the last time Jax had been in Tierney Bay, he'd done the thing he regretted most in his life. And maybe he'd always known he'd have to face up to it at some point. You could only keep the piper at bay for so long before you had to pay.

He put the truck in drive and drove from Portland out to Tierney Bay in under an hour and half, keeping an eye out for speed traps. And here he was, pulling into town, still raging hot under the collar at his brother. Because Jax had done everything he could to make sure Evan got a good life and didn't end up like their parents.

And what had Evan done? He'd taken his tuition money and opened a board game shop.

Jax turned onto the street that Evan's friend had directed him to and pulled into a parking space in front of the park. Like the town, the park had gotten quite a facelift, but its bones were the same, as were the distinctive smells of cool, green grass and dirty metal. He remembered walking across the woodchips, Chiara's warm hand in his, her voice drifting to him as she told him about her day—

He shut down the memories; replaced them with his anger at Evan.

He turned and walked toward the shop. There was a sign, hung at a slight angle, just a cheap printed fabric banner. *Oh, Evan*, he thought. *You pissed away your college education, and you couldn't even make it look classy.*

He pulled open the front door of the shop, mouth already open to tell Evan what a dumbass he was. But it wasn't Evan behind the desk. It was someone smaller, slimmer, dark-haired.

Beautiful.

She looked up, and God, it was like having someone slide a knife between two of his ribs. That deep and that sharp.

How pretty she was, those blue eyes, and the way they made him feel like she could see into him. After what he'd done, it wasn't fair that she still made him feel anything.

She, on the other hand, looked pretty much like he'd just punched her. Which he deserved. He'd never had to look her in the face, tell her he was leaving, see the hurt. So this was as close as he'd get. And it sucked.

He opened his mouth to say something that made sense, but the only thing that came out was, "Evan."

She shook her head. "He's not here."

"Where—?"

She hesitated. "If he wanted you to know that, don't you think he would've told you?"

"Look. I didn't come here to fight with you. I didn't even know you'd be here."

"If you had, you wouldn't have come," she challenged.

It was true, and he deserved it. He deserved whatever she wanted to dish out. It felt good in a way, like finally letting out a breath. He almost hoped she would yell at him. Maybe then he could set down the guilt.

"Did you know he was supposed to be at college?" he asked.

He could tell from the way her big blue eyes got bigger that she hadn't known.

"Yeah," he said. "Portland Community Yamhill. Summer session. I showed up today for a surprise visit. Thought I'd, you know, take him out to dinner, see his place. He'd sent me *photos* of his place. In fucking Portland. And photos of the campus." He pulled out his phone, pushed it across the counter to her.

She took it, looked. "That's his apartment here. I don't

know where he got the campus photos, but anyone could pull them from online."

"So I tracked him here. His friend Asher told me where to find him."

Chiara nodded at that. She apparently knew Asher.

"Where is he?"

She shook her head. "I can't—"

"Where is he?"

"It's not my place to tell you that."

"He's my brother."

Against his better judgment, his voice had risen, and her eyes narrowed. "You can't just show up here and talk to me like that—after what you did—" She stopped. "Did it occur to you that maybe he doesn't want to see you?"

The anger in her voice cut through the thickness of his own frustration, shut him right down. He took a deep breath. There were freckles across the bridge of her nose that he didn't remember. A smattering on her cheeks, the fair skin underneath bright pink with the heat of her emotion. Her eyes flashed with it.

And suddenly he was so ashamed of himself that he could barely stand it. She was right, of course. After what he'd done to her, he had no right to speak to her at all, let alone demand anything of her.

"He doesn't want to see me?" he asked. "Or you don't?"

She stood very still. Only her fingers moved, fidgeting with something on the counter. A game piece, he thought. She turned it over in her hand, moved it between her fingers, set it down again.

"Both," she said. The heat had gone out of her voice. Which made him feel worse. She said it calmly, like she'd had ten years to get used to the idea. Like she didn't much care anymore. Which he deserved, but still.

He almost told her right that second, just blurted it all out. He'd always been a little bit afraid that the first time he laid eyes on her it would all come spilling out. The whole story—why he'd left, why he'd never gotten in touch. Right after he'd left, he'd fantasized that he'd be able to tell her someday. He'd pictured her listening—angry at first, but then, somehow, willing to forgive.

That had been ten years ago, and he still couldn't tell her.

She was texting.

"What are you doing?"

"I'm asking Evan if I can tell you."

His heart started to pound. He wasn't sure why. Something about the serious expression on Chiara's face. "Tell me what?"

"Tell you, uh, where he is."

"Why wouldn't you be able to tell me?"

She looked at her phone, then up at him. Her eyes were softer now.

"He says I can tell you. He's okay—but—he had to have emergency surgery. He's recovering in the hospital."

"Oh, Jesus," he said. It was possible his heart had actually stopped and restarted, and now it was beating some kind of jerky tap dance that couldn't be normal. "That—*fucker*." He exhaled a ragged sigh. "He better fucking be okay—because if he's not, I'm going to kill him myself." He unclenched his fists.

"That's probably why he didn't tell you, huh?" She crossed her arms.

"Apparently he's not telling me much of anything these days," Jax said darkly. "So. Is he at North Coast Hospital?"

She hesitated.

"What?" he demanded.

She texted something else.

"Are you seriously asking him if you can tell me where he is?"

Her expression tightened again. "I'm just warning him. That you're fired up. And that you know about the store."

For the first time he really looked around. From where he stood, he couldn't see most of the shelves, but the ones he could see were pathetic and barren—comics spaced out too widely, games squatting too far apart. The window was filthy; the corners were dusty; the carpet was worn and rucked up in places.

"Oh, shit," he said. "This is where my money went."

"Your—?"

"My tuition money."

Her mouth fell open.

"Yeah," Jax said. "I know he's your friend, but he's my *brother*. And he used the money I gave him for college to fund this—" Words failed him.

"Shithole," Chiara said quietly.

"Yeah," Jax said again.

They looked at each other, and a flicker of understanding jumped the gap between them. Her face softened, got pained. He'd always loved that about her, that her face was like a mirror. Back in high school, when he felt sad, she looked sad. When he felt angry, she looked angry. You couldn't feel alone when there was someone willing to feel it with you.

Not that this was anything like that. You couldn't be lucky enough to have that, fuck it up, and expect it to happen again.

She crossed her arms and stared at him. "You can't yell at him."

She was still fierce. It made him want to laugh. "I raised him," he said simply. "'Course I fucking can. But, if it'll make you feel better, I'll wait till he's healed up before I *really* rip him a new one."

"Just go easy on him. He's had a tough time." She reached for a stack of comic books. "He's at North Coast, yeah."

She came out from behind the counter and headed away from him, toward the shelves. She turned her back on him and started shelving the comics. They didn't want to cooperate. Some of them slid down, or folded in on themselves. She patiently straightened them.

There were so many things he wanted to say. *I'm sorry. I had to. I wanted to explain, but—*

Instead, he said, "Thanks for watching the store for him."

He saw and heard her draw a quick breath, but she didn't turn around.

He watched her back for a moment. The tilt of her head, her long, slender neck, the skin creamy. He still remembered the feel of that skin under his lips.

He made himself walk away.

Those goddamned bells tinkled on his way out.

## 3

She was still shaky when she walked into Beachcrest. She paused outside the dining room of the inn her sister owned and ran, took a deep breath, smoothed her hair down—it frizzed easily and tended to reflect her mood. Then she stepped inside. "Hey, guys!"

Five heads swiveled, four pairs of cobalt eyes and one pair of slate eyes fixed on her face. They were all there—her two brothers, Levi and Mason; her two sisters, Auburn and Hannah; and Trey, Auburn's new but very serious boyfriend. And she could tell from their faces that whatever expression she was wearing on her face, it wasn't fooling any of them.

"What's wrong?" Auburn asked her.

There was no point in evading. They'd all find out quickly enough. It was a small town, and Auburn and Levi were both connected deep into the heart of it. And then there was the fact that Chiara was apparently an open book.

"Jax is here."

"Nooo," whispered Auburn, all instant sympathy. "To visit Evan in the hospital?"

Chiara nodded, wincing. She gave them a quick recap of what she'd learned about Evan's deception and Jax's detective work.

Levi, their oldest sibling, whistled. "I don't blame the guy for being pissed. I'd be pissed too if I gave one of you tuition money and you spent it on comic books."

Auburn glared at him. He shrugged. "I would."

Hannah, the youngest, at sixteen, wrinkled up her face. "Who's Jax?"

"You remember Jax," Auburn said. "He used to sometimes come to dinner with Evan—"

"Ohhhh," said Hannah. "Was Jax the one who helped Evan and me that one time when we made the really huge sandcastle?"

*A perfect sunny day, already hot for early May. Six-year-old Hannah, eight-year-old Evan, Jax and Chiara had gone down to the beach with sand molds. They'd built an elaborate castle, with turrets and bridges and deep moats, and Jax and Chiara had been laughing and jostling each other, trying to shore up a wall that was sliding into the moat as fast as they could rebuild it. They'd given up and sat back in the wet sand, and he'd turned to her and grinned, all tanned face, green eyes, and straight white teeth, and said, "One day it'll be us and our kids doing this."*

She'd boxed up all those memories and folded them away in the attic of her mind. She had planned never to take them out again.

"Yeah," she said. "That's Jax."

Trey was slowly absorbing the Campbell family reactions. "Long story?" he asked.

Auburn and Chiara exchanged glances. Auburn's said, *Want me to?* And Chiara's said, *No, I got it.* "He worked for my dad at Cape House when I was a senior. He and I got—involved. And then he moved out of town, and I never saw him again."

"He disappeared off the face of the fucking earth without another word. It was a total dick move. To Chiara and our dad." Levi's voice was hard.

When Jax had first left, she'd barely eaten for weeks. She'd lost eleven pounds. And cried until her eyes burned and her chest hurt. As bad as it had felt on the inside, she knew it hadn't been easy for her family to watch her suffer, either.

Trey raised an eyebrow. "Your dad?"

Chiara's throat tightened. "Dad kind of took him under his wing. Jax was—" She took a breath. "He was a good worker. Dad really liked him. And he found out that Jax was struggling with school and his family—"

"Dad was a sucker for anyone who needed help," Auburn said. "Our family pets were all strays. There was always someone at Thanksgiving dinner who didn't have anywhere else to go."

Chiara picked up the thread. "Jax was basically supporting his mom and his brother, trying to get through school, barely holding on, in danger of not graduating, and Dad found out, and he started doing all this stuff for Jax. Giving him extra projects with big bonuses, arranging tutoring for him that was magically at these super-low rates, because Dad was supplementing. He called it all workplace benefits."

"Your dad sounds like a good guy," Trey said. They hadn't talked about the Campbell's parents that often since Trey had started coming to family dinners. They had died in a boating accident during Chiara's freshman year of college—Auburn's junior year of high school. Levi had left behind his med school dreams to be there for Auburn and Mason and to raise Hannah.

"He was," Chiara said. "The very best." She knew, after ten years, that she would never stop missing both her parents like a piece of her soul was gone.

Trey's eyebrows drew together. "So he must have been pretty upset when Jax left, too."

"Oh, he was," Chiara said. "He was really hurt by it."

"And you and Jax—" Trey winced, seeing her expression, although she hadn't even realized she'd reacted. "Sorry, sore subject?"

She didn't want it to be, not after all this time. "Not anymore. Jax was always around—around Cape House"— Cape House was the hotel her parents had run and Levi had inherited—"and around our house. He and I got pretty serious." It was her turn to wince, at her own understatement. Because *serious* didn't even begin to describe how close they'd been, how happy they'd made each other—or at least, how happy he'd made her. "He skipped town with his family without telling me—or anyone—they were leaving. And ghosted me."

That was all she was going to say about that.

"That's—"

She'd managed to strike Trey speechless. "Yeah," she said. "It sucked."

"And it sucks he's back," Levi said. "Let me know if you want me to kick the shit out of him."

"Thanks," Chiara said wryly. "He can't be planning to be here very long, right? I mean, he visits Evan, yells at him, goes home? I'm sure he has no more desire to stick around now than he did then."

They were all silent for a moment, thinking about that.

"Well," Auburn said. "We have your back for as long as he's here."

"Hell, yeah," Levi said.

Hannah, Mason, and Trey were all nodding.

Chiara got hit with a big dose of the warm fuzzies—her siblings were such terrific human beings—and that, in turn, abruptly, reminded her that she was about to tell them something they weren't going to like. Her stomach lurched. But she couldn't put it off. It wouldn't be fair. She took a deep breath and confessed, "I might be moving to Seattle."

Five mouths dropped open.

"You *what*?" Hannah demanded.

"I interviewed for a job in Seattle."

"Why. Would. You. Do. That?"

"*Shh,* Han," Auburn said. "Let her tell us."

"But—"

"Let her tell us."

"I love my job. You know I do."

She owned her own business, doing books and accounting for small businesses in town—and a few clients she'd won online.

"But lately, I've been bored. That's the only way I can say it. It doesn't feel like a challenge. I've been feeling like I need something—bigger."

Auburn was nodding. Levi was, too.

"You know how Dad always felt like he gave up too much. He had all those big dreams, but he had to give them up to take over Cape House from his dad."

Auburn and Levi absolutely knew; for the three oldest kids, it had been one of the soundtracks to their childhood, their father talking about how he never wanted them to give up their dreams, not even for family obligation. How they should think big and dream big and act big. Mason had been old enough to remember his parents clearly, but by the time he'd come along, their dad's refrain had mostly been aimed at the two eldest, not him. And Hannah, who'd been six when her parents died, barely remembered them at all.

"And I guess I'm feeling like with Hannah old enough to really be independent, and Auburn back in town to help with anything she needs—"

"I can take care of myself," Hannah said.

"Well, exactly," Chiara said. "So I saw this job that was absolutely one hundred percent perfect for me, director of finance and planning at Buyathon—"

"Buyathon!" Hannah said reverently. The corporation was one of the U.S.'s ten biggest tech companies, a household name. When Chiara had heard about the job opening from an old business school friend, she'd jumped on it like a late bus.

Levi whistled. "And that's no slouch of a title, either."

"Yeah," Chiara said. "Reports to the CFO. I didn't say anything at first because I didn't know what was going to happen, but the first round of interviews went really well, and they told me they'll be calling me back for a second round."

There was a deafening silence. Then they all started talking at once. "That's amazing!" "That's terrific, Kee!" "Such good news!" "We're really happy for you!" "It's definitely your time." "It's your turn to get out and do something for yourself!"

She let herself relax a little bit. Of course they were supportive. She should have known it. They were the best family a girl could ask for.

"Dad would be thrilled," Levi said. "I can practically hear him crowing about your head for numbers. And your Stanford and Wharton credentials not 'going to waste.'" He made air quotes.

She'd been thinking about her dad a lot, ever since the interview process started. Speaking of bittersweet. On one hand, interviewing for this job had made her father feel more alive to her than he'd been in the decade since they'd lost him. As she'd sold herself to the HR rep and the hiring manager, she'd heard her father telling her, *Be bold,* and, *That's my girl.* She'd felt him watching over her shoulder, approving and instructing.

But she'd also missed him more than she'd missed him in years. Levi was right—he would have been proud. And she wished so, so much that he'd lived to see her going after this job.

*Getting* this job.

She would get it. For him.

One doubt clouded her excitement. She wasn't the only Campbell who had put her dreams on hold. Levi had dropped out of med school for the good of their whole family —because he'd had exactly zero choice. And before she could pursue this job, she needed to make sure she wasn't standing between Levi and the future he'd deferred for them.

"I guess what I wonder is, isn't it really Levi's turn?" she asked. "If I go, does it make it harder for Levi—?"

Right after her parents' deaths, she'd tried to convince Levi to let her drop out of Stanford to help him with

Hannah's upbringing. And he'd told her in no uncertain terms that she was forbidden to sacrifice her education. But it was different now. This wasn't about dropping out of college. And Levi had waited a long time. If he wanted his turn, Chiara would give it to him in a heartbeat.

"He can't leave until I graduate," Hannah said. It was barely more than a whisper. But they all heard her.

"Hannah," Levi said firmly. "I want to be here. You are not holding me up or keeping me here or anything like that. There will be plenty of time for me to figure out what comes next when we get there." He turned to Chiara. "And don't be ridiculous. If you're making a killer salary and lining up to be Buyathon's next CFO, it's going to make things easier for all of us. You know that."

"But I won't be here to help you guys—"

"We'll just make Trey do twice as much work," Levi said. "He's still earning his place."

Trey flipped Levi off, out of Hannah's line of vision. These days, he was helping Auburn renovate Beachcrest, while also commuting back and forth to keep tabs on his San Francisco tech company. In the short time since he'd been accepted into the family, Chiara had already come to believe he would do everything in his power to help not just Auburn—whom he adored—but all her siblings.

"Oh, Kee, I will miss you so much," Auburn said. "I can't believe I'm just back and you might be leaving. But of course this is exactly the right thing! You have to do this, for sure. Go for it!"

Hannah still looked a little shell-shocked.

"It's only four hours away," Chiara said. "I'll be able to come back pretty much any weekend you need me. And if I get the job, I could negotiate for some work-from-home time, too, so I can do longer weekends or even a week here, here and there. And when I'm here I'll really be here, not working or going to Chamber of Commerce meetings or reunion committee—"

"Or the food pantry or the affordable housing board," Auburn added dryly.

"Right," Chiara said. "And anyway, it was just a first interview, so this is all premature. I just wanted you guys to know it might happen."

"*Of course* they'll hire you."

Every head at the table turned, because it had been Mason who'd spoken. Mason hardly ever talked, and when he did, it was short and to the point. Unemotional. But he was unflinchingly loyal to the people he loved. Chiara suspected he'd take one of their secrets to the grave, if it were called for.

"And *of course* you should accept it."

"Oh, Mason," Chiara said, tears springing to her eyes.

They were all nodding and smiling, except Mason. Even Hannah was coming around now, looking less worried and more excited.

This was the best response Chiara could possibly have hoped for.

So if that was true, that they'd told her exactly what she'd wanted to hear, why didn't she feel relieved? And what was that heavy sensation in the middle of her chest?

Jax poked his head into Evan's hospital room the next
morning. He'd missed visiting hours the day before,
but he'd made sure to be here right on time today.
He wished he'd been smart enough to think of
buying a couple of comic books from Chiara while he was at
the shop—Meeples, what kind of name was that?—but then
he hadn't wanted to go back in. So he'd gone to Tierney Bay
Book Shop instead and asked if they had some graphic novels
or something else an eighteen-year-old boy would like. He
had two graphic novels in a brown bag in one hand and an
iTunes gift card in the other.

A lean, shaggy-haired kid with an indoor-white
complexion got up from a chair beside Evan's bed. Jax recognized Asher, the kid who'd outed Evan's game store plan. He
hoped he hadn't made any trouble for him.

"Hey," he said.

"Hey, Jax," Asher said. "I was just heading out." He cut
Evan a sympathetic look and made for the door before
anyone could object.

His brother looked like shit. Not just because he was lying in a hospital bed and no one looked good under white sheets with fluorescent lighting. But also because he had started to grow a beard, and he was, like, nine-tenths of the way to having enough scraggly reddish facial hair to pull it off. But not there yet.

"Hey."

Evan's greeting held all the sheepishness and guilt Jax thought he'd wanted to hear, but truth was, he was just so fucking glad his brother was okay. "So what the hell happened, my dude?"

"Lost a little bit of intestine, that's all," Evan said.

"You know that's not all, right?" Jax said. "You know you need to take care of yourself and call the fucking doctor if something hurts or there's blood or anything, right?"

"Chiara said you promised not to yell at me yet."

"Oh, my dude, this is not fucking yelling," Jax said. It took all his self-control to manage a civilized tone. "Wait until you're up and about, and then you will find out what yelling is all about."

"I'm looking forward to it," Evan said dryly.

"Call the fucking doctor next time. Please. For the love of God."

Evan was quiet. Then he said, "I promise."

"Thank you." Jax settled himself into an uncomfortable vinyl chair with wooden arms. "Here. I brought you stuff." He took the books out of the bag and handed them to Evan. The gift card, too.

Evan thumbed through the books. "Oh, wow. These look good. Thank you."

"You don't have them?"

"I read the first one in this series, but not this one. Never heard of this one. And the gift card'll be good. I'm sick of all my music already." He gestured at the nightstand. "Mom sent flowers. This is way better."

"That's what Moms do, though. And she's not the chicken soup type or anything."

"She wanted to fly up, but I told her not to. She got into some really big curated craft show and she was all excited about some adjustable-waist skirt she was going to sell a million of. And I figure, if she's making money, that makes your life easier, right?"

There was a puppy dog look on Evan's face that made Jax's chest hurt. It was those brown eyes—legacy of Evan's dad. Evan's dad had stuck around their mom just about as long as Jax's own had—a couple of years—before disappearing without a trace. "Don't you worry about that," Jax said.

The puppy dog look got worse, not better. "I thought it would help," his brother said.

"You thought—what would help?"

"The game store. If I could make some money. Instead of just spending it. Like an investment."

Oh. And ohhh. "That's why it was a big secret."

"I was going to surprise you with it."

It clobbered him, how much people could screw things up while trying to get them right. Human beings were such a beautiful mess. And how the hell did you tell a puppy dog that chewing up your shoe wasn't the best way to show love?

"The whole point of college," Jax said carefully, "is that it was supposed to be an investment in *you*."

"But it wasn't what I wanted to do," Evan said. "I told you that, and you wouldn't listen."

"Because 'I want to open a game-and-comic book shop' isn't a real life plan! Those things never succeed! They're like restaurants."

"Some do," Evan said.

"Yeah, man, I know, some do, but—" He heaved a sigh. He wasn't going to yell at his baby brother while the guy had a gut full of stitches. "Let me ask you this. How's it going with the store? And—" He crossed his arms. "I'm looking for the truth here, bud."

Evan closed his eyes and screwed up his face.

"Not so good, then," Jax said, for him.

"Not so good," Evan confirmed. "I'm behind on the rent and I haven't actually—made any money."

Jax made himself breathe. Deep, full breaths.

Even after Jax had convinced Evan to go to college—or *thought* he had—they kept fighting. Jax had wanted Evan to go to school near home. Evan wanted to go to school outside of California. But out-of-state tuition was twice the cost of in-state.

*I just want to* live *a little*, Evan had said.

Jax had closed his eyes, because he'd known exactly what Evan was talking about. Evan had missed almost all of seventh grade when he'd first been diagnosed with Crohn's. He had been too sick for the eighth grade banquet, so Jax had stayed up with him and they'd watched B-grade action movies. Evan hadn't made it to his high school prom because he'd landed in the hospital, which had necessitated another round of action movies. And the coveted school-sponsored Peru trip he'd wanted to go on the summer after junior year of high school had been a no-go because it wasn't possible to control Evan's diet to the extent necessary. That time, Jax had taken Evan camping as a consolation prize.

He would always be there for his brother when he was sick, but what he really wanted was to make him *less* sick.

For years Jax had been trying to save for one of the experimental treatments that were helping patients with harder-to-treat Crohn's. There was an immuno-therapy that had shown signs of changing lives, but Evan's insurance sucked, and the cost was prohibitive.

Sending Evan to an out-of-state school would eat up more money and put off treatment longer. But Evan *would* go to college. And then he'd be able to get a better job, and between Evan and Jax they could save up for the treatment faster.

Instead, there was no college and no money.

Jax was about to ask Evan if he'd consider just giving up —returning what inventory he could, enrolling in the fall semester—when Evan said, "I want this, Jax. And I guess I just got sick of people telling me what I can't do."

Jax took one more deep breath. And for some reason, that one worked.

It was *Evan's* life he was trying to make better. And all Evan was asking was for a little bit of control over his own destiny.

It was something Jax could do.

"Maybe you shoulda called me when you realized you were in over your head?" Jax said quietly.

"I know I screwed up," Evan said. "And I'll make it right."

He was in no condition to make it right, though. That

store needed help ASAP, not when Evan could be on his feet again.

His brother sank back against the pillow; he looked exhausted. A little defeated, maybe.

And suddenly Jax knew: He was going to fucking make it work for Evan. It might not have been his plan, but it was Evan's plan.

"You have to let me help you, then."

He'd shocked his brother. "You—"

"I'm between projects. Just finished up a house, next one doesn't need me for a few more days." He didn't say that he'd been thinking about a trip somewhere—somewhere where he wouldn't have to think for a while. Not about his mother, who refused to apply for steady work because she knew Jax would bail her out if she ran into trouble. And not about his brother, who was supposed to be safely away at college. He'd wanted a trip that was just about putting his own feet up. He wanted to pretend he was the kind of guy who could drink a beer without worrying that someone he loved was one bad day away from financial disaster.

Someday he'd take that trip. But right now he was going to make things right for Evan. "We can fix up the place to help defray rent. And that'll make the shop more inviting, too. I can burn a better sign and build some better shelves— and get rid of that carpet, which can't be good for your immune system."

"You—you don't have to do that, Jax."

Jax was well aware that Evan hadn't told him not to. Or even asked him not to. So all he said was, "Yeah. I don't have to. But I want to. And it's *my* investment, so you owe me the right to make it pay off."

Despite the harshness of Jax's words, Evan suddenly relaxed. Gave a sigh that could have been anything, but sounded a lot like relief. And—even better—the defeated look slipped away. He was—maybe not smiling, but there was a lightness in his expression that hadn't been there before.

Jax was a sucker, maybe, but you would never convince him that Evan wasn't worth being a sucker for.

"I'm on it. You just rest up and get better. We're gonna make this happen for you."

"You and Chiara," Evan said.

"What?" Jax said.

"That's what you meant, right? 'We'?"

"I meant you and me."

"Well, you can get her help, too, until I'm stronger. She's full of good ideas. And she's there every day until I'm ready to come back. She promised."

Evan's eyes had drifted closed, and his last few words blurred together.

"I can't work with her," Jax said. What he really meant was that she would never, in a million years, work with him.

No response from Evan, except steady, deep breathing. He'd always been able to fall asleep at the drop of a hat. In a moving car, in the middle of a sentence.

"You're not really asleep, dude," Jax said.

Nothing.

"It's a bad idea."

More nothing.

He got up slowly, arranging the books and gift cards neatly on the nightstand, folding the paper bag and tossing it in the trash.

He was in trouble. He understood that. Because working

with Chiara was just a plain old bad idea. What he'd done to her would constantly be between them—and he'd never be able to explain it. The terrible things that had happened, the events that had sent him reeling and driven him and his family to California—he'd vowed he'd never tell anyone the truth. Including the woman he'd left behind.

Work in the store? With Chiara?

He should hate the idea.

But he didn't hate it. He didn't hate it at all.

It was the first thing he'd really wanted in a long time.

## 5

Chiara was reviewing the rules of how to play Terraforming Mars, one of her favorite games, in case anyone came into the shop and wanted her to demo it. And the process of doing so was showing her something very important about the game shop: It needed a bigger table. There was only one little table with two chairs, and it was *just not big enough for Terraforming Mars*. What had Evan been thinking?

Probably that he had only enough money for the shoddy card table that he'd set up.

She sighed and carefully stacked up the ocean hexes. The rulebook was blurring in front of her eyes. She had slept badly last night, tossing and turning, still processing her siblings' responses to her possible move.

But mostly she'd been unable to stop thinking about Jax. Not the worst parts. Not how she'd felt after he left—afraid, then confused, then hurt, then angry. Even ashamed, because how was it possible to have felt what she'd felt for him—

believed what she'd believed about him—and for it to have come to *this*?

But it wasn't bad memories that had ruined her sleep. What had kept her awake was trying to hold back a tide of *good* memories. Jax, mowing the Cape House lawn, shirt off, smooth and summer-tanned and glistening with sweat. Jax, the first time he'd really, really looked at her with those green eyes, the softness and curiosity that had surprised her. Jax, the way he listened so intently that she felt like what she was saying mattered, the way he pointed at her drawings and asked just the right questions. Jax, the first time he'd leaned in close enough that she could smell soap and shampoo and deodorant and *skin*. *Him*. Jax, eyes startled and dark, leaning in to capture her mouth—

She'd catch herself and try to put it all back in the attic storage, and it would slumber there for a few minutes and then it would come out again, like a jack-in-the-box that wouldn't stay put.

It wouldn't last forever, though. He would be gone soon and she would get her amazing, executive-level Buyathon job and move to Seattle and meet a great guy, someone whose ambitions matched hers, and they would live happily ever after. Screw Jax, because she really, truly, did not give a crap about him anymore.

The bell tinkled, the door opened, and *shit*.

"Hey," he said. And unfortunately, in real life, he beat the hell out of her memories last night. He was broader and better-built than he'd been in high school, his shoulders and biceps straining his black t-shirt. His sandy hair was rumpled, probably because he'd been running his hands through it.

She wished she didn't know that.

She really, really wanted not to be attracted to him anymore. And she was really, really out of luck.

"Hey," she finally managed. *Please say,* I'm just stopping by to say goodbye before I head out of town.

"I just visited Evan."

"How's he doing?"

"He's okay. We talked about the shop."

His hands were bigger than they'd been in high school. Everything about him was bigger, including his presence. He'd seemed so masculine to her then, but he'd been just a boy compared to now. The stubble clinging to his strong jaw. The appealing roughness of his skin. The way he filled the room.

"I told him I'd fix it up while he was in the hospital."

"Wait, what? What do you mean?"

"I mean, I'm going to fix up the store. He's going to be in the hospital a couple more days, right? So I'll stick around and clean up this place. Deal with the paint, the carpet, all that."

Her insides locked up. That meant he wasn't leaving—he was *staying*. For at least as long as "while he was in the hospital" lasted. And that he'd be here. In the shop.

She must have been staring at him dumbly, because he gave a short, not-very-amused laugh and said, "Yeah. I know. I'm sure it wasn't your plan to spend quality time with me. If you want, you could leave. I can watch the store. I know you can't be super happy to see me, and I get it, believe me, I get it—"

"If you got it," she said shortly, "you wouldn't have left in the first place without telling me you were moving, or why, or where you were going, or where I could find you."

Damn it, she hadn't meant to say that. To admit how abandoned she'd felt. She hadn't wanted him to know she had ever given a shit about his leaving, let alone that she still did.

Well, too late for that. Now he knew. Now they both knew she still cared.

She took a deep breath and said, "I'm over it, okay? But that doesn't mean we can be friends."

"I didn't ask."

"I'm just setting boundaries," she said, drawing walls around herself as she said it.

"I see them," he said. He sounded a little bit amused, which pissed her off even more. He didn't get to be amused by any of this.

"And one of those boundaries is that I don't want you in the shop while I'm in the shop."

He squinted. "Technically, it's Evan's shop. And Evan wants me in the shop. Actually, if you want to get super technical, I think that since Evan used my money to rent the shop and buy the inventory, it's *my* shop. And I want me in the shop. So if you don't like that, you could get out of the shop."

Screw him! He hadn't wanted to be honest in the past, and now he was going to bully her in the present? Uh-uh. No way. A strong stubborn streak ran in the Campbell veins, and Chiara could feel it settling in for the long haul. "Evan asked *me* to take care of the shop. I'm not walking away from that. I'm the one who's seen the books, who knows the financials and who knows what they mean. And I'm the one who knows comics and games. I'm not going anywhere."

"Then I guess we're both going to be in the shop," Jax said with a shrug.

"Not at the same time," Chiara said. "You can't be 'fixing stuff up'"—she made air quotes—"while the shop's open."

"Because I might drive customers away?" he asked darkly.

They both looked toward the door.

"There *are* customers," she said.

"How about I promise no messy projects during business hours, and if customers come in and I'm doing something that makes noise, I'll take a break. I just don't have forever to get this done. I've got to get back and start my next project."

She knew from Evan he was a general contractor, a good one with a great reputation. That didn't surprise her. He'd been a hard worker, strong as an ox. Always on time. Super organized. He'd had to be, to work the hours he'd put in at Cape House, make sure his brother stayed on track with schoolwork, clean up after his mother when she was on a bender, and still, somehow, manage to more or less pass his classes.

Sometimes less. He'd had a few teachers cut him extra slack, she knew. And in the end—had he ever actually graduated from high school?

She wasn't going to ask.

She sighed. She'd wished for someone handy to remake the shop; now she had someone. Unfortunately, he was not the someone she would have chosen. But beggars couldn't be choosers. "Okay. No messy projects during business hours— no sawdust, sanding, finishing, nothing that's going to irritate customers. Keep your work self-contained and tidy. And yeah, no noise when there are people in the shop."

"*My* shop," he reminded her.

"Evan's shop," she countered. "And I'm minding it."

"What's that sound?" he asked, glancing around the shop.

It took her a second to register that he'd changed the subject. "What sound?" And then, "Oh, shit."

It was the sound of her phone vibrating in her purse. She plucked it out and said, "Damn, I'm late for my Chamber of Commerce meeting."

He tilted his head, considering her. "You the treasurer?"

"Yeah, so?"

"What else are you the treasurer of?"

The answer was effectively *everything*. Every association she was on the board of, all the companies whose books she was doing. But she knew better than to tell him that. Instead, she rolled her eyes at him. "Come on. I need you out of here so I can lock up."

"I can lock up," he said.

"I have the key."

"We'll need a copy," he pointed out. "Leave me with the key, I'll make a copy."

She hesitated.

"What do you think I'm going to do, leave town with it?"

She raised her eyebrows. "You do have a history."

There was utter silence between them.

"I deserved that," he said with a sigh. "Look. Shop's closed tomorrow, right? I'm planning to be here working tonight and all day tomorrow. So I'll make a copy of the key first thing and you can grab it from me anytime you want."

"You'll be here the whole day?"

"I might make a few trips for materials, but you can text me first, make sure I'm here."

She squinted at that. "That would require you to unblock me."

His gaze skittered away from hers, and she thought she

saw his jaw tighten. "I have a new number. Here. Give me your phone."

She handed it over. He tapped in his name and number and handed it back.

She sent him a text. She started to type *Kee's number,* but that was way too intimate. *Chiara's number,* she typed instead. It felt strange. For almost two years after he'd left, she would have given anything to be able to exchange texts with him. But now? He was just a good-looking stranger. Because the boy she'd thought she knew wouldn't have left the way he left. Which meant that she'd never really known him at all.

"Make sure you buy local," she told him. "No big box stores for materials. There's a great local hardware shop and a great local lumberyard."

"Yes, ma'am," he said, and she rolled her eyes again.

"Don't make a mess. And make sure the shop is neat by Wednesday at ten."

He saluted her, and she turned and left before she could think too much or too hard about what she'd just agreed to.

## 6

"What are you doing?"

He hadn't heard her come in, but there she was, standing in the shop staring at the progress he'd made. He'd texted her a little while ago to say he'd be in the shop for the next few hours if she wanted to come get the key.

She was so fucking pretty. Black hair and fair skin and those blue eyes, which were the exact color of cobalt glass. All five Campbell siblings had those eyes, and Chiara was no exception, except that her eyes were different. Deep set, fringed with long lashes, and as warm as the color was cool.

Well. Not now. Right now, she was glaring at him.

"I'm painting."

Specifically, he was putting a coat of primer on the bookcases, which were a total eyesore.

"Yeah, I can see that. And you tore out the carpet."

"Yeah. I've got the new stuff in my truck. And clean padding that's not riddled with mildew. Sorry. I think I might have created a bit of a toxic waste situation over there—" he pointed to where the old padding was heaped up.

"But—" She seemed to be struggling. "Okay. I don't know how to say this."

"Just say it." He had zero patience with bullshit.

"I mean—I am grateful. I really am. And it's—obviously, paint, carpet, that's all going to help. For sure. But—that's not going to do it. I thought—" She took a deep breath. "Okay, I don't know why I thought we were on the same page. You said 'fix it up,' I thought you meant the same thing I meant. Which is totally unfair. You can't read minds, and I should have clarified."

"What did you mean?"

"Not this. This is like, I don't know, a bandaid on a bullet wound. This place—if it's going survive—it's got to be all different. A bookstore isn't a game store. It's different. Comic books go on racks, not shelves. And games, they need shelves that are deep enough to hold the whole box and tall enough to use for display. There has to be a library for demo games, and people have to be able to play at tables."

"So, like, a complete renovation. Tearing out the shelves, building new ones— You know how much work that is, right?"

"All I know is, we have to do something. Something big. He has to be on track by Labor Day weekend. That's what I worked out," she said.

"What do you mean, that's what you worked out?"

"I mean, I looked at the books, and if the shop's going to survive, he has to be going strong by Labor Day weekend at the absolute latest. You know Tierney Bay."

He did and he didn't. He'd lived here just under two years,

one of the many places he and his mom and, later, Evan, had drifted through. He shrugged.

"It's a tourist town. Retail is all seasonal," she said. "You sell all summer and into the fall. Maybe till Christmas if you're lucky, if you've got stuff people want. And then it's January, and *nothing*. Nothing till March at least, and that's in a good year. If Evan is going to survive his first year, he has to be ramped up no later than Labor Day."

She bit her lip again. He had a sudden, visceral memory of that lower lip. It was soft and plump and when Jax's tongue had first flicked over it, she had whimpered and he had felt it in every nerve ending.

It sucked that he couldn't always remember his computer passwords but he still remembered that. For all the fucking good it would ever do him.

"And you think that means tearing this place down to the walls and floor."

"I *know* that's what it means," she said.

He took a deep breath, tried to pull together his emotions. "You want a complete renovation, but you don't want me to make a mess. You don't want me to dirty up your pretty little shop during business hours. You don't want me making noise or dust. And you don't want me in your space. How the hell am I supposed to do that and get back to Bakersfield to start my next project inside of two weeks?"

That shut her up. She looked around the space, frowning at the carpet padding. He couldn't blame her. He had a strong stomach and that stuff was vile.

"I don't know," she said quietly. Her chin dipped, which made his stomach hurt. He hadn't meant to be a dick about it. It was a real question, though. There wasn't enough time, and there sure as hell wasn't any way to do what she was talking about without interfering with the shop's open hours.

Something buzzed; she dug in her purse and pulled out her phone. "Oh, whoops," she said. "I'm supposed to be at Beans by the Beach in five minutes."

"Late to another meeting?" he asked. She'd been the queen of it in high school. On every committee, a member of what seemed to him—the ultimate non-joiner—like, every club. National Honor Society and Yearbook Committee and Environmental Justice—ticking boxes like crazy to get herself into college. He'd been proud of her, but also jealous of all the things that ate her time, when time was the thing he had the least of. It made him crazy when he had an hour off and she couldn't get free. A chance to sneak away, to be alone together, lost.

She gave him a guilty look that told him the answer had to be yes.

"What is it this time? Tierney Bay Rotary Club?"

"Reunion committee."

That gave him a nasty jolt. He'd forgotten their ten-year was this summer. Was he going to be in town during it? He sure as fuck hoped not. "When is reunion?" he asked, trying to hide his dread.

"September," she said.

No, he'd be long gone by then. Thank God. "What are you doing for reunion committee?"

She looked at him and narrowed her eyes. "Helping with planning."

"And keeping track of the money."

"Yeah, so?"

"Still doing everyone else's math homework, huh?" That's

what he'd called it in high school, when she'd been the treasurer of everything. She'd had it in her head that math was her thing, and she'd gone after it with her whole self, which was the way she did everything.

Everything.

He closed his eyes, trying to get the images out of his head.

"Well." She shrugged. "It's what I'm good at."

"You were good at lots of things."

He'd been thinking of her art, hadn't meant it to come out suggestive—but it did, dripping with innuendo. She cast him a look he couldn't read, then tucked her phone away.

"Look." Her voice softened. "I get it. You don't live here. Bottom line, this shop isn't your problem. If you can't do it, I can help Evan find someone who can."

"And pay them with what? Monopoly money?"

Her face flushed, and he instantly regretted being so flip.

"You know what?" She crossed her arms. "Go ahead. Be snarky about it. But this isn't about me. None of this is about me. It's about Evan." She slung her purse over her shoulder. "Where's my key?"

He handed it to her.

"Make sure that shit is out of here by tomorrow morning at 10," she said, gesturing at the pile of padding.

When she was gone, he rested his head in his hands.

She was right. This was about Evan.

But she was also wrong. Because, yeah, he wanted to help Evan. But he also wanted to make things right between him and Chiara. He could never tell her everything, but he could try to repay a fraction of the emotional debt he owed her, work off some of the guilt he carried.

Doing what she was asking would take longer than a few days. Much longer than he'd planned. And it wouldn't work the way she'd pictured. There was no way they could arrange never to be in the store at the same time. It would be disruptive. He would be in her space.

But if it meant he could make things right for Evan *and* make things up to her?

He'd be willing to try.

## 7

"Okay, so let's just go over the list of people who haven't RSVP'd. I'm pretty sure I've dropped a text message here and there, and maybe this'll jog our memories." Chiara's friend Willa Beecham, tall and slim with warm brown skin and hair in twists, pushed her reunion folder aside and drew a single sheet towards her. "Julian Kincaid." Willa eyed Chiara and their reunion-planning buddy, Vannah Ewing, a pale-as-milk redhead sporting a messy bun. "No? Nothing from Julian? Gabriela Jimenez? I think she's on the East Coast now. Most of our East Coast classmates can't swing it. Lauren Spinak. Oh, shit, Lauren told me she's coming. Not sure how I lost that one. Stupid texts. Donelle Robinson."

"He's in Atlanta. He's a hotshot lawyer, in the middle of a big case. He can't make it," Chiara said.

Willa marked her sheet. "Erik Kim?"

"Erik's in L.A. No response from him yet. Last I heard he had landed a lead in a feature film, so maybe he's filming," Vannah said.

"Jax Walker. Huh," Willa said. "I didn't even realize he'd graduated. Or did he? I figured he dropped out. Or got his GED or graduated somewhere else. But I guess he somehow managed to finish up and wrangle a degree from Tierney Bay High School."

That answered *that* question.

"Do you know if he's planning on coming?" Willa asked.

A day ago, Chiara could have truthfully said she hadn't heard from him in ten years, but now she was stuck with just shaking her head *no*. Should she tell them he was in town? There were some excellent reasons not to. For one, he'd be pissed if she sicced the reunion committee on him. And for another, she knew there'd be loads of follow-up questions. She and Willa and Vannah hadn't run in the same circles in high school, but it was a small enough school that when someone got stood up for prom, everyone knew. The three women had gotten pretty chummy while working on reunion planning, but that didn't mean the subject of her getting dumped had ever come up. And while she wouldn't mind talking about Jax with them, it just felt too weird and raw right now.

She was having trouble making sense out of it herself: Jax was back in town. And not just in town. In her space. Literally.

"Maybe that's for the best, hmm?" Willa said, misreading the expression on Chiara's face.

"I'll definitely have a better time if he's not there," Chiara said—there, that was entirely true and completely honest—and unlike Auburn, Willa and Vannah didn't seem to know her well enough to see through her, given that both women nodded and laughed.

"Yeah. I wish Bryce Avers wasn't coming," Vannah said. "He was so nerdy and awkward in high school. And he had that weird crush on me."

"He's had a lot of time to chill out and grow up," Chiara said. "And rumor has it he runs his own tech company and is pretty successful."

Vannah gave a little shudder. "Which is adult-speak for nerdy and awkward! You guys have to run interference for me."

"Of course!" Chiara said. "What are friends for? You'll be busy any time he tries to come talk to you."

"Or dance with me."

"Definitely," Willa said. She held out her fists for simultaneous bumps.

Chiara returned the fist bump, smiling. Her sister would like Willa and Vannah. Still newly returned to town, Auburn needed a posse that extended beyond her siblings. Obeying instinct, Chiara said, "Auburn's taking me shopping for a new dress for reunion soon. Wanna come?"

"Hell yeah," Willa said.

Vannah nodded. "I'm in."

"I'll let you know when we're going."

Important business thus dispensed with, they packed up their stuff, waved at Em, the pink-, purple- and blue-haired owner/barista of Beans at the Beach, and left. Chiara headed back to use the restroom.

When she came out, she did a double take. There was Jax, ordering a coffee, like they'd made him appear by reading his name off that list.

Except if she'd had the power to conjure him, she sure as hell would have done it ten years ago.

He looked up, saw her, smiled, and waved for her to come over.

She refused to smile back. His pine-green t-shirt called out the green in his eyes—and she was mad at him for looking so good. For being able to smile at her like he'd never left town without a word.

There was no way to avoid him short of total rudeness, and Em was watching them curiously. If she ignored him, the whole town would know about it.

She headed toward him, dredging up a neutral smile as she approached.

"I was a dick, and I'm sorry," he said. No *hello* or *hey*, just right to the point.

That made her smile for real. She'd always liked his bluntness. So many people made things more complicated than they had to be. If Jax had a flaw, it was that he made things simpler than they actually were.

He raked his hair back and got to the point. "You're right about Evan. We both love Evan. We can work together on this. I pushed my project out a bit, got my guys doing some things that can get done without me. If we sit down together and work out what we need to do, I think we can whip the shop into shape by Labor Day."

She wanted desperately to make the shop work for Evan. But Jax was talking about them working together. He was using the word "we." It made her dizzy.

"Sir—"

She watched Jax realize Em was still waiting for payment. "Oh, God, sorry."

It was endearing to see him flustered. He hastily paid up.

"Hey, Kee," Em said cheerfully.

"Hey, Em," Chiara said. "Love the new ink." She gestured at Em's full-arm sleeve, a complicated whirl of abstract color vivid against Em's pale-gold skin.

"Thanks! Got it done at the new place in Caledona. He's great."

Chiara admired the work—clean, sharp, bright. "It looks amazing." She gestured at the cafe. "How's business?"

"It's been a great week. I love August, you know?" She opened her eyes wide, rolling them towards Jax in an obvious "who's the hottie?" inquiry.

"Em, this is Jax Walker. His brother owns that new game shop, Meeples."

"New game shop?" Em asked, illustrating one of Evan's marketing problems. He should have visited every shop in town and dropped off business cards—or *something*. Every shop owner in Tierney Bay should know he was here.

"It's across from the park. Come check it out."

"We're about to do some renovations on it," Jax said. "Wait a couple of weeks. It's going to be amazing."

*A couple of weeks.* Jax Walker was going to be in and out of her line of sight for a couple of weeks. She closed her eyes in despair.

The door opened and a large group came in, toting beach bags.

"We'll get out of your hair," Chiara said to Em.

"Good to see you! Great to meet you, Jax." Em waved over their heads at her assistant—who'd been wiping down tables—to get himself back behind the counter.

"Take care, Em," Chiara said.

"You, too, hon."

Chiara drifted down the counter to wait for Jax's order with him.

"That stuff you were talking about. Shelves, racks, tables, even. I think I can build most of that, and fast. Chairs—might be cheaper to barter or buy."

"Those don't matter so much," she said. "We can grab some mismatched ones from wherever."

Somehow, she was going along with him. Without quite meaning to. Like she was rolling down a big grassy hill, gathering speed.

He gathered a cup sleeve, a lid, a napkin. "I can do some of the actual work in Evan's apartment. To stay out of your way. And maybe I can find somewhere else to work on the bigger pieces."

She thought about that for a sec. "Maybe you could work in one of the sheds at Cape House. I'll talk to Levi."

He didn't love that idea—she could tell—but he didn't say no, either. Instead he took a deep breath. "I don't know shit about game stores. You're right about that. But I do know a lot about renovation. And building. And I'm good at swallowing my pride. I'm good at listening to someone's vision and making it happen. So you're in charge. You tell me what we need to do, and I'll do my damnedest to make it happen."

She was pretty sure her mouth was hanging open, but before she could speak, Em called Jax's name. He grabbed his drink, capped it, dropped it in the sleeve, and said, "Shit, I should have asked if you wanted anything."

"I just drank a venti latte. I may never want coffee again."

He cocked his head. "So, what do you say? Are we partners?"

She'd said it herself. It wasn't about her. It was about

Evan. Evan, who'd played with Hannah even though she was two years younger and a girl. Evan, whose brain was full of the strangest ideas. *What would happen if you had a tournament where the NFL and the NHL had to play alternating hockey and football games against each other?* Evan, who'd spent his eighth birthday in the hospital, and had been one hell of a good sport about it; sweet, even.

She looked at the man towering over her, and surprised to find he was waiting patiently. Even more surprised to see that foreign softness in his eyes. A kind of —hope.

Oh, God, what was she doing?

She had no idea; she only knew she was doing it.

"Sure," she said. "We're...partners."

8

———

They went back to the store and sat at the table. It was too small for comfort. Her knees didn't quite touch his, but he could *feel* them. She grabbed some paper from the printer and spread it out, and then they both started drawing. She had her phone out, too, and after a few minutes, she started pulling up photos up to show him.

"I'm going to make a Pinterest account for the store," she said. "That way we can both collect things we find."

"I'm not going to add things to a Pinterest board."

"You never know."

"I know."

"Well. I made one. It's called Meeples, and the password is —" She spelled it out for him.

He wrote it down, despite himself.

She sketched the outside of the store, shingles repaired, window box replanted. A big wooden sign that stretched the whole length. Meeples. With two little gingerbread-style people on either side.

"What are those?"

"Those are Meeples," she said. "They're game pieces."

"Oh."

She got up and went to find a game, which she brought back to the table and set next to him. It was called Fresco. She opened it, pulled out two tiny ziplocs, and shook the little wooden people out onto the table.

"Got it," he said. He peered into the box. "That's a lot of plastic bags. Why can't it all go in one big one?"

"Well. You don't want the pieces getting mixed up or it takes forever to set up the game when you want to play." She carefully replaced the small yellow people in their zip bag, returned the game to its shelf, and went back to sketching. She sketched the front counter and a row of comic racks. She sketched a wall of shelves for games that were for sale and another wall of games that were for demo. She filled the center of the store with tables and chairs. There was a small back room in the shop, and she reshelved it with deeper, taller shelves for holding game inventory, holding comic inventory and for files. "Not that we want to store a lot. We don't. Only the most popular items. We want to keep things moving."

She kept passing him pages, and he kept passing them back. "You're going to want drawers here," he said, pointing. "And—you'll need more space here. You want people to be able to stand behind the chairs and look at the shelves without feeling crowded."

"Oh. God. You're right." She erased and redrew, scattering shavings with a sweep of her hand. She'd always done that.

Her cheeks were bright pink. Her mouth was red. Her eyes were so blue it hurt to look at her. He could feel the shimmer of her skin, that vibration, that buzz that lit into him. She loved what she was doing.

When he first met her, she was just one of the Cape House kids. Just his boss's kid. He thought she was boring. She dressed in clothes that didn't draw attention in any way. Jeans and t-shirts—pop bands and famous musicals and TV shows. Nothing that would get you in trouble. She hung out with kids who took hard classes and got good grades. Once when he'd been on shift, her friends had come over and they'd done homework together, and then gone into the TV room and watched some teen movie. She and her friends sat together at a lunch table and didn't make waves. She wouldn't stand out anywhere.

And then one day he was wiping down the tables in the lobby and she was sitting where she always sat, doing her homework. Except when he got close he saw she *wasn't*. She was drawing. She had earbuds in and was singing quietly to herself and shading in something with a colored pencil. He got closer so he could see. It was a superhero, a girl. Or woman, actually—hourglass curves. She wore a cape, and on her chest—swooping over an exceptional set of tits—was the letter K. The drawing was really fucking good—like, you could see the expression on the girl's face: surprise.

But it was the expression on Chiara's face that made Jax stop breathing. She looked so dreamy. Happy. And not ordinary at all. Lit up, on fire.

It was the first time he felt the tug in his chest that later became as familiar as hunger or thirst.

Just then, something clued her in that he was standing in her space and she looked up and covered her drawing with her arm. Everything about her posture told him that he needed to keep on cleaning and pretend he hadn't seen anything, so he did.

But he *had* seen. And he couldn't think of her the same way again.

"What?" Chiara asked. She'd looked up—in Meeples, right damn now—and caught him watching her.

"Just—" He almost said, *I was just remembering...* But it would be so far out of line. "What about colors? You have colored pencils?"

"What? No. No colored pencils. We can just, you know, label the colors. Bright colors, definitely. Because we want everything to appeal to families. And the games should be organized by youngest to oldest."

"You used to always have colored pencils." It popped out, against his will, against his better judgment.

She didn't respond. She was labeling the shelves with colors and age-levels. "That was a long time ago," she said, finally, when he'd stopped waiting for her to answer.

"Do you still draw?"

"I'm drawing now," she said, not looking at him.

"You know what I mean. Do you still draw, you know, the comic book characters?"

She shrank in on herself, shoulders curving, chin dropping. Her face shuttered.

"What do you think? Could you do something like this for the racks?" She pushed a sheet of paper across the table to him. "I mean, I could probably find some used ones somewhere for cheap, but—"

"Yeah. I could do that."

She wasn't going to answer him, and who the hell could blame her? Drawing had brought them together. It had been special, between them. As special as kissing or sex, that inti-mate. He couldn't just bring it up like it was fair game. He'd ruined that, like everything else, when he'd left. Even though he'd had his reasons.

So he changed the subject. He started breaking the work down for her. Order of operations—draw plans; spec materi-als; build what he could outside the shop; paint and finish; paint the interior; build what couldn't be built outside the shop; install the rest; carpet; paint. He'd try to work around the weekends. Sunny days would be for exterior work—which, he'd decided, might need to include reshingling the roof. They needed to get in touch with the landlord—she wrote that down on her list.

After a while, she relaxed, and her face opened up, at least a little. But she didn't let him see the brightly lit, focused version he'd caught just a glimpse of.

And God, he wanted to see her again. His Chiara.

## 9

"Um, I need to get a few measurements back here—you mind?"

Jax had poked his head into the shop late Wednesday, taking measurements, asking questions. Now he was behind the counter with her.

"No. Go ahead."

He knelt, playing out the tape measure, then standing up. He was close enough that she could smell his laundry detergent, fresh and bright. He stepped back—thankfully.

"How's the height for you? It's technically a little low for counter height. I could boost it up. Might make it more comfortable for working when you're standing."

"Huh. Yeah, it *is* uncomfortable to work on, now that you mention it. I thought it was just me."

"No—a lot of people don't know this, but there's a standard table height and a standard counter height. And this is somewhere in between. It'll feel awkward no matter what you try to do at it. It was probably custom-built this way for the original owner."

"Yeah. A little higher would be nice. I mean, we can ask Evan, but—"

"I'll ask him," Jax said.

He was wearing a soft gray cotton t-shirt that fit him like a second skin. It was tight around his biceps, and she was having trouble taking her eyes off the shadowed cut that defined the bulge of muscle above.

"What about the length?"

"What?" She yanked her gaze away from his upper arm and found him watching her, one eyebrow hiked in amusement. She looked away, cheeks hot.

"The length of the counter. I'm building the new one from scratch, so I can do it any way you think would work. You want enough room for two register stations? I know Evan doesn't need it now, but he could, right?"

"Definitely," she said.

Her phone rang and, grateful, she answered it, face still warm.

"Chiara?"

"Yes?"

"This is Lyra at Buyathon."

*Buyathon!* "Hi, Lyra."

"I'm calling because we'd love to get you back here to meet some of the team."

She'd been expecting the call but it still gave her a little thrill of accomplishment. She'd done it. She'd made it to the second round. "Absolutely. When do you want me?"

"Would a week from this Friday work? The sixteenth? Early afternoon? Scheduling is a disaster here right now. Somehow everyone booked August vacations, so there are, like, two days in all of August that everyone is in the office together."

Jax reached up to examine the small window behind the counter. His t-shirt rode up, leaving smooth, tanned skin exposed, above a thin strip of white, untouched by the sun, and the gray waistband of...

"Chiara?" Lyra said.

"Sorry!" Chiara said. "I was just looking at my...calendar and thinking about some logistics. Friday the sixteenth should work perfectly."

"I'll get it on everyone's calendar."

"Please let them know I'm really looking forward to meeting them," Chiara said.

When she hung up, Jax said, "Friday the 16th should work perfectly for what?"

There was no harm in telling him the truth, and he was, in fact, the most logical person for her to ask to cover the store. "I have to go up to Seattle. I'm interviewing for a job. This is the second interview, so I'm meeting with a bunch of people. If you're still around by then and Evan's not back in the shop, any chance I could convince you to take over for me that day?"

"Sure," he said, with a shrug. "A job in Seattle, huh? Don't you have your own business?"

She hadn't told him what she did. She gave him a quizzical look.

He shrugged. "I googled you."

She immediately wanted to know more. When—and how often—had he googled her? What exactly had he found?

Funny, that she had spent so many years deliberately *not* googling him, when he'd been doing it to her. That was the privilege of the dumper; you didn't have to guard your heart —or your pride.

"I do have my own business."

"And your brothers and sisters are here. So why would you want to work for someone else, and in Seattle?"

"I never meant to freelance forever. It was a way to be here for Hannah when she was growing up. Decent money, flexible hours—but it was never the dream."

"I remember when I first met you back in high school you said you wanted to be—what was it again? The business brains for a big company. The one who makes the numbers add up."

"CFO."

"But then I thought you changed your mind. You weren't sure. You thought you wanted to do something more creative."

She'd almost forgotten that. There *had* been a time. When she'd thought maybe she would be happier doing something with illustration or animation or storyboarding. But that had really just been a teenaged fantasy. Just because you liked to draw didn't make you an artist.

"It takes creativity to be a CFO."

"Sure," he said. "I'm not knocking it. Obviously it takes all kinds of skills, or they wouldn't get paid the big bucks. I'm not saying you wouldn't be great at it, either. I'm just wondering if it's what you love."

"Do you love being a general contractor?" she countered.

He nodded. "I do, actually. I love being able to take what someone wants for a project and make it real in the world. And I love being hands-on with stuff. I could never sit in an office."

Jax had a way of looking at her like he could see what she was thinking. "Not everyone's like that, though."

"Well, sure, no, but—you have this creative streak—" He gestured down at the counter in front of them, where she'd been doodling again. Refining designs. Unable to stop herself, she flipped over the paper, hiding it from his eyes.

"That's just messing around," she said. "It's nothing that could ever *be* anything. I'm good with numbers. Great with numbers. And Buyathon apparently thinks I could make a competent director of finance and planning. You know what?" she said. She was suddenly, unexpectedly, irritated with the direction of this conversation. "This is none of your business. You blew your chance to express any opinion about my life a long time ago."

He stiffened. "You're—" He took a breath. "You're right. I'm sorry. And—" He sighed, this time. "Actually, you know what? I've been meaning to do this, and it's never the perfect moment, but I—I'm sorry, period. I know it's too little too late, but I've been realizing I owe you a big apology. For what I did. For leaving with no explanation. There's no excuse. I'm sorry."

She froze. Of all the things she'd been expecting, this was the last. An honest-to-God apology.

And by most standards, it was perfect. No excuses, no explanations, just: apology. And God, he really sounded like he meant it. The expression on his face was open, contrite. Almost—pained. He was *sorry*.

"I—"

She tried. She opened her mouth, and she tried to say something that made sense. Maybe, "It's okay"—although it wasn't. Or "I forgive you"—which at some level, she did, because she believed in forgiveness. She really did.

But she couldn't do it. She couldn't just let him off the hook. Because she still needed to understand. She wanted to know why he'd done it.

That explanation, the one he'd left without offering? She still craved it.

But she didn't want him to know how much.

"You don't have to say anything," he said. The silence had dragged on long enough that it was clear she wasn't going to fill it. "I just needed to say that. But don't feel like you have to say anything back. I know there's nothing *to* say."

Finally, she found her voice. "No," she said. "There isn't."

## 10

H e shut up for a while after that, because she was one hundred percent right: Her life was none of his business. But he stayed aware of her—where she was, what she was doing—even when he was busy with other things. He checked to make sure there wasn't wallpaper buried under the layers of peeling interior paint, prodded the subfloor to make sure it was all sound, tried to figure out how much of the trim and built-ins he could reuse or repurpose.

Inspired by Chiara's sketches and enthusiasm, he'd spent the week filling Evan's apartment with tools and materials and working every free moment when he wasn't at the hospital with Evan. He'd drawn plans, built racks and shelves, started in on the parts of the counter he could do off site, sketched out to-do lists. He'd caught himself whistling as he worked—which wasn't something he'd done in years. Something about this project had gotten under his skin, and he liked it.

A few minutes later, a paying customer came in—a mom and her son, who looked like he was around eight or nine.

They were visiting family in Arch Cape, and whenever they went on vacation anywhere, they always checked out all the game and toy stores, the mom explained.

"Sorry about the chaos," Chiara said. "It's temporary. We're renovating."

The mom waved a hand. "We're just happy to be here. But just so you know, your store didn't pop up in our online search for board game shops. We would have missed it completely except that Cade wanted to check out the playground, and we happened to spot you guys."

Chiara sighed. Another thing Evan needed to remedy. "So you guys like game stores?"

"We love game stores. I'm Sadie," the woman said.

"I'm Chiara."

"Do you have demo games? That's our favorite thing to do, sit and play demo games. We left our non-gamer family members home so they wouldn't rush us."

"We *do*," Chiara said.

Jax was basically done with his inspection. He should leave. He should go back to Evan's apartment and dig in again. He wanted to be able to have most of the built-ins ready to install by Friday, so he could do it while she was gone.

Instead, he began a careful—and mostly unnecessary—inspection of the interior trim.

"So, Cade, you're, what, ten?" Chiara asked the boy.

"Nine." He wore square-framed black-rimmed glasses and his hair hung in his eyes.

"Tell me what games you guys usually play together."

"Catan," the boy replied.

Even Jax had heard of *that* game.

"Agricola. Puerto Rico. Dominion."

"Okay," Chiara said. "That helps. So you're not a typical nine-year-old gamer."

Sadie laughed at that. "No. He's pretty advanced."

Chiara went to the shelves and pulled out a game. "This is my current favorite," she said conspiratorially. "In this one, each of you is a corporation, trying to make the most money on Mars. The game is exactly what it sounds like. You're literally terraforming Mars—raising the temperature, upping the oxygen levels, and creating oceans. And meanwhile, you have these cards that let you earn money and other resources, and you build an empire that way."

"Ohhh, that sounds *cool*," Cade said.

Jax felt that way, too. It was the enthusiasm in Chiara's voice. It was infectious. He hadn't played a board game since —well, since the last one he'd played at the Campbell kitchen table—and he was ready to sit down and join in.

Chiara got the mom and son seated at the table and set up the game for them. It was immediately obvious that the table was too small, but Chiara managed to fit it all, somehow. Things looked precariously balanced, and Jax couldn't help thinking that one swipe of that kid's sleeve would send pieces everywhere.

Leaving the mother and son to their game, Chiara went back behind the counter.

Jax came over. "Table's way too small, huh?"

She nodded. "When I play with Auburn we sometimes use muffin tins to hold the pieces, but there's not even room for that."

"Muffin tins," he repeated. "Clever."

She was watching her customers with a thoughtful look

on her face. "You know," she said. "I think that's the key."

"Muffin tins?"

"No. Demos. Events. Getting people in here. And not at teeny tiny tables, either. God. It could be great. We could— Evan could—have Magic the Gathering Nights. D&D. But also family game nights. Math game nights. And weekend stuff, for tourist traffic. Beach games and puzzles..."

She was bouncing a little, on the tips of her toes, with excitement. He tried not to notice the way the bounce vibrated through her curves, but hell; he noticed. He noticed the flush in her cheeks, too.

*Focus, Jax.*

"You work on the events," he told her. "Leave the tables to me."

The chimes over the door rang again and they both looked over. "Two customers at once?" Chiara whispered. "Say it isn't so."

But it wasn't. It was Chiara's siblings, minus Mason, plus a man Jax had never seen before. They came through the door with typical Campbell energy, like a litter of puppies, chattering and jostling.

"Keeeee," Auburn sang. "It is *perfect* kite-flying weather and these lunatics just convinced me to play hooky and leave Beachcrest in Carl's capable hands for an hour so we can get down on the beach. You have to come, too. You can leave the store with Jax," she said, turning to him. "Good to see you."

Her tone managed to convey the exact opposite of her words. "You, too," he said. Only he actually meant it. He'd always liked Auburn. She was a louder, curvier, curlier, more extravagant Chiara, minus whatever chemical ingredient made Chiara irresistible to him.

Levi gave him a look that conveyed more or less what Auburn's tone had—plus a helping of *watch out*—and he didn't bother with the niceties. But Hannah, who looked a hell of a lot like her sisters had at sixteen, came forward and held her arms out for a hug.

He hugged her. Her hair still smelled like strawberry shampoo, like it had when she was six, and he was suddenly in the Campbell's kitchen, watching Hannah on the floor with her dolls spread out.

He let Hannah go, and she stepped back, telling him she'd missed him and was glad he was here, even if her dumbass brother and sister wouldn't say so—

But the memory didn't want to let go.

Maggie, the Campbell siblings' mom, would have been at the stove, cooking something that smelled amazing, usually a stew or chili or spaghetti sauce. One of the kids would be helping her out—sometimes voluntarily, sometimes because she'd enlisted them against their will to chop onions for her, which made her cry too hard. Someone would have cued up a playlist, and everyone whose playlist it *wasn't* would be griping about the music. At least one sibling would be doing homework at the table, often accompanied by him and Chiara.

Despite the bickering over music, the siblings were super close. He loved watching them together. The way they cared for each other and worked together and, yes, even fought, made him feel good and bad at the same time. Good because for this moment, just this moment, he felt part of it. Bad because this wasn't really his.

At his house, he cooked—not like Mrs. Campbell, but enough to get by; he could boil water for pasta, bake chicken, grill burgers, and scramble eggs. He cleaned up—after dinner and after his mother, who sometimes disappeared at dinnertime or afterwards on dates, and other times passed out in the early evening, leaving a wake behind her—empties and cigarettes, mail she'd opened and left, books she'd started but never finished, clothes she'd shed, wrappers, dishes.... He drove Evan where he needed to go because he didn't trust his mother to drive, and he helped Evan with his homework because his mother...well, most nights, somewhere between *didn't* and *couldn't*.

"This is Trey," Auburn was saying, gesturing at the unfamiliar man, and Trey, with an easy smile, stuck a hand out. Jax took it; the guy had a firm shake, but not asshole-firm, and Jax liked him on sight.

"Where's Mace?" Chiara asked.

"Some work thing. We couldn't spring him."

Chiara was looking at him, a question on her face, and he got himself grounded back in the moment and said, "Yeah. Go."

"You sure? This, and Friday, you don't mind?"

"Nah," he said. It was less than an hour till closing. "But what if they want to buy that?" He gestured to where the mom and kid were still—happily—terraforming Mars.

She showed him how to ring it up—he wrote it down so he'd have it for Friday, too. "It'll be your first sale," she said.

"You're very sure of yourself," he said.

"I just know that if I can get them in here, I can sell them games," she said.

That made him smile.

"Go," he said. "Fly your kite. Hang with your family. I'll hold down the fort."

## 11

I t *was* perfect kite-flying weather, and because it was midweek and almost dinnertime, the beach was crowded but not mobbed. Levi had brought along his favorite kite, a dual-line dragon in flame colors. He let Hannah get it aloft—she was still the baby, even at sixteen. The wind threatened to disappear just as the kite took wing, then returned with a vengeance, and the dragon's oranges, yellows and reds lit up against the cloudless blue of the sky. Chiara squinted up at it and felt happy.

"What was Jax doing in the shop?" Auburn demanded, coming up alongside her sister and bumping her with one shoulder.

She'd been waiting for it. They'd left her alone on the walk to the beach, maybe because Hannah was hanging on every word, and, even though sixteen was pretty mature, it wasn't all grown up, not yet.

Levi joined them on her other side. "The offer to kick his ass still stands."

"You don't need to kick his ass."

"That worries me," Levi said.

"You also don't need to worry about me."

Levi frowned, squinting into the sun. "Convince me."

"I told you Evan's store's in trouble," she said to Auburn.

"You'd have to be blind not to see that," Levi said. "What the fuck was that kid thinking?"

"He was thinking ten thousand dollars would go a lot further than it did," Chiara said.

Levi nodded.

"So Jax and I are going to get him back on track," Chiara said. "My brains, Jax's brawn."

"Has Jax heard that description?" Levi asked, one eyebrow sky high.

"I'm not serious," she said. "We just agreed, I'd provide the vision, he'd do the contracting work."

Levi pursed his lips. "Makes sense."

Hannah ran up, kite spools extended to Chiara. "You want it?"

She took the spools, feeling the kite tug. She dipped it one way, then the other.

"Can you turn a loop?"

She did, then handed it off to Levi. She and Auburn strolled toward the water, where the sand was damp, and stood staring out at the horizon. The water was vivid and sparkling, the lighthouse visible in the distance to the right. Breaker Rock loomed over them, off to their left. She felt a brief, sharp moment of grief: She'd be leaving this behind if she went to Seattle.

But there were always opportunity costs. She remembered her father talking about what he'd given up to run the family business, take over Cape House hotel. He'd sometimes look at business magazines, the ones with lists of influential people, and he'd say—half-joking, in a Brando voice—*I coulda been a contender.*

*You'll be on one of these lists one day. That's my consolation. My money's on youngest female CFO of a Fortune 500 company.*

There were always opportunity costs.

"So you're going to be in the shop with him all day every day for—?"

"A couple weeks. That's all."

"And he's going to have his shirt off, running the sander."

"No. He's not going to have his shirt off. Or be running the sander. He's going to do the dirty work somewhere else."

Auburn waggled her eyebrows.

"Shut. Up."

"He looks good," Auburn said, abruptly. "I'm sorry to say it, but he does. He's aged well."

Chiara sighed. "Yes. He has." She had stored up some nice visuals from the morning. The way that gray t-shirt clung to the planes and contours of Jax's bad-ass body. And those few scraps of bare skin—the dips and dives of bicep and that stolen glimpse of his back.

Also the uncertainty on his face the one time she'd looked up and caught him staring at her. What the hell had he been thinking?

Hannah drew even with them, kicking sand up as she did. "You have homework, bebe?" Chiara asked her.

"Keeeee," Hannah moaned. "I can take care of my own homework. I'm sixteeeeen."

"Tough habit to break," Chiara said. She'd been in charge of making Hannah do her homework for most of Hannah's life. And Hannah hadn't always been a good student. She'd had trouble in school until this last year, when suddenly she got interested in pretty much everything. Math still gave her hell—go figure; genetics were weird—but it was like something got turned on in her brain sophomore year and suddenly she wanted to tell her siblings about government and history and psychology and philosophy and whatever her teachers fed her. Auburn had been the same way, except her indifference to school had ended in late high school when she realized she wanted to run her own hotel one day.

Chiara suddenly thought of Jax and his crack about helping other people with math homework. That did describe her life—all of it—pretty damn well.

*Is it what you love?*

"Earth to Keee-aaah-raaa."

Chiara surfaced to find both her sisters staring at her.

"Something on your mind?" Auburn asked innocently.

Hannah squinted. "Do you have a crush on Jax?"

"No," Chiara said. "I most certainly do not have a crush on Jax."

"Methinks the lady doth protest too much," Hannah said.

Chiara rolled her eyes. "School is ruining your brain."

# 12

---

J ax was at Meeples when she got there the next morning—and on a ladder. Her gaze climbed the rungs; he was standing three-quarters of the way up. It was a good look for him. He had a spectacular ass. It should be illegal, or at least a controlled substance, especially in those well-worn jeans. With the small hole at the base of the pocket, through which she could see a flash of gray.

He'd been a boxer-briefs guy, as a teenager. Was that one of those things that stayed consistent throughout life?

Why was she thinking about his underwear?

Any minute, she'd start thinking about what was *under* his underwear. And damn, now she was. Well-formed, smooth, soft as velvet under her hand, but steel to the core. And he'd felt so good inside her, the one time she'd gotten to experience it.

Gah!

It took her a minute, because of the distraction, to understand what he was doing. He was hanging a new sign. It was made of wood and said *MEEPLES* in big, burned-in letters. On either side of the shop's name, there were game pieces—a chess queen, a checkers piece, a simple pawn, and one of the meeple people she'd showed him.

It was fantastic. He'd taken her vision and made it even better.

They'd been like that, in high school. When she'd drawn and he'd leaned over her shoulder and dreamed up the story with her. She sometimes felt like he was inside her head, following the story as the film played out on the screen in her mind.

He must have sensed her eyes on his work—or his ass—because he looked down and smiled at her. "You like it?"

"I love it."

That made his smile even bigger. And Jax, full-on smiling, was something to see. He had smile wrinkles at the corners of his eyes, an almost-dimple in one cheek, and very white, slightly crooked teeth, every one of which was familiar to her: the canted front tooth, one vampirish canine, and the just-a-little-bit crowded bottom teeth that made him look impish.

Damn him, his illegal ass, and his impish teeth. Also, his perfect sign.

He came down the ladder and stood next to her. "I did it last night."

She wanted to hug him, but resisted the urge. That way lay...madness. "It's really, really great," she said. "It looks just like I would have imagined. But better."

His face got very serious all of a sudden, and he was looking at her in a way that made her feel like she needed to get out of there immediately.

"Gotta get to work," she said, sliding under the ladder and into the shop.

A few minutes later he came in. "I finished the plan for the checkout counter, too."

"Did you sleep?"

"Not much."

Funny. She hadn't slept much either. Partly because she'd also had a game-store fire lit under her. She'd spent hours strategizing events for the store, for Labor Day weekend, for this fall. She'd made a plan to publicize them with social media and the North Coast Gazette—Willa, her reunion committee friend, was the newspaper's editor and would help.

But even after she'd gone to bed, she'd tossed and turned, unable to get herself the right temperature. Finally, after midnight, she'd given in and employed the single best, tried-and-true method, Mr. Buzz.

It was *possible*, although she wouldn't admit it even if you tortured her, that she had fantasized about Jax.

"Where'd Terraforming Mars go?" she asked.

"I put it away."

She tried, she really tried, but she couldn't stop herself from crossing the room to the bookshelf that was serving as a demo shelf.

"Really," he said. It wasn't a question. "You're going to *check* to make sure I put it away right."

"It's not you," she said. "I would check if anyone had put it away right."

"Evan?"

"Not Evan. But he's a gamer."

She took the box out and set it on the table. "There are

extra plastic bags," she said. "That's usually a sign that you didn't separate out everything I would separate out."

He was shaking his head, but also smiling. "Seriously, Campbell, you know you have a problem, right?"

She glared at him and sorted the resource cubes into three piles—gold, silver, and copper—and put each in its own plastic bag. Then she separated the oceans from the greenery and the cities. She put the flat stuff in the box first, then the cards, then the plastic bags full of pieces.

"Feel better?" he asked, smirking.

"I'll have you know," she said, mock-primly, "that in the scheme of gamers, I don't even register on the neurotic game-piece management front."

He raised his eyebrows. "I'm finding that hard to believe."

"No, *seriously*. There are gamers who build insert trays out of cardboard or balsa wood—hand built, custom-built—for each of their games."

"You're kidding."

"Swear to God. And there's a whole cottage industry for 3D printing—and sometimes even machining—better game pieces. Like upgrades." She got out her phone and showed him, on Etsy. "Look at these. Aren't they adorable?" She'd been coveting the Terraforming Mars pieces for a long time —plastic hexes to replace her cardboard ones, with teeny-tiny trees and teeny-tiny buildings.

"Adorable," he said dryly, but when she looked up, his eyes were on her. He had an expression on his face that made her shove her phone in her pocket and put a couple of feet between them.

Her heart was beating too fast. She hurried behind the

counter and began setting up for the day, jiggling the mouse to bring the computer to life and initializing the card reader.

"Can I show you my plan for the counter?"

Whatever she thought she'd seen on his face was gone. "Sure," she said.

"It's in my truck. I'll run and get it."

"Yeah. Perfect."

As soon as the door shut behind him, she let out a breath.

It felt like she'd been holding it for hours.

## 13

H e took his time getting the counter plan from the truck, giving his body time to recover. His systems had gone into overdrive when she'd said she loved his sign—and meant it. And fuck, he shouldn't give a shit. He hadn't made the sign for her, he'd made it for Evan.

Or so he'd told himself, but if that was true, why had it meant so much to him that she'd loved it? That she'd looked at him like he'd done something worthwhile?

Then he'd teased her about the game pieces and she hadn't shut down. She'd teased back. It was like the old days, like they were friends. And then she'd come close with her phone in her hand, and her arm had brushed his. Her apple-cinnamon scent had filled his brain, and every single nerve in his body had blazed to life.

He remembered once telling a girlfriend—one of his longer-term relationships, lasting a whopping two or three months—that getting an erection wasn't like flipping a switch but more like pouring a good glass of beer. (Except for in high school. Because in high school, Chiara had been a reliable source of insta-hard.)

Apparently, insta-hard was still a thing. So apparently it was Chiara, not high school, that was the key.

And then he'd made her uncomfortable, damn it, which was the last thing he wanted to do now that maybe, just maybe, they were sort of kind of a little bit friends. She'd run away from him so fast that she'd set some kind of land-speed record on banged-up subflooring.

He grabbed the plan and headed back inside. She looked up at him and smiled, so that was good. He hadn't blown everything.

Although—what the fuck did he think was going on here? He couldn't *really* be friends with her. You couldn't be friends with someone when you knew something big you were never, ever going to tell them.

Could you? If your motives were good, then could you?

"This is *great*," she said, spreading the plan out on the counter.

He kept his distance this time. He didn't need another hard-on that fierce. Those kinds of erections made you do stupid shit you would regret later, like all the blood in your head really *had* run right into your dick.

"Oh, wow. I love this." She pointed at the drawers and shelves below the counter.

He'd known she'd be excited about that. He had a few other surprises up his sleeve, too—

For *Evan*. Surprises for *Evan*.

When he'd visited Evan yesterday and updated him on what was going on with the store, Evan was thrilled that he and Chiara were working together. So much so that Jax had felt like he had to say, "It's not a big deal, Ev. It was ten years ago and as far as I can tell she doesn't actually give a shit anymore."

Evan had said, shrugging, "Okay. But I'm glad anyway." And then, brow wrinkling, "You should tell her why we left."

"Pretty sure she doesn't care," Jax said.

"Well. You can tell her if you want to."

"I'll bear that in mind."

He'd go back to the hospital again today, as he had every day since he'd been here, sometimes more than once, and show Evan photos of what he'd done, the plan for the counter. He probably should have shown Evan the plan first, but he'd wanted to get here early and get the sign up so it was the first thing Chiara saw when she showed up.

"What's this?" she asked, pointing to the lines in Jax's sketch that represented the wall behind the front counter. In the shop, that spot was hung with an unmatched montage of framed maps, old photographs, book covers, and book leaves. In Jax's plan, he'd drawn only a big, blank rectangle.

"Your mural," he said.

"What mural?"

"Whatever you want it to be."

She squinted at him. "What are you talking about?"

"Something fun. Family-friendly. Bright colored. Something to do with games and comics."

She was shaking her head. "I wouldn't know how to do something like that."

"Sure you would. It's just like the stuff you used to draw in high school, but bigger."

She looked at him like he was stark raving mad. "I haven't

drawn since high school. And I wouldn't know how to scale it up, anyway."

"You draw it, I'll scale it up," Jax said. "We can do that thing where we transfer it square by square."

"I wouldn't know what to draw."

"Superheroes playing board games." Then he was sorry, because her face closed down in a big hurry. Like a door slamming.

She pushed the plans across the counter to him. "These look good. We can hang some fun posters behind the register. We'll find something."

He didn't push. He wasn't willing to scare her off. He'd come close enough as it was. "I'll work on this," he said. "And I'll let you know when I need to be in the store for built-in installation and carpet and paint and all."

"Sounds good." Her tone was businesslike. He half expected her to stick out her hand to shake, but she didn't. She just went back to messing with the computer.

On the walk back to the truck, he chastised himself. What had made him suggest superheroes for a mural? Of all things?

Back in high school, a couple of weeks after Jax had seen Chiara drawing at Cape House, she left a stack of notebooks behind when she went home with Levi and her dad. He told himself he was only opening the top notebook—which looked like a sketchbook—so he could confirm they belonged to her before he returned them.

But once he had it open, he couldn't put it down. Many of Chiara's drawings were one-frame cartoons—funny scenes, captioned. A woman at the grocery store, laying her items on the belt—donuts, donut holes, and a tube of superglue. The caption read, *When the grocery checker calls her manager.* He laughed out loud.

There was one recurring character—that superhero she'd drawn, with the slammin' bod and the "K" swerving across her chest. She was everywhere. In one drawing, she was singing into a mic. In another, she was at the top of the Eiffel tower, looking out over Paris. In yet another, she seemed to have shoved a skinny blond chick to the ground and was standing with one foot on the skinny girl's chest.

"What do you think you're doing?"

He had looked up to find Chiara staring at him over the notebook.

"You—left this."

She grabbed it out of his hands. "You shouldn't have looked in it."

"It's really good," he'd said. Maybe he should have shut up, tried to pretend he hadn't seen a whole lot of her drawings, but he couldn't.

"It's really not. I can't draw so it looks like real life." She flipped it shut and turned to walk away.

"Who's the girl?"

"Which girl?"

"The one with the 'K' on her shirt."

"None of your business."

He stayed quiet, and then realized he was holding still, too. Praying, or what passed for it in his world.

She turned back. Her face was bright pink. "SuperKee," she said.

"Super—Kee?"

"Kee. For Chiara."

"She's *you*?"

She looked like she was either going to hit him or run. He wanted to take it back—the shock in his voice. Then she said, "Yeah."

"Why's she—?" At a loss for how to ask it diplomatically, he fell back on: "She doesn't look like you. Why'd you draw her like that?" He didn't mean to do it, but his hands unconsciously traced a woman's curves in the air.

She got even pinker. "She's how I wish I looked."

"I like the way you look."

Sometimes words jumped out of Jax's mouth without his permission. He wanted to reel them back in, hand over hand, but it was *definitely* too late for that.

"Um, thanks," she said. And she smiled. A small, very shy, but definitely very pleased smile.

Something shifted seismically in Jax's chest.

"I'd, uh, better go," she'd said, gesturing behind her. "They're waiting for me in the car."

"Yeah, you better go."

He remembered that she'd looked back once, right before she reached the door. And given him another one of those smiles.

It occurred to him that he would do just about anything for those smiles. And that scared him. Because there was no space, anywhere in his life, to feel that way.

## 14

At the hardware store Friday morning, Jax worked his way methodically through the items on his list. Straight metal attachment plates, toggle bolts, swivel casters with locks—he wanted Chiara to be able to move the tables around.

Correction: He wanted *Evan* to be able to move the tables around. Chiara would be in Seattle. Technically, she didn't have the job, but he knew that she'd get it. She'd always gotten what she went after. Valedictorian, the college of her choice, a top business school.

*Except you*, a voice told him.

*She wasn't really after me*, he argued back. *She thought she was, but I wasn't right for her.*

In that regard, Chiara's dad had done them both a favor. Jax hated to admit it, but the man had seen the truth of it, even if his delivery of the message had sucked.

His phone rang, jangling him out of the past. He pulled it out of his pocket and saw that it was his mother. Well, shit. With Evan in the hospital, he couldn't ignore her calls.

"Hey," he said.

"Hello, Jax."

"I just have a few minutes."

She sighed, which he knew was because he only ever had a few minutes. He loved his mother. He was devoted to helping her out any way he could. But at the same time, he wouldn't say that he exactly enjoyed spending time with her.

"I had a long talk with Evan," she said.

That, too, was code: *Evan talks to me.*

He didn't rise to the bait. "I'm glad you guys got a chance to talk."

"I told him all about the craft fair."

Right, the craft fair. "How did it go?" he asked.

"It was great. I made more money there, with these skirts, than I have at any other single event. I think I'm finally onto something."

His mother had gotten sober shortly after their move to California. Jax wasn't sure what had finally made sobriety stick. Maybe she'd understood, however incompletely, how much she'd taken away from him. Or how her misjudgments had grossly affected Evan. Or maybe she'd finally seen that it was only a matter of time before she did something that couldn't be undone.

He'd asked her once, but she'd given him a typically vague answer, something about energies aligning or it being the right season.

Even sober, his mother had trouble staying anchored in the world. And often Jax had felt like he was still the parent, and she was more like Evan's sister than a mother. She took an intermittent interest in Evan's well-being, but didn't stay focused for long, abandoning him for projects that snared her full attention. She moved from project to project and scheme to scheme and was only ever barely solvent. He was constantly rescuing her from herself. Bailing her out "just this once" or for "just a few hundred."

*I'm onto something* was probably also code for, *I need a hundred bucks.*

"That's great, Mom."

"I was wondering if it would help Evan if I sent him a little bit of this money."

He nearly dropped his phone.

"Hang on, Mom, give me a sec." He switched his phone to the other hand. Maybe some people were ambidextrous, but he definitely wasn't one of them. Wait, hang on—he suddenly zeroed in on his task. Not straight metal attachment plate; he needed the angled one. Had he already checked all the drawers on this row?

He gave up on doing both things at the same time and wandered into a corner of the hardware store to give his mother his undivided attention. "How much money are we talking, Mom?"

"Twenty-five, fifty bucks?"

Oh. Right. He let the foolish hope that had bubbled up in him settle back down again. Not the kind of money that would help pay for an expensive experimental treatment. And she'd be asking him for a hundred two weeks from now when she realized that she hadn't set aside money for supplies to make the next batch of skirts.

He suppressed a sigh. "Hang onto it, Mom. You'll need it for something. I've got Evan."

He did. He always had, and he always would. He'd moved several states away, lost the woman he cared about, upended the hope for a life of his own, and he couldn't fully regret it, because it had all been for Evan.

"You sound busy," his mom said—code for: *You sound impatient.*

"I'm at the hardware store. I'm helping Evan with some stuff."

He could see why Chiara had urged him to shop local. This hardware store had some of everything, and right now he was standing in a corner reserved for arts and crafts materials. His hand drifted, idly, to a set of colored pencils that were open, on display. Seventy-two of them, arranged in rainbow order. Chiara in high school would have gone nuts over them. If she'd let herself enjoy them. She might also have gotten hung up about whether drawing was a waste of time. Whether she should be concentrating instead on activities that her father had decided would help her get into college. Her father had treated the drawing like a charming, self-indulgent little hobby. And Chiara herself had vacillated about whether she was any good at it or should give it up. She'd taken some art class and gotten dissed by the teacher, and she'd taken it to heart.

Without making a conscious decision, he picked up one of the closed, packaged sets beside the display and added it to his basket.

"Just make sure you're taking time to take care of yourself, too," his mother said.

He rolled his eyes. His mother was a big proponent of self-care. Self-compassion.

He mostly thought all that was selfishness. You did what needed doing, and then you did what needed doing next, and you put other people first, especially family.

"I'm fine, Mom. But I'd better go."

He had tables to build. A brother to visit. A store to rescue.

"I love you, Jax."

"I love you, too, Mom."

He almost put the pencils back on the table. Who was he fooling? This wasn't an eight-pack of Crayolas. This was an expensive gift.

But he could see the look on her face, that lit-up, alive expression, and he couldn't make himself leave them behind.

## 15

"I'm kicking you out."

Jax had come in, crossed his arms, and made the pronouncement.

"Out of the shop?"

"At least away from the counter. I'm building the new counter today."

"You know we're open."

He swept a critical look around the empty shop.

"Okay," she said, with a sigh, and yielded the space to him.

She decided to use the time to rethink what was on display. Evan needed to lead with fun family and party games that would pull tourists in. Then he could upsell people to high-end games like Agricola or Scythe or Terraforming Mars. But he wasn't going to grab walk-in traffic with that stuff. It just didn't work that way.

Also, people didn't buy what they didn't understand. Especially with those more complicated games, Evan would have to keep demos on the tables to lure people in.

She spent half an hour rearranging stock and furniture to appeal more to moms, dads, kids, and groups of casual-gamer friends, then realized she'd frozen in place and was staring at Jax while he worked.

Because, who wouldn't have?

At some point, when she wasn't watching, he'd stripped down to the waist—just like Auburn had said.

Damn her for being right.

He was wearing a pair of jeans that fit him like they'd been made for his butt and thighs, but that wasn't where her eyes wanted to go. They were fixated on the taut skin stretched over acres of muscles in his chest, stomach, and back. Oh, my *God*, he looked good. All golden tan and glistening just the tiniest bit with sweat, and every time he moved to drill or hammer or screw or whatever the hell he was doing with that other thing, his body bunched and flexed and made something go loose and liquid low in her belly.

He looked up and caught her looking. They both looked away at the same time.

Ten itchy minutes later—ten minutes of very deliberately not looking his way—she realized it was time for her to get the hell out of the shop.

"Mind if I run out?"

"Nope," he said, not looking at her.

She headed into town and found Lily herself behind the counter at Tierney Bay Diner. She walked Chiara's order for two lasagnas back, then came out to chat.

"Are the lasagnas for you and Auburn?" she asked.

"Um, no. One's for me and one's for the contractor who's working at Meeples."

"Oh, *that* guy," Lily said, eyes going wide. "He was here for breakfast this morning. He is—a nice addition to the landscape."

"Uh. Yeah. He is."

Lily raised an eyebrow. "So he's new in town?"

"You didn't get the whole story out of him?"

"I was on the grill this morning. I saw him but didn't get to give him the third degree."

"He's Evan's brother, actually. The kid who owns Meeples, you know?"

Lily nodded. "Another excellent customer."

Chiara squinted at that; she was pretty sure there wasn't much Evan could safely eat at the diner.

"I do special meals for him," Lily said, seeing Chiara's eyebrows rise.

"You're a saint," Chiara said.

Lily shrugged. "I just appreciate a kid who appreciates good cooking, you know?" she said.

The lasagnas came out—Lily had put a friend-rush on them—and Chiara hugged Lily across the countertop, then walked the hot food back to Meeples.

"Here," she said, setting Jax's on the counter and trying not to ogle the lovely hollows in the muscles of his shoulders, the grooves to either side of his spine.

He looked up from what he was doing, and when he saw the boxes she had laid out, a smile lit him up.

"You got me *lunch?*"

"I was getting myself some, so I figured—yeah, I got you lunch."

"Wow. That's—thank you."

He looked like she'd brought him Christmas, not lunch. She remembered him being like that in high school, too. So damn grateful to her mother, thanking her five times a night for having him and Evan over, for cooking for them.

Back then it had been because no one ever cooked for him.

Was it possible that was still true? Because if so, the women of Bakersfield were missing out in a big way.

"Oh, man—oh, God, that smells unbelievably good."

"Tierney Bay Diner," she said.

"That place!"

"Hang on," she said. "You know this is a no shoes, no shirt, no service establishment, right?"

Mainly because there was no way she could eat while he looked like that. It was too distracting.

He laughed, grabbed for his shirt, and tugged it back on. "Hey. Um. I have something for you, too."

"You—what?"

"Hang on. Give me a second."

He went out of the shop, was gone a few minutes, and came back in with a small brown paper bag. "Here," he said.

The package was flat and made a strange subdued rattle, like the rustle of leaves. She opened the bag and pulled out a box of seventy-two colored pencils. Something lurched in her chest. These must have cost him a fortune. And she'd never use them.

"You shouldn't have. Seriously, Jax. I don't draw anymore. I haven't since high school. It was just a passing phase."

He frowned. "It shouldn't have been."

"It was just a kid's hobby. I never had the eye for it."

And once Jax had left, she hadn't had the heart for it. But even if she had, being practical had become even more important after her parents' death—and numbers sure beat the hell out of pretty pictures in being employable.

"You only believe that because some art teacher who was probably jealous of you said it."

"I just—I don't have time." She tried to hand the pencils back to him. "Jax. I can't accept this. It must have cost you a hundred bucks or more."

"I want you to have them." He put his hands up in the universal gesture of refusal. "I won't take them back. It's fine if you can't use them. Maybe Hannah can. Or you can keep them in the shop for kids to use."

"These aren't kid colored pencils." Against her own better judgment, she opened the box, stroked a finger over the pencils. They wiggled in their little grooves, and she *wanted*. She wanted to use them. Just like she wanted all the things that Jax made her think about, all things that didn't make any sense to her life now.

It touched her that he'd gone to the trouble of buying the pencils for her, even though money must have been tight for him, especially with his brother blowing the college funds and him having to buy materials for a reno. It moved her more than she wanted to admit.

And why could he still do that to her? She wished, more than anything, that she could put up a wall around her heart. So he couldn't mess with her, even unintentionally. He was so bad for her sanity. She was still as vulnerable to him as ever.

Thank God he was leaving soon.

H is belt sander quit spinning mid-morning. Which sucked, because he'd been making great progress.

"God *damn*," he said. It wasn't the sander's power, because the pile of shit was still vibrating, which meant it was the drive belt. He could try to repair it, but it had been a while since he'd messed around in the innards of a sander. It would be a hell of a lot easier if he could borrow someone's....

And maybe he could.

"Do you think Levi has a belt sander?"

"What's a belt sander?"

"This thing." He held it up, although he could tell it made about as much sense to her as Terraforming Mars made to him.

"Probably?" She shrugged. "Want me to text him?"

"Sure?"

She grabbed her phone, dashed one out, then said, "He said come on up."

A few minutes later he pulled into the Cape House parking lot and found himself staring at the hotel where his life had changed completely.

Eleven and a half years ago, he'd climbed this hill on foot to ask for a job. Back then, Cape House had been a popular Oregon coast destination, but definitely still a beach hotel, with all the scrappy charm that went with it. Weathered cedar shingles, exterior staircases with indoor-outdoor carpeting, balconies on the beach side with cast iron railings, and metal and plastic furniture. As soon as he'd stepped into the shabby lobby, he'd felt at home—like he and Cape House were old friends.

Sometime since then the hotel had come up in the world. The stairwells had been closed off, the whole building reclad in siding and freshly painted, the trim and windows upgraded and in perfect repair. There was a new wing, too, whose one glass wall exposed a full-size swimming pool. He was pretty sure that if he walked around to the beach side, he'd find well-crafted wood railings and upgraded furniture.

Levi Campbell had grafted a new entrance on the front of the building, and Jax couldn't help but feel that the new-and-improved Cape House was watching him warily to see if he measured up.

Or maybe he still felt like Rich Campbell was watching him and finding him not-quite-good-enough.

He sighed and heaved himself out of the truck, striding up towards the lobby and main office.

Levi wasn't behind the desk—Jax didn't recognize the middle-aged man who was—but the man ducked into an office and Levi came out.

"Walker," Levi said. It wasn't exactly friendly. "You need a belt sander? What for?"

"I don't know if Chiara told you—" Jax felt the weight of Levi's hostile scrutiny, but hid his immediate defensiveness behind the friendliest tone he could muster "—but she and I are fixing up Meeples. Evan's store. I'm working on new built-ins—front counter, shelves, racks—and my sander just died."

Levi's gaze assessed him. "There are some good reasons I shouldn't give a shit about your problems."

He was a big guy; Jax could probably take him in a fair fight, but Jax guessed pissed off big brothers hit extra hard. He gave Levi a tight nod, holding his own temper—he deserved the wrath, after all. "Fair enough."

"But you came through with Dad's loan money, and that meant something to me."

Startled, Jax said, "Oh, Jesus. That." He'd almost forgotten. He'd returned the money Rich had given him when he left town, sent it to Levi with interest and told Levi in a note that it was repayment on a loan. "I owed you that money." He wasn't going to take any credit from any member of the Campbell family for zeroing out that particular ledger.

Levi assessed him a moment more, then seemed to arrive at a decision. "Come with me," he said. He led Jax out a back entrance of Cape House and around to a utility shed. He threw open the door, to display a treasure trove of equipment in a neat workshop. Jax immediately spotted the jointer, thickness planer, circular saw, router—and a couple of belt sanders.

Levi tilted his head. "Whatever's in here is yours to use. You can take a sander with you. Just leave the pneumatic. That's mine."

Jax didn't want to push his luck, but it was the perfect segue. He took a chance. "One thing I need is space."

Levi appeared to think it over, then nodded. "As long as my guys aren't working in here, you're welcome to it. You get out of the way if they need it."

"For sure." Jax bet Levi was a good boss—like Rich had been.

"I'll get you a key. So I don't have to see your ugly mug every time you want in."

Jax wasn't sure if Levi was joking or not, but figured he'd err on the side of laughing.

Levi didn't laugh. "The generosity doesn't extend to my sister. She's not yours to mess with. You had your chance, and you blew it. We understand each other?"

Levi's tone had barely changed. They might still be discussing use of the sander. Which pissed Jax off. Chiara wasn't an object to be bargained over. But at the same time... he got it. From Levi's perspective, Jax had treated Chiara like crap, and Levi wanted to make damn sure it didn't happen again.

Jax nodded. "We understand each other."

Levi was turning to leave when Jax remembered another question he'd meant to ask. "Hey," he said. "You guys still own the house you lived in when I was in high school?"

Levi looked surprised at the change of topic, but shook his head. "Nope. Sold it in the early days when we didn't know how we were going to keep the hotel running. I live at Cape House with Han and Mason. Auburn lives at Beachcrest. Chiara has her own place."

"Sorry about the house, man," Jax said.

Levi shrugged. "The past's the past." And he raised his

eyebrows in Jax's direction, as if to say, *And don't you fucking forget it.*

There was no danger of that.

## 17

On his way back to the shop, the belt sander in the back of his truck, Jax took a detour by the house where the Campbells had once lived.

He turned up the dirt-and-gravel lane, hoping he wasn't about to get arrested for trespassing—but there weren't any other cars in the driveway. He sat, looking at the house. It was a run-of-the-mill Northwest contemporary. Nothing special, but even just staring at it gave him a bad case of feelings.

After Jax had gotten the Cape House job, Rich Campbell had taken it upon himself to turn what could have been another year of drudge and hardship into a pretty decent senior year. Jax had tried to keep his home life out of Rich's view—he tried to keep it out of everyone's view, because the last thing he wanted was for adults to decide they needed to meddle. He knew that was how kids ended up in foster homes. But Rich was a smart guy. There had been enough times that Jax had asked to leave early, or showed up late, or swapped a shift to "help his brother" with something. Jax could make up wild excuses until he was blue in the face, but sooner or later Rich would get the lay of the land.

"You have a lot of responsibilities at home, huh?" he'd asked casually one day.

There wasn't much Jax could say, other than, "Yeah."

After that, Rich's dinner invitations started including Evan. At first Jax said no, because he still didn't trust Rich not to get up in his business. But the Campbells were too great, and it was too tempting to show Evan how a real family lived.

Plus, for Jax, not having to eat dinner with his drunk mother—or worse still, not having to eat dinner while his mother was passed out in the other room—had been a breath of relief in a life packed too tight with responsibilities.

And then there was Chiara.

In the beginning, Jax and Evan had always left promptly after dinner. But once Jax started getting to know Chiara, things changed.

Because once he started getting to know her, he wanted to know her better.

One night, at dinner, he let it drop that he was having trouble with precalculus.

He *was* having trouble. He was so tired at the end of every night that doing his math homework was a joke. He fell asleep over and over again with his cheek pressed against the page. He woke up with pencil imprinted on his skin and drool on the paper. He handed in maybe twenty percent of his assignments on time. He was going to be lucky if he managed a C-.

But he also knew how Rich and his family worked well enough to guess who'd be his tutor if he hinted that he was going to fail math.

"Chiara," Rich said. "You still remember your pre-calc, don't you?"

She snuck a glance at Jax across the table, squinting one eye. She'd sensed a ploy. Which made him happy, too. She was no dummy.

"Yeah," she said cautiously.

"Maybe you could give Jax a little help after dinner."

So after dinner they sat at the Campbell family table, and Chiara eased him through his math homework. With Evan playing happily with Hannah in the living room and the other Campbells making happy Campbell family background noise, pre-calc didn't seem so daunting. And there was no danger of his falling asleep with Chiara that close to him. He could smell her hair. Her arm occasionally brushed his, and every last hair on that side of his body would stand on end. Along with some other things he tried not to think about.

Having a tutor should have made him better at math. And yet he managed, for months, not to improve at all. Once, after he and Chiara were together-together, she said something about being a crappy math tutor and he confessed that he'd deliberately never learned anything so he could keep sitting next to her.

She'd swatted him on the arm. And then kissed him and said she'd sort of hoped he would keep sucking at math, too.

He could ask her if she remembered that.

No, goddamnit, he couldn't. Not after the way she'd reacted to the colored pencils. She obviously did not want to take a trip down memory lane with him.

Speaking of which...he backed out of the driveway of the

Campbells' old house, because getting caught there would be creepy.

Impulsively, he made one more stop on his way back to town.

He had to brace himself for it—the house had been falling down when he, his mom, and Evan had lived there. He'd done his best to keep it up, repainting and repairing trim, doing yardwork, when he wasn't picking up Evan from an activity or taking him to a doctor's appointment. He wondered if the current owners had also let it fall to shit, or whether they were doing a better job of taking care of it.

But when he reached the street where he'd lived, the house was gone. In its place was what Jax could only call a mansion. It loomed over the smaller houses on either side.

You couldn't go home again. He'd heard that somewhere. And it was apparently true.

Not that he would have wanted to. Not to that house.

The Campbells' house, though, had felt like home.

Well, until it hadn't.

He started the truck again. He needed to get the hell back to work so he could get the hell out of town, before he started wishing for things that couldn't be, ever again.

---

## 18

For the rest of Friday, Jax worked in a whirlwind of hammer blows and sawdust, and Chiara stayed as far out of his way as she could, catching up on work for her own business, rearranging Meeples stock, placing orders, and designing social media posts.

By the end of the day, the check-out counter was done, and at closing time, he sent her away to go visit Evan so he could spray paint it without suffocating her. They'd agreed on white with red flourishes—shelves and drawers.

When she came in Saturday morning there was a note from Jax telling her that she shouldn't use the counter, but that it would be good to go by Sunday. He'd built her a temporary stand for the register from the remnants of the old counter.

Her first impulse was to be annoyed, but the counter looked so goddamned cute, she couldn't find it in her. Plus, she didn't need to use the counter, because they didn't get a customer all morning. In the afternoon, a few families drifted in, and Chiara did several hundred in sales. It was great, but not enough for a Saturday.

She'd planned the shop's first event to bring in families, a "Gaming with Kids of All Ages" workshop, for next weekend. She was *really* hoping it paid off, because otherwise Evan would be screwed.

Speaking of Evan, where was Jax? Every time the door opened, she looked up, but it was never him.

Finally it was too much for her. *Where are you?*

It was more than forty-five minutes until she got an answer back. *Building.*

*Are you at Evan's?*

*No.*

*Where?*

Silence.

*Cape House?*

*Yes. But don't come up here.*

*Why not?*

*You'll see it when I'm ready for you to see it.*

*Should I be scared?*

*No. You should be excited.*

That sent a waterfall of tingles down her spine. *Can you send me a picture? Or give me hints?*

*Nope.*

*Jax! I don't like surprises.*

*You'll like this one.*

She thought about defying him, about showing up at Levi's workshop to see for herself, but something stopped her.

Maybe she didn't hate surprises as much as she thought.

Sunday morning, she went to see Evan again.

"When are they springing you?" she asked, setting Shards of Infinity and Innovation, two of Evan's favorite games, on his nightstand.

He frowned. "Things still aren't...copacetic." He made a face. "They think there's scar tissue blockage, so I may have to have another surgery. They're going to do some imaging. But no matter what, I'm not leaving before next weekend."

"Oh, hon," she said, and took his hand.

They sat for a moment, and then she said, "Jax built an amazing counter for the store." She pulled out her phone and showed him.

"Niice!" Evan said. "Man. I gotta get him to show me how to do that while he's here."

"I'm sure he would love to. He's working on other stuff but he won't tell me exactly what."

"Yeah. He won't tell me either. He gets like this sometimes. He really loves surprises."

For some reason, that made Chiara smile.

They played a long game of Shards of Infinity, and Chiara told him about the sales she'd made the day before, and the mom and son pair who'd been in a couple more times. And her newest plans for demos and events.

"I didn't schedule anything out past when I know I'll be around," she said. "I didn't want you to feel locked into anything. And I know that until we turn things around, you can't afford to hire someone to do events. But I have faith you'll feel better by then."

"At least someone does," he said gloomily. He sighed. "Kee. I really don't want to lose so much intestine that I have to have a colostomy bag."

"Oh, Evan," she said, her heart giving a terrible lurch. "I don't think that's going to happen."

"Your mouth, God's ear," he said.

She reached over and hugged him, tight. His beard—now officially a *thing*—was surprisingly soft against her cheek, and he felt strong, despite the time in the hospital. Even so, her voice choked with tenderness. "You're going to be fine, bud."

She went out twice as determined to make the shop work.

After she left the hospital, she went straight to Meeples, hoping Jax would be there, maybe with part of his surprise to unveil—but no. He didn't show up until mid-afternoon—empty-handed. He was wearing paint-spattered jeans and an equally stained t-shirt. There was a smudge of paint on his cheek—white. She wanted to reach up and wipe it away—even though it was dry. Instead, she eyed him narrowly.

"I don't understand," she said. "You're supposed to be renovating the store—"

"And I am," he said. "You'll see."

"So mysterious."

"You aren't good with surprises, are you?"

"I'm *fine* with surprises," she protested. "So why are you here?"

"So suspicious! I'm just here to see how things are going."

"Quiet. Too quiet. My own business has slowed way down because I put marketing on hold until I knew where things were going with Buyathon. I burned through what I needed to do, and now I'm bored."

He looked around the store. "You could read comics."

"I've read them all. Twice."

"You could play a game."

"I'm tired of paying games by myself."

"I could play a game with you."

"Would you?" She didn't mean to sound so shocked, but she was genuinely surprised. He'd said he wasn't a game guy —and even back in high school, he'd mostly sat out Campbell games of Taboo and Scrabble.

"Sure, why not?"

"Want me to teach you the game I just played with Evan?"

"You visited Evan?"

She nodded.

"How was he? I'm going over later."

"He was..." She sighed. "Honestly? He seemed kind of discouraged. And I think he's scared. He said—"

She hesitated, worried she would be breaking Evan's confidence.

"I know," Jax said, and the sadness in his voice and on his face made Chiara's stomach hurt. "He's totally freaked out about where this is going. And the thing that sucks is, they've made these huge strides in immunotherapies, and his insurance won't pay for it."

Impulsively, she touched his hand, slipped hers around his. It was as big and warm as she remembered, and calloused now; she reflexively ran her fingers over a callous and he made a soft little sound that she felt all the way down to her toes.

Oh. Oh, she liked that way too much. She dropped his hand and retreated to where she'd set down Shards. "Here. This one."

They sat at the demo table together. God, this table really *was* small. His knees were so close to hers that she could feel the heat coming off them—and knees weren't even a known heat-generating body part.

She should probably stop thinking about heat-generating body parts.

She dealt the cards, set up the marketplace, showed him how to reset his counters, and taught him to play.

He caught on fast, and in twenty minutes, he was beating her. And crowing about it.

"Seriously, Jax?" she said. "Did you hustle me? Do you secretly come in here at night and practice."

"No. I just have that competitive fire," he said, lining up his cards. "Sixteen attack."

"Sixteen—"

"You're down to five."

"Yes. I can see that."

He beat her handily and wanted to play again, so they did. And then he said, "You need to teach me Terraforming Mars."

"You can't *handle* Terraforming Mars."

"Try me."

So she got out the game. Once again, he was a quick study.

"You don't have to let me win," he said, right around the time the oxygen level on Mars maxed out.

She scowled at him. "I'm not letting you win."

He raised an eyebrow.

"Go to hell, Walker."

"I don't need to go to hell," he said. "I own the red planet!" Then he sobered up. "I'm sorry. I'm being a terrible winner."

That made her laugh. "Can I tell you something?"

"Yeah, of course."

"I don't care if I win."

"You don't—you don't *what*?"

She shrugged. "I don't care if I win. I just like playing."

"Who doesn't care if they win?"

"I don't. I like everything about playing. I like the cards and the game art and the little pieces and setting up and putting things away. I just like games."

He stared at her until the intensity of his gaze made her face hot and she had to look away.

"You know what I think?" he said. "I think you would make an amazing game designer."

For a beat, she let herself entertain the thought—she'd done a lot of play-testing—it wasn't the craziest idea ever. But then she wrinkled up her nose at him. "Are you trying to find me yet another alternate career?"

He shrugged. "No."

"Good. Because I like mine."

He didn't say anything else.

"And speaking of which, looks like you might still be around on Friday when I go for my Seattle interview. You up for holding down the fort?"

"Sure am."

He put another two cards in play, set a greenery hex on the surface of Mars, and sealed his victory. Then he said, "Just don't go into alternate-Earth-building. You're not cut out for it." He regarded his conquest with a smirk. "Also, loser puts the game away."

"You would do it wrong anyway."

But when it came time to clean up the game, he let her instruct him about which pieces went in which bag and didn't even give her a hard time about it.

## 19

He worked his ass off that week, building and painting racks and shelves and tables in Levi's workshop. Occasionally Levi wandered out to check on his progress, and Jax cautioned him—for the hundredth time—not to say anything to Evan. Or, for that matter, Chiara.

"You do great work," Levi said, running his hands over Jax's creations. "I wish I'd had you here when I did the hotel reno. So much shoddy shit, man, I tell you. I could probably give you full-time work for weeks undoing the fucking mess those guys made."

"Thanks, man," Jax said. "But I'm outta here as soon as this is done."

"She knows that, right?"

They didn't have to identify "she" by name. They both knew who they were talking about.

"A, she knows," Jax said. "B, there's absolutely *nothing* going on between us. Swear on—"

Really, he should swear on Levi's dad's grave, but that

would be the height of crassness, and he didn't have it in him. "Swear to God," he amended.

There *was* nothing going on between them, but he had to say that it didn't feel as much like the truth as he would have wished.

Maybe Levi saw it in his face, because he just said, "Don't make me kill you." And then he wandered out again.

Meanwhile, Chiara had been working like crazy in the shop. Jax was finally starting to feel hopeful that between the completed work he was about to spring on her and the work she was doing, they'd get Evan pointed in the right direction. He went down to the shop a couple times a day to recheck measurements, make sure he was going to be able to fit stuff through the door—and—he wasn't going to lie to himself— to see her. It didn't matter whether she was puttering around the store, doing work for her own business on the computer, or chatting a mile a minute with customers, she was like a hummingbird. That kind of constant energy whirring under her skin made him feel more awake. More alive.

He was ten times more productive after he saw her. He got more done in the hour after he dropped by the store than in the two hours before. It was like a drug. They should bottle her.

Plus she was bringing him lunch every day now. Sometimes she brought it up to him at Cape House, but she was respectful of his rules; she knocked and he came out and they walked to the beach to eat. Or she'd text him that she had lunch at the shop and he'd use that opportunity to head over. Often it was something she'd gotten at Tierney Bay Diner, but occasionally it was leftovers from her dinner the night before. She cooked stuff he liked—comfort food—lots of pasta and risottos and stews and chilis, even though it was summer. No salad-y bullshit. He loved it. He loved it way too damn much.

Tuesday and Wednesday, she brought him dinner, too. Because he was working pretty much from sunrise until he fell into bed, exhausted. His breaks were visiting Evan and grabbing food with Chiara.

Then somehow it was Thursday, and tomorrow was the day she was going for her interview in Seattle. And he was close to where he'd wanted to be, but not quite there. But that was fine. He had a plan.

He brought dinner to the shop for the two of them. Because he wasn't an asshole, and as good as it made him feel to let her take care of him, he was never going to be the kind of guy who took that for granted. He had asked Lily, at Tierney Bay Diner, what Chiara's favorite was, and Lily had told him Chiara loved the heck out of a good bolognese and that last year she'd gone nuts for Lily's lamb version. After that, Lily had put some lamb in the freezer, saving it for Chiara's birthday or another special occasion, but she said she'd happily whip it up for Jax to bring to Chiara. And she made him a molten chocolate cake, too. "It's her favorite," Lily said.

Lily didn't ask questions, raise her eyebrows, or make snide comments, and Jax was grateful.

Chiara did go nuts over the lamb bolognese. "Oh my God!" she said. "This is my favorite. How did you *know*?"

"I didn't," he said. "But Lily did."

"Oh, Lily. She is a Tierney Bay *treasure*." She said it through a big mouthful, an expression of bliss on her face.

He was a huge fan of that expression of bliss. He'd seen it in another context a long time ago, and he hadn't forgotten it.

Damn, he was suddenly not hungry at all. Or at least not for Lily's lamb.

"What?" she asked, looking up and catching him staring. She swiped at her face.

"Nothing," he lied.

After she'd demolished the chocolate cake, he drove her home and dropped her off. Then he took the truck back to the workshop, filled the bed, and headed to Meeples.

On the sixth trip, Tierney Bay's chief of police, Alfie Rains, pulled up alongside his truck outside the shop and got out of the patrol car.

"Jax Walker," Alfie said. "Ran your plates. Kept seeing a vehicle I didn't recognize. But I knew your name, and I know your face, now that I see it."

When Alfie was a beat cop, he had once brought Jax's mother home, extremely drunk, from Bob's Tavern. He'd helped her into the house and onto the couch. And then he'd pulled Jax aside and said, in a voice so fierce it had scared Jax almost more than the close call with law enforcement: *You ever need anything, you call me. Not one of the other cops.*

Jax, of course, had made it a personal goal never to call any cop. Ever. Cops were one step away from child protective services and losing Evan.

"Hi, Chief Rains," Jax said.

"What are you up to? And can I safely assume it's with your brother's knowledge? And/or Ms. Campbell's?"

"You can."

Alfie took a look in the back of the truck, then came

around and leaned near where Jax was standing. "That's nice work."

"Thanks." Jax said. "I appreciate it."

"You turned out okay." He didn't say, *despite everything*, but they both knew it.

Jax laughed—a short, humorless laugh. "Guess I did."

"And your mama?"

"She's doing better," Jax said.

Alfie nodded, tight and knowing. "Glad to hear it. I'll let you get back to work."

"Can you maybe—?" Asking a favor of the chief all these years later made his belly tight with remembered shame, but he didn't want to risk ruining the surprise. "Can you not let the Campbells know I'm here tonight? This is a surprise for Evan and Chiara."

Alfie thought about that a minute, looked from the contents of the truck to the new sign above the shop. "Yeah. I think I can do that." Then he surprised Jax by extending his hand for a shake. "Glad to see you back here, Jax."

"Glad to be here, Chief."

He realized, watching Alfie turn the car and spin away, that it was true.

## 20

C hiara was having a beast of a time concentrating.

It was probably because she was now on her fourth—or was it fifth?—interview of the day, part of the lineup Buyathon had prepared for her second round of interviews.

First, she'd met again with the Buyathon CFO, the guy who would be her boss if she got this job. His name was Greg Pepper. He was thirty-five-ish, with a neatly trimmed beard, a man bun over shaved sides, slim fit pants, and a button-down with rolled sleeves. Chiara had liked him right away when she'd met him two weeks ago. And this time, he welcomed her like an old friend.

He set her up in a conference room overlooking Lake Union—dotted with boats and sparkling in the Seattle summer sun—and led a succession of finance team employees in to meet with her. Somewhere around the third interview, she'd lost her edge, and her focus. She'd managed to answer all their questions, but her mind kept wandering.

She wanted to blame the gorgeous view outside, but the

truth was that she was thinking about Meeples. And Evan. And Jax. She was worrying that whatever Jax's surprise was, it wasn't going to be big enough to save Meeples. And she didn't know what she would do if she had to deliver that news to Evan.

Not to mention that she thought her own heart would break if the store had to close.

Even though she was probably moving to Seattle. If she didn't blow this interview.

"Chiara?"

The COO had apparently just asked her something, because he was looking at her impatiently. Well, *shit*. She needed to concentrate.

*Pull it together, Kee.*

It was her dad's voice, pushing her to ignore distractions so she could succeed—as he'd always wanted her to do. If he were here, he'd tell her to keep her eyes on the prize and nail this thing to the wall. *Stay strong. Swat unhelpful thoughts away like mosquitoes.*

She sat up straight. "I'm so sorry. Could you repeat the question?"

"You describe yourself as detail-oriented—tell me what that means to you."

She winced at the irony of zoning out in the middle of that question. It was a softball, and she had a hundred stories she could tell. She chose her favorite, about how she'd caught an invisible two-cent error that had repeated itself enough times to cost a client nearly six thousand dollars.

She thought of Jax, giving her shit as she rearranged the Terraforming Mars game pieces. No one who'd watched her do that would question her commitment to detail.

She wondered what would happen if she told *that* story.

She didn't think the COO would be impressed.

At the end of the interview session, Greg Pepper came back to wrap up the day. He chatted casually with her for a while, then threw her a zinger.

"Tierney Bay's an awfully beautiful place to live," Greg said. "Why would you leave it for Seattle? Especially when you've got a pretty cushy gig, working for yourself? What if I'm a cruel taskmaster?"

She'd done her homework on that last point. "A friend of a friend of mine—Damien Howers—worked for you at Meridian, and he says you're smart, funny, and the kind of boss who would throw yourself under a bus for your employees."

He raised an eyebrow. "That last part is probably an exaggeration. Maybe a Segway scooter."

They both laughed.

"But seriously," he said. "I wouldn't leave Tierney Bay, ever, if I had a job that let me live there."

*Go for it, Kee,* her dad said. *You've got this.*

"I've always wanted to work for a big company. And I'm not going to lie. I'm ambitious. I promised myself as a little kid that I'd be the CFO of something one day."

He grinned. "Funny that," he said. "I promised myself I'd be the CEO of something one day. And I respect ambition in my people. Damien probably told you that, too."

She smiled. "Sure did."

"Did he say I had good coattails?"

"He did."

"Sounds like we'll get along very well," he said. "There are a few more people we need to you to meet, but unfortunately,

August is a rotten time for hiring, and getting them lined up might take a few weeks. Are you in a hurry for a decision?"

She shook her head.

"I'm guessing we'll be able to call you within two weeks to set up the final round of interviews."

"Perfect," she said.

They chatted for a bit longer, and then he showed her out, promising to call "with news" as soon as he could.

*That's my girl!* said her dad's voice in her head, as she climbed back into the driver's seat of her aging VW Passat and pulled out of the parking garage. *Strong work!*

"It couldn't have gone any better, could it?" she said out loud.

*I'm so proud of you.*

He would have been, too. She knew it to her soul. She wished—so much—that she could call him right now. Or better yet, drive home, find him, throw her arms around him, and tell him all about it.

Her eyes filled with tears. The adrenaline that had propelled her through the interview now slowly leached out, and she leaned her head back against the seat, suddenly almost too tired to move.

It was going to be a long drive home.

She cranked her psych-up playlist, pulled herself together, and backed out of the parking space.

## 21

J ax didn't leave the shop, except to get food, from Thursday at dinnertime all the way through closing on Friday.

The trickiest part was Friday during store hours. He did everything he could to keep the disruption to a minimum during those hours. And when customers wandered in, he made them collaborators, explaining the situation and making them promise not to post anything about Meeples to social media or mention anything to the Campbell family. A few seemed confused or irritated, but most of them thought it was cute and were excited to be in on the secret.

He wanted to make them sign a contract in blood so no one would spoil the surprise.

He couldn't wait to see Evan's reaction to the shop. His brother was long overdue for news to celebrate. The idea of being the one to put a smile on his face was reason enough to work overtime.

But Jax knew he had another reason, too.

Chiara.

He wanted to see her face when she saw the shop. He wanted to watch her eyes light and her expression open up. He wanted her to look at him like he'd performed a miracle.

*Walker, you're screwed,* he thought.

Luckily, he had hours and hours of backbreaking work to distract him from his own idiocy. Although it didn't staunch the flow of memories. Something about being back in Tierney Bay, about spending time with Chiara, had unleashed them, and they were coming thick and fast now.

Like the night long ago when SuperJax met SuperKee, for example.

It had been a bad week. Evan had been sick, and the doctors had been trying—again—to figure out what might be wrong with him. Jax had barely made it to school that week, because Evan hadn't been able to go to school, and their mother—

Well, she had been waking up in the late afternoon and having a mimosa. Or a Bloody Mary. She'd actually explained to him that a Bloody Mary was a good breakfast because it had vegetables in it, and no sugar.

She'd tried to hug him but her breath smelled of Clamato juice, and he pulled away.

That week, between work shifts and what school he could manage, plus shopping and cooking to try to entice Evan to eat, Jax was exhausted. He hadn't been able to accept any of Rich's dinner invitations, and Chiara hadn't been at Cape House during his shifts.

But this afternoon, Chiara was working in the Cape House lobby and Jax was drawn straight to her. He drifted over to where she was working and even though he knew he couldn't pull out a chair and sit down—Rich was a generous boss, but not that generous—he knelt on the floor and leaned on the table and said the thing that set the world in motion.

"I want a superhero, too."

She raised both eyebrows. "Okay." She tugged her notebook close. "Does he look like you?"

"More or less," he said. "Bigger shoulders. More muscles."

"I like the way you look," she said. She sounded like she was kind of teasing him, because that was what he'd said to her. But the way she was looking at him wasn't teasing at all. She was staring at him. Not just his eyes, not just his face, but all of him. He wasn't sure a girl had ever looked at him, like that, like she liked what she saw. It made him hard, which made every useful thought go out of his head. He had to look away.

"They should have an adventure," Jax said, to fill the awkward silence that followed.

She was still looking at him. Her eyes were very big and her cheeks were very pink and he wondered if their eye contact just now had messed her up, too.

That thought did *not* help with the brain fog.

She dug into her backpack and pulled out her notebook and her pencils. She set them out, opened to a blank page, and said, "What kind of adventure?"

"What does SuperKee do?"

"Anything I wouldn't do," she said promptly.

"Like what?"

"Skip school. Deface public property. Smoke pot."

Jax laughed, a short bark of surprise.

"Yeah, I know. None of that probably sounds like an adventure to you."

He shrugged. "Not so much. I skipped school Monday, Tuesday, and Thursday this week. I've probably skipped more school than I've attended. And when I was in Virginia—we've moved around a lot. I've never lived a single place more than two years."

She was watching him. There was no judgment in her eyes, just curiosity.

"My mom gets herself tangled up in things. Or screws stuff up. And she gets antsy. She doesn't like sorting things out. They get messy and she runs. Finds a new place to live."

He could tell she was having trouble understanding. The Campbells, they were people who would stay and clean up their messes, no matter how ugly or complicated. But still, there was no judgment in her eyes, which made it easy to keep going.

"Anyway, I guess it was a couple of years ago, we were in Virginia. My mom was still with Evan's dad. He wasn't a perfect guy, but he had a good effect on my mom. She sort of held things together, and he always had a job. And then...I don't know, he met someone else, and moved to France. That was when my mom got bad, and I did, too, for a while." He sighed. "Until I figured out no one was going to take care of Evan if I didn't. Anyway, during that time, I did all kinds of stuff. Spray painted the side of a school, shoplifted, ate my weight in pot gummies, stole my mom's liquor. And then one day I came home really late. It was after midnight. And Evan was awake and watching TV. There was a crime show rerun on and it was really violent. He was four, and he was scared— big eyes, tears running down his face, but he was just sitting there, like he didn't know what else to do. My mom was passed out in a chair. And I don't know, I just kind of knew.

That I had a choice to make, and I was going to be making it for both of us. Evan and me. So I pulled it together." He grinned. "I did still miss a lot of school."

"Not for fun, though."

"No," he said. Her sympathy carved out a hollow spot in his chest. "Not for fun."

She just looked at him for a while with those vivid blue eyes. Then she sighed and turned back to the blank page. "SuperJax and SuperKee need to have an adventure that's an adventure for both of them."

"What if they solve a mystery?"

She pursed her lips. "Okay." She thought for a moment, then began sketching.

Jax's shitty pre-calc teacher got murdered and SuperKee found the dead body. Chiara drew it for him—the classroom, Mr. Mueller's body draped over his desk, the murder weapon a blackboard pointer. SuperKee, distraught, in the doorway of the classroom, laying eyes on the slain teacher.

She bit her lip while she drew. Her eyes were bright and her breath came fast, like she was—

He made himself unthink that. If he thought about her that way, then he would want to kiss her (even more than he already did), and if he kissed her then she would have expectations for him, and if she had expectations for him there would be another thing in his life that he would be responsible for. And he would drop a ball, and it might be her.

And she did not deserve to be a dropped ball.

"Okay. So then what happens?" she demanded.

"SuperKee starts investigating."

She was drawing again, sending SuperKee and SuperJax fingerprinting, DNA testing, and interviewing through the halls of the high school. He found himself leaning in closer to see. A strand of her hair tickled his cheek. She smelled like apple pie.

Jax wanted to push the strand behind her ear. He wanted to bury his face in her hair to find out if that's where the apple pie smell was coming from.

He was a breath from doing it, when something caught his eye and he looked up to see the kitchen clock.

"*Shit*," he said. "I was supposed to get Evan fifteen minutes ago."

Right. That was why he was not supposed to get distracted by Chiara's hair or cinnamon scent or drawings. Because he had responsibilities.

He left her sitting at the table, absorbed in the drawing. As he went out, he wanted to tell her, *Wait for me. Don't draw it without me.*

But he didn't. Because leaning over the paper, sketching as fast as she could, she looked vividly happy, and he didn't want to take that away from her.

Now, ten years later and in the game store, Jax leaned against the wall beside one of the comic book racks and rested his head in his hands.

*Something had taken away her joy, though, hadn't it?* he thought, as he finished toggle-bolting the last of the game shelves into the wall. She didn't draw anymore. Even though he'd seen the longing in her face as she'd looked at those colored pencils.

For that brief time in high school, something had given her space to be herself. But over time she'd shaped herself back into the mold her father had laid out for her. Had Jax's leaving thrown that switch, pushed her to clamp down on the parts of herself that didn't check boxes or toe the line? If so, it was another sin he'd lay at his own feet. And Rich Campbell's, too.

If he told her the truth, would it set her free again?

For a moment, hope scrabbled at the door. Then he shook himself and reset.

No. It might set *him* free, but he wouldn't take that freedom if it would cause her pain. No way.

He looked at his watch. It was getting late, and he hadn't heard anything from Chiara about how her interview had gone. Not that he'd expected a blow by blow. Maybe he'd text her and ask for an update.

He reached for his phone.

## 22

Well, this *sucked*.

Ten minutes ago, in the middle of an unexpected summer downpour, the acceleration in Chiara's car had suddenly gone wonky—like the power had just dropped out from under her as she was going 55 miles per hour. A moment later, a wisp of white smoke seeped out, like fog, from under the hood. One glance at the temperature gauge told her that she wasn't imagining things—it was climbing rapidly toward the danger zone.

Panicked, she pulled over to the side of Highway 101 and tucked the car as best she could onto the tiny shoulder, overlooking a drop-off into a forested gully. The wind was whipping around and the car shuddered a little. So did Chiara.

She called AAA and waited a long time as the rain lashed the windshield. Finally they came and towed her to a garage in Aberdeen—twenty minutes out of her way, on top of everything else. Her driver was a tall, thin man named Joe who had four daughters under the age of six and said that the only time it was quiet was in the truck.

They didn't talk much after that.

The garage was just closing for the weekend when they got there.

"I'm sorry, sweetheart," said the garage owner, a petite woman named Jess in coveralls and a ponytail. "Pretty sure it's a blown head gasket. Not a tough fix when I'm in the shop, but we're closed on the weekend—and even if I wanted to help you out, this weekend I've got to move my mother-in-law into a nursing home. I can have it ready for you by the end of the day Monday."

"Can I drive it back to Tierney Bay as is?" The car hadn't ever died completely, so *maybe*?

The garage owner shook her head. "Nope. Sorry. Not unless you want to be looking at a hell of a lot more expensive repairs."

"God, no."

"You *could* get it towed. If you've got the long-distance towing option on your AAA, it's covered—?"

Chiara shook her head.

She took a deep breath. She was two hours from Seattle and two hours from home, but she wasn't in the middle of nowhere. Aberdeen was a decent-sized town with shops, restaurants, and hotels. She'd spend the night, get one of her siblings to pick her up in the morning, then have another sibling drive her back on Monday or Tuesday to retrieve her car. Not fun, but—well, as she frequently told herself, life was what happened while you were busy making other plans.

Her phone told her there was a hotel within walking distance—not likely to be a pleasant walk, considering the weather, but she had grown up walking the Oregon coast beaches in rainy fall, and she wasn't going to let a summer storm get the best of her. She called the hotel and made a reservation, then, assured of a place to sleep, she turned her attention to food.

"Where should I eat?" she asked Jessie, who was lingering to make sure she was taken care of for the evening.

"There's a great Italian place a block over."

After thanking Jessie for her time and help, Chiara headed that way, got seated, ordered a plate of spaghetti and meatballs, and pulled out her phone to text Jax.

*Can you cover the shop tomorrow morning, too? Stranded in Aberdeen—car troubles.*

The text came back right away. *What???*

*Blew a head gasket. The car did, that is.*

*LOL. That sucks. Where are you?*

*In an Italian restaurant. I have a hotel room.*

*I'll come get you.*

*What? No!*

*Sure. It's not that far.*

*It's two hours!*

*Whatever, I like driving. Evan's good—I just saw him. Give me your address and stay put.*

She didn't reply right away. She was struggling with herself. It would be so nice to sleep in her own bed tonight. She wouldn't have to drag one of her siblings all the way up here to get her. And she'd be able to open the shop herself tomorrow morning.

But she'd have to spend two hours in the car with Jax.

Disturbingly, that didn't feel like a "con." It felt like a "pro." Which was the best reason of all for her to spend the night in a hotel.

*I'm fine. Don't come.*

It took five minutes for him to reply.

*I'm already on the road. You can text me the address whenever you get a chance.*

She wasn't going to tell him to turn around. That would be—

*Prudent,* said the practical side of her brain.

*Ungrateful,* said the other half.

She didn't tell him to turn around. She texted him her address. And, *Don't text and drive.*

*I won't.*

She rolled her eyes, laughed, and called the hotel to cancel her reservation.

Two hours later, almost to the minute, he texted her from the front of the restaurant. She dashed out and climbed up.

"Hey," he said. He was wearing a tight black t-shirt that featured a picture of a hammer, with the caption underneath, "This is not a drill."

She was tired and frustrated and cold—she'd never really gotten warm again after her long wait on the side of 101. The restaurant had been chilly, and she was bare-legged under her pencil skirt. The truck was warm and he was—beautiful. His hair looked like he'd been running his fingers through it all day. It was speckled with sawdust, and his strong jaw sported two-day's scruff.

And of course he was such a good guy. How many guys would make a four-hour round trip to pick up a stranded friend—if he even thought of her that way? In her experience, not many.

She wondered if there were people in his life now who took care of him the way he took care of other people. There hadn't been in high school—or not, anyway, until her father had semi-adopted him.

He had soaked up every ounce of care and love that Rich and Maggie had bestowed on him. And when he'd finally let Chiara love him—

Loving him had been the most gratifying thing she'd ever done. No one had ever made her feel like her love was such a gift.

She shoved down the wave of longing that washed in with those memories.

"How'd it go?" he asked.

She hesitated. "You really want to hear the whole story?"

"Why wouldn't I?"

"Other people's job interview stories are maybe a little bit like other people's dream stories."

"We have two hours," he pointed out. "No shortage of time for stories."

So she told him. About Greg Pepper, the executive suite members, directors, and managers she'd met, including the CTO who'd mumbled his way through the interview until she'd stumbled on the magic question, about local brew pubs, and then he'd come to life and given her an in-depth guide to Seattle's beer scene. She told Jax about the conversations she'd had, and that she thought she'd made a good impression. She didn't tell Jax about the moment with the COO, when she'd lost her focus. That had been a fluke, and she'd gotten back on track. "I'm, like, ninety percent sure they're going to call me for a third interview."

"And you want that."

He sounded so damn *doubtful*. "Yeah. I do. Why do you keep doing that?"

"Doing what?"

"Making it sound like you think I'm making a mistake."

He took his eyes off the road long enough for her to see the flash of green. "Because the way you talk about this job isn't—"

He stopped.

She should let it go. He didn't want to finish the sentence, and probably, she didn't want him to finish it. But something wouldn't let her drop it. "Isn't *what*?"

"I've seen you. When you're excited about something."

Her body reacted to that as if it were a come-on, but she knew—could tell from his tone of voice—that he hadn't meant it that way. He meant something else. Something *more*.

"In the shop, even. Getting excited about the plans. You were all lit up. You were so into it. Doubly so when you have a pencil in your hand."

She didn't want to talk about how she was with a pencil in her hand. It was too close to the heart of what mattered.

"Do you remember SuperKee?"

Of course she did. But why the hell was he doing this? He was the one who'd walked—no, run—away from what they'd had, so how dare he bring it up?

But yes, she remembered.

He glanced her way again and saw it on her face.

"You were so sure you wanted to study math or accounting or business, but then you'd draw SuperKee and you let her be whoever *you* really wanted to be. And that made you more you."

Her heart was pounding.

"I don't know what you're talking about."

"I think you do. No. I know you do."

The night that came back to her was in late winter senior year. It was one of the nights that Jax and Evan had come to dinner at her parents' house, and then stayed afterwards for the bullshit math tutoring he'd engineered. Which she hadn't called him out on, because she'd wanted it, too. She'd wanted to sit next to him in the kitchen while her mom and dad washed and dried the dishes—the homey memory of the two of them brought tears to her eyes, but that was nothing new, and she brushed the tears away.

So there they'd been, in the Campbell kitchen, side by side at the table. His body had given off heat like a furnace. She'd figured maybe it was because he was all muscle and it chewed through calories every minute of every day. Certainly he ate like several grown men and still had zero body fat.

She'd been able to feel the heat even when he was six inches away. She could smell laundry soap and deodorant and something musky and personal that was *Jax*.

Her parents had dispensed with the dishes and gone into the living room. Shortly after that, she and Jax had finished up his math homework, and he'd pushed back his chair, ready to round up Evan and go home.

And then he turned back.

"Who was the girl that SuperKee was standing on?"

"What?"

"In that picture in your notebook, she knocked someone down and was standing on her chest."

"No one. Just a girl I hate."

"What did she do?"

"She said something shitty about Mason."

Jax nodded, like that required no further explanation, which—she liked that. There was no more unforgivable sin, in Chiara's book, than going after her younger brother, who would not speak to defend himself. "So, like, she does stuff for you that you wouldn't do yourself."

She hadn't really put it into words, but that was exactly it. "Yeah."

"She's *brave* you."

"Yeah, I guess." She blushed. It was true, but it also felt like too much, him knowing that. So she said, "And SuperJax is brave *you*, right?"

For a second, she thought he was going to deny it, but then he said, "Yeah. So what?"

"What would he do that you can't do for yourself?"

She met his eyes. His eyelashes were ridiculously long. His bottom lip was soft and full. His eyes were green, but with streaks of gold and amber. And he was tired. There were big circles under his eyes and a gray slackness that she associated with her parents when they'd been working too hard to keep the hotel afloat.

"Maybe not things I can't do," Jax said. He sounded as tired as he looked. "Things I don't want to do. Vacuum. Mow the lawn. Empty ashtrays. Clean up around the toilet when someone throws up and misses."

Her chest hurt.

"Carry my mom to bed when she passes out."

Her chest hurt *bad*. Like really bad.

He kept looking at her, which was how she understood that he was *telling* her this. He was telling her through Super-Jax, just like she'd told him about Mason and the girl who'd called him something cruel.

Jax was ticking things off on his fingers now. "Take Evan to the doctor. Do my homework when I'm too tired."

She couldn't help herself. She reached out a hand and touched his arm. As she'd known it would be, it was a million degrees, even through his flannel shirt. She felt the heat travel all the way up her arm. It filled her whole body.

She wanted more of it.

But instead she took her hand away and opened her notebook to a fresh page.

"What happens next?" she asked. "In their adventure?"

Because it felt far, far easier—and safer—to imagine that than to ask herself what was going to happen next in the Campbell kitchen.

Or, now, in the present, in the truck, hurtling along 101. There were a lot more than six inches between them, but she thought she could feel the heat of his body anyway.

"You were different when you drew," he said. "You were so happy."

"We were just kids," she said. "We were just fooling around."

He shook his head. "No."

He was quiet for a long time, and she almost thought that was it. That he'd said what he was going to say, and they'd moved on. But then he took a deep breath, and she saw his hand grip the wheel, tight enough that his knuckles flared white.

"Maybe we were just kids, but we weren't just fooling around."

He looked at her, long enough that the car wavered, briefly, on the road, before he fixed his eyes forward and said:

"We knew exactly what mattered."

---

## 23

After he dropped Chiara off at her house, he went back to the shop. He thought he could finish up in another three or four hours of work. He even made himself place a call to Chief Rains. "I'm going to be in the shop until three a.m. again," he said. "Mostly painting, so I don't think noise will be an issue, but just in case someone sees the light on—"

"Thanks for letting me know," the police chief had said, no muss, no fuss.

Jax hung up the phone and poured paint into his roller tray, started working the big wall behind the front counter, the one that he'd hoped Chiara would turn into a mural. He should just fucking leave her alone already.

Except he *couldn't*.

Despite what he'd more or less promised Levi, the past wasn't just the past. He'd made sure of it. As long as he was in Tierney Bay, what he'd done was going to creep around him like a ghost and make it impossible for him to forget.

One night, during the spring of senior year, Jax and

Chiara were sitting at the Campbell kitchen table. Evan was playing with Hannah, and Maggie and Auburn and Mason were in the living room watching the first season of *West Wing* on Blu-Ray. Rich had gone back to Cape House to grab some paperwork he needed.

They were supposed to be working on Jax's pre-calc homework, but Jax's brain felt sluggish. He'd erased and rewritten the same problem three times already, and the paper was starting to wear thin in that spot.

It didn't help that the day had been unseasonably warm for March and Chiara was wearing shorts and a tank top. Most of her was bare, soft and pale—the white flesh of her inner thighs and the lightly freckled curves of her shoulders and upper arms.

He wanted to know if the skin was as soft as it looked.

"I've been thinking," Chiara said. She'd opened the sketchbook when he wasn't paying attention, and she was doodling something.

He leaned over to look.

"What if something bad happens to SuperKee and SuperJax has to rescue her? Like, she figures out that it's Mr. Barker, the chem teacher, who offed Mr. Mueller, and she has proof. Fingerprints, or whatever."

"DNA," Jax offered.

"DNA's good. She has his hair, or whatever."

"And he knows she has it."

"Yeah. And he gets her to stay after school for something, and then he has a syringe with some evil concoction in it and he's got her trapped in the chem lab—"

She started drawing. The chem lab took shape, with SuperKee tied up against the gas hood.

SuperKee's proportions had changed since he'd first seen her. The new SuperKee looked an awful lot like Chiara herself—lean and athletic, with perfectly proportioned curves that would feel just right under Jax's hands. There were ropes around her ankles and around her wrists, and Jax wondered exactly how messed up it was that he liked them there.

"SuperJax knows something's wrong. She said she was going to meet him for coffee, and she's never late. Plus he has a sixth sense with her. So he shows up at the school. Everything's locked up, so he breaks a window."

Chiara drew it: SuperJax, his shirt wrapped around his fist, going after one of the windows in the science wing. "He knows it has to be Barker."

Under Chiara's pencil, SuperJax overpowered Barker and knocked him unconscious.

"He runs over to where she is. He's breathing hard, he's bruised and bloody and his hair is all messed up," Chiara said.

He waited for her drawing to catch up. She took a long time over SuperJax, and sometimes she looked at him while she was drawing. He liked that best, when she stared at him for a long time and then drew SuperJax, looking too perfect to be human. Because then, just for a second, he could believe that was what she saw.

She was looking at him now, her eyes moving over his face in a way that made his breath freeze.

"When he sees her like that, he realizes how worried he was for her. And he realizes that if anything ever happened to SuperKee, he—"

"He wouldn't be able to stand it," Jax said. He just knew

that was how the sentence ended. Because they were both there, inside the story. That was how it worked.

He could hear Chiara breathing. "And he realized, right then," she said, "that he was in love with her."

Jax froze. Or, his outsides froze. Inside, everything was super-heated and rushing, and he couldn't catch his breath.

"So he didn't even wait to get her untied. He just stepped in, and—"

Jax finally recovered the ability to move. He reached over and took the pencil out of her hand. "Kee," he said.

She slowly turned her head. Her pupils were huge. She bit her lip. It was like watching someone bite into a peach; his mouth watered. Her gaze fell to his mouth. He set the pencil down and leaned toward her.

"Chiara," a voice said. "That doesn't look like homework."

It was Rich, standing two or three feet away. Jax couldn't make out his expression. Concern, and—anger? He'd never seen his boss angry.

Chiara closed the notebook and pushed it away. "Sorry," she said. "I got off track there for a bit."

She didn't look at Jax when she said it.

"'Distraction wastes our energy, concentration restores it,'" Rich said. "Sharon Salzberg." His eyes moved from Chiara's face to Jax's, his frown intensifying. There was something in his eyes, some message that Jax couldn't read—but he was pretty sure it wasn't anything good.

"Sorry, Daddy. I was—we were—"

"It's my fault," Jax said quickly. "She was working, and I distracted her."

A small twitch moved through Rich's mouth, but it wasn't

laughter. Jax felt a chill. "Well," Rich said. "Back to work with both of you."

His voice was cheerful, and he'd turned and walked away.

The whole interaction was almost nothing, but Jax felt, somewhere in his gut, that it wasn't.

Just because nothing had happened—nothing that you could point to or record or photograph—didn't mean the world hadn't changed.

## 24

He wanted the timing to be perfect. So he got to the shop before Chiara the next morning and intercepted her outside the front door.

She looked so damn good, her hair around her shoulders like a cape, smiling all the way up to her eyes at him. And in her hands, she held something that he was pretty sure was food.

"Is that—?"

"Lily's French toast."

"I would have gone with you to get it fresh there."

"Another day," she said, shrugging. "I couldn't get myself up early enough."

He let himself imagine them waking up together in the morning—then squashed the thought as flat as a pancake. That was not ever going to happen. He'd made sure of it.

She tried to get past him to the door, but he blocked her.

"I have something to show you," he said.

"Am I finally going to get to see what you were working on?" Her face lit up, eyes bright, cheeks pink.

God, she was going to kill him.

"Yup."

There was still work to be done. He hadn't been able to get all the painting done. There were a few areas where the carpet wasn't down. There was no art or signage on the walls ... But you could see the bones now of the new shop, the shape of it. He'd set the games in their shelves and the comics in their racks. You could see the finished product like a photographic image rising on an old Polaroid.

And really, it was the tables that he wanted her to see most. The rest had been her design, her vision; he'd only executed it. But the tables ...

He finally opened the door and let her in.

Her mouth opened as she looked around. Her eyes got huge.

"Oh, my God," she said. "This is—amazing." She took a step forward, to one side, then the other, like she didn't know what to touch first. Finally, she set the French toast down on the front counter and went to the racks, touching the comics displayed there, then to the shelves. "Oh, my God, Jax, it's so beautiful—it's better than I even imagined."

Then she spotted the tables. "Oh. Oh, wow." She hurried over, reached out and stroked the surface of the wood, and he felt it like a caress.

The new tables were bigger than the old ones, and each one had cutouts in the surface to hold game pieces, and shelves underneath that would slide out to make extra room for individual player's boards, cards, and other fiddly bits. He showed her how the shelf pulled out, and she put her hand to her mouth. Her eyes filled up with tears.

"Jax. I—I *love* them."

It was the tears, or his name on her lips, or the soft gratitude all over her face that did him in, he thought later.

She turned toward him. Her eyes were full of that thank-
fulness and amazement, and he could see that she'd forgotten
that she was supposed to be careful around him. She was
going to hug him, and he was going to let her.

She came into his arms, and she was the same combina-
tion of strong and soft that had totally wrecked him ten years
ago. She smelled exactly the same, too.

Holding Chiara, he was overwhelmingly, almost painfully,
aware of how alive she was. How her heart beat and her
blood rushed and her body was filled with the energy that
made her Chiara. Every time he'd ever held her like this, his
body had instantly reacted to hers, like two voices finding a
shared pitch. Right now was no exception. His heart thun-
dered, his blood pulsed, and his body was about to make it
abundantly clear how much he wanted her.

She'd gotten very still in his arms.

She felt their connection, too. He knew she did. He knew
her stillness as well as he knew her liveness.

Her head came up in slow motion, her face tipped toward
his, her lips parted in welcome. All he needed to do was
lower his head, and he'd catch her mouth in the sweetest,
hottest kiss ever.

His body craved that kiss so much, a fierce ache.

*It's a terrible idea.*

*I don't give a shit.*

He could feel her breath on his lips when sudden aware-
ness moved through her body. A subtle change. The temperature dropping. Her lips were gone, her face tilted away, and

then she was stepping back, reaching up to smooth her hair into place.

Putting everything back in order.

He opened his mouth to say her name. Plead with her, maybe, but just then a shadow passed in front of the game shop door and the bells jangled and the moment was lost.

## 25

She was shaking all over, if she was honest with herself.

Because he'd brought her vision almost perfectly to life. Everything she'd seen—the shelves, the racks, the paint colors, the new carpet—and things she hadn't been able to imagine, like those beautiful tables.

He must have been working every waking hour when they weren't together. Laboring with her vision—with her—in his head.

And then—

His body against hers had been the best thing she'd felt in years. Hard and warm and supple, the flex of muscle against her clothing and her skin.

She'd registered a longing so fierce it had knocked common sense straight out of her head. She'd only recovered a functional brain cell at the very last minute, just before they'd hit "oops" and "I'm really sorry" territory.

Because that's what it would have been. A mistake. Obviously the chemistry between them was alive and well, but that didn't mean she had to fold like a cheap fan.

Thank *God* she'd nipped that one in the bud. So, so many reasons that sucking face with Jax would be a bad idea. One, he was leaving town any minute now. Two, *she* was leaving town any minute now, assuming she got her dream job. And three, the last time she'd kissed Jax, she'd ended up with a broken heart.

So. Catastrophe avoided. Doomed kiss averted. And here they were, eating French toast.

They had helped their customers find a copy of Machi Koro, wrapped the board game for a birthday present, and sent them on their way, and then they'd sat at the new demo table with French toast, even though it made Chiara super nervous. But Jax said it would be fine; he'd deliberately varnished the tables to within an inch of their lives to withstand all manner of sticky kid touching. "Maple syrup will wipe right off."

"How did you do all this? I literally don't think there are enough hours in the day." She swept her arm out to indicate everything in the shop. New racks, new shelves, the counter he'd already built, which she understood now was the one thing too big to transport from Levi's workshop to here. And the tables, which every time she looked at them made her chest hurt, for reasons she wasn't sure she could even put into words.

"I didn't sleep much," he admitted. "Which was partly to get it done in time and partly because it was so damn much fun. More fun than I've had in years. It felt like—"

He clammed up, then.

What had he been about to say?

"It felt good. And doing something for Evan felt super satisfying."

Right. *Right.* For *Evan.* She was glad he'd said that, glad he'd reminded her of the fundamentals of the situation. If only he'd reminded her before she'd tilted her face up to his like a flower turning toward the sun—but you couldn't have everything.

"He'll be out tomorrow," Jax said. "I'll bring him in here and show him."

"He's going to love it," Chiara said. "He's going to be crazy about it."

And it would also mark the end of this—this weird, awkward, wonderful, crazy period of her and Jax collaborating. And then he really *would* leave. "Are you going to take off once he's home from the hospital?"

He shifted uneasily, one foot to the other. "Yeah. I'll stick around a day or two to get him settled, make sure he's okay, then head out. I have to get back and start things up down there, or I'll be behind on my next project."

And she was supposed to be glad of that. She was supposed to be glad that he was going to take his attractive, denim-clad, tool-belt-garlanded ass out of her field of vision, so she could stop doing stupid things that would eventually land her in a world of hurt.

"Did you get this done today, on purpose, so it would be finished for the 'Gaming with Kids of All Ages' workshop?"

He nodded.

"You're amazing, Jax Walker."

He was looking at her in a way that made her throat hurt and her chest tight and, yes, she would admit it, her low belly achy. So, of course, she looked away.

She finished her French toast and got up and tossed out the take-out box. And when she looked back at him, he was focused completely on his food.

"I'm going to set up for the event," she said.

"Let me know if you want my help. If I won't mess with your genius."

She smiled at that. "I'll yell if I can use newbie assistance."

---

## 26

The event was a bust.

Not from the perspective of the people who attended. The four families who participated had a great time. One came with an eighty-year-old Grandma and two teenagers. One with four kids, ages three through fourteen. The other two had two kids each, but widely spaced in age. She'd definitely identified an important audience—people who couldn't get all their family members together at one game table without a world war breaking out.

And she found games for all of them—like, the family with the eighty-year-old Grandma and two teenagers played Taboo—and Grandma was, hands-down, the reigning champ. She sent every family home with games.

It wasn't enough, though. Evan needed more people in the store.

She was going to figure this out. Somehow.

First, though, she had a date with Auburn, Willa, and Vannah to go dress shopping. Willa had convinced her friend Erin Mackey, who owned Bay Boutique, to keep her shop open for a couple of bonus hours so the four of them could look for dresses.

As she walked into town, she found herself desperately wanting to tell Auburn what had happened—or, well, *almost* happened—with Jax.

She had almost kissed him. She still couldn't believe it.

The longer it stayed true, the more she couldn't stop thinking about it—his arms around her, his breath brushing across her face, the expression in his eyes. Lust, yes, but something else.

If loving Jax had been the most rewarding thing she'd ever done, being loved by him—

She couldn't let herself think about it, because it wasn't an option.

Only Auburn understood both pieces—how much Jax had meant to her, and why she couldn't let it happen again.

Which also meant that as much as she wanted to tell Auburn the story, she was also scared of Auburn's reaction. Her sister could be fierce when one of her siblings was in danger, whether emotional or physical, and almost kissing Jax was definitely danger territory.

She was suddenly so glad that she'd roped Willa and Vannah into the evening, because with them there—and Erin, too—there was at least a passing chance that the subject of Jax would never come up.

She stepped inside the shop to find all her girls already there. Her heart leapt to see them together.

Willa had clearly taken care of introductions. She and Vannah were standing with Erin and Auburn at the front desk, sipping wine, chatting animatedly. The shop had a breezy, open vibe, even as the sun was setting outside, with white walls, light wood, and muted, gorgeous colors. Erin had pulled all her dresses onto one rack for them and wheeled it next to the fitting rooms, which were curtained, with pretty beaded tiebacks.

The door of the shop was propped open, and as she entered, she could hear that Willa was asking questions of Auburn a mile a minute—when had she bought Beachcrest and what changes was she making and how was inn ownership? Willa said that she had sometimes wanted to own an inn herself, but she wasn't sure she wanted to quit her job at the North Coast Gazette—it was true it paid shit, but she loved being at the center of things. Auburn was eating up the attention, Vannah was sipping her wine and munching brie on a cracker, and everyone was happy.

Auburn glanced over, saw her, and called out her name. Everyone looked up, gave her warm smiles, and folded her into hugs and greetings.

"Oh, Chi*ahhhhhhhra* ... " Vannah sang out. "Is there something you'd like to tell us?"

"No?" Chiara attempted. But she had a bad feeling she knew where this was going.

"Jax Walker is back in town."

Auburn's gaze flashed to hers—alarmed and sympathetic. "He's not back in town," Auburn told Vannah. "He's just *in town*. For a very short visit."

Having her sister on her side made Chiara able to catch her breath again. She shot her sister a grateful look, and Auburn telegraphed back, *Gotcha, babe.*

"And you didn't think that was maybe a fact you should mention to Willa and me? As reunion planners? Or, say, your *friends*?" Vannah crossed her arms. She didn't look hurt or mad. Just schoolteacher stern, and her voice was *definitely* amused.

"There's nothing to tell."

Willa and Erin were looking back and forth from Vannah to Chiara to Auburn, clearly starting to grasp that something was up.

"That's not what *I* hear," Vannah said brightly. "*I* hear he spends all his time either up at Cape House or at his brother's shop—where, as we know, you are currently working."

"He was building stuff for the shop."

"Yeah?" Vannah teased.

"She doesn't want to talk about it," Auburn said fiercely, looping an arm around Chiara's shoulders. The affection and support made tears burn behind her eyes.

Auburn's tone had gotten through to Vannah, who looked stricken. "Shit," Vannah said. "I put my foot in my big mouth, didn't I? I knew things didn't end the greatest, but I didn't realize—I'm sorry. That was insensitive of me."

"I thought I was over it," Chiara admitted. "But it's apparently still a sore spot."

"Just ignore me. I can be so oblivious."

All four women were looking at her with soft eyes. And it wasn't that Chiara had wanted to keep this a secret from her friends. It was more like she wanted to talk about it so badly that she knew she shouldn't. Like, if she opened her mouth, it would all come pouring out.

So of course, she opened her mouth.

"His being here has nothing to do with me. He's building for his brother. Who's in the hospital. It's his brother's shop, you know? And he just wants to fix it up for him. With, like, new shelves and racks and tables and stuff. And paint and flooring. And I try to stay out of his way—"

They were all listening sympathetically.

"Not so easy, huh?" Willa asked gently.

And that was it. She cracked. "God, no. It's not. He's right there in the shop, and he's being unbelievably nice. And he's *hot*, like all shirt-off and tool-belt and—gah! He's built all this amazing stuff for the shop. You should see the tables. They're gorgeous. And then Friday night my car broke down on the way back from Seattle—"

Auburn's eyes got huge. "You should have called me!"

"I—"

They were all watching her.

"I didn't want anyone to have to come get me. I was going to just stay over and wait for the car to get fixed. But I texted Jax because I needed him to watch the shop on Saturday...."

"He gave you a ride?" Auburn hazarded.

Chiara nodded, biting her lip. She took a deep breath. She might as well get it all out there.

"AndthenthismorninghealmostkissedmeandIalmostlethim."

"What?" Willa asked.

But Auburn appeared to have heard perfectly well. "Oh, honey."

"I didn't. I didn't kiss him."

"That's—good?" Willa said uncertainly.

"Yes! It's good that I didn't!"

They were all looking at her.

"What happened after you didn't kiss him?" Auburn asked.

"I pretended nothing had happened. I'm going to keep

pretending it never happened. Forever. And he seems perfectly happy to go along with that."

Auburn closed one eye. "Sooo much easier said than done."

"It's just stupid lust!" Chiara discovered that her voice had risen in pitch, and she hastily tamped it back down. "It means absolutely nothing, and it will only cause trouble."

"How can you tell it's just stupid lust?" Willa asked. She sounded genuinely curious.

"I can tell the difference between stupid lust and real emotion."

"I'm glad someone can," Willa muttered.

Auburn swept a hand through her curls, which were—in a rare move—unbound and wild around her face. "I've never met someone who actually can. People claim they can. But they turn out to be wrong. Usually in the thinking-it's-lust-but-really-it's-more direction. Especially if there's history," she said pointedly. "Because sometimes I think stupid lust is your body's way of telling you that there's some real emotion in there. Sometimes I think your body knows first. Or, you know, your snake brain. That deep-down part of you that's smarter than all the thinking you can do."

Chiara sighed. "Well, whatever part of me it is that wanted to climb Jax Walker like a tree, it wasn't a smart part. It's the stupidest idea I can imagine. I mean, let's get real. Who'd be dumb enough to give someone a second chance after what he did to me?"

Auburn nibbled her thumbnail. "Mmm. What happened to 'past performance doesn't indicate future results?'"

"Romance is *not* finance," Chiara said.

Auburn smiled wryly. "No. No, it is not."

"Seriously. I'm turning over a new leaf. Starting now. Well, starting, technically, right after I didn't let him kiss me. No more letting him drive me around. No more admiring his—"

"Forearms?" Willa suggested.

"Shoulders?" Vannah proposed.

"Racks?" Auburn said innocently.

"Can we please talk about something else?"

"Yes," Erin said. "I've got some beautiful dresses for you ladies to try on."

It was a very effective subject change, mainly because Erin's dresses were gorgeous. And there was something for everyone—an adorable cap-sleeved wrap dress for Auburn's curves, a mermaid sheath for Willa, who was tall enough to pull it off, and a full-skirted dress with sweetheart neckline for Vannah, who looked adorable in everything.

Chiara tried on six dresses before she found one she loved. It was a periwinkle blue empire-waist, delicately beaded.

Willa gasped gratifyingly when she came out of the dressing room.

"That's the one I'd pictured for you!" Erin said.

"It reminds me a little—" Auburn stopped. She surveyed the dress from top to bottom, and then her gaze landed on her sister's face.

"What?" Erin asked.

"My prom dress," Chiara said, waving it off. "It's really nothing like it. Maybe the color. And the beading."

"And the fabric," Auburn whispered.

"I always tell my customers, we know what we love," Erin said. "I have people who literally, every time I get a gray sweater in stock, buy it, then come in the next time and laugh at themselves and say, 'I always buy gray sweaters!' We buy what we love, over and over."

"I did love that dress," Chiara said. "Whatever happened to that dress?"

"I think Mom consigned it that fall," Auburn said. "Along with all our homecoming and Sadie Hawkins dresses."

That would have been one of the last things she'd done before she died, then.

"She loved that dress, too," Auburn said.

The three of them had gone shopping together, and when Chiara had tried it on, her mother's eyes had gotten big and bright. "Oh, Kee," she'd said. "It's *perfect*."

Chiara's eyes found Auburn's. Auburn's were filled with tears, and Chiara felt her own flood. Auburn reached out and clasped her hand, and Chiara hung on tight.

"She almost didn't consign it. But I convinced her to. Because it had bad memories attached to it."

"But here it is. Back in our lives anyway."

"It's not the same dress," Auburn said pragmatically, but Chiara could see her wavering.

"I know, but..."

Neither of them finished the thought, but Auburn's face softened, tears overflowing, and Chiara knew her sister was thinking much the same thing that she was, that if the dress *could* have been resurrected, their mom would have wanted her to have it. To wear it and enjoy it and redeem it from the bad memories.

Chiara went back into the dressing room, took off the dress, hung it up, and put her own clothes back on. She was tying her shoes when Auburn spoke from behind the thick drape.

"Can I come in for a sec?"

Chiara pushed the curtain aside and Auburn sat on the small soda fountain chair in the corner. She shifted uneasily. "I'm feeling like kind of an idiot, but I never really thought until now about how much you lost that year. More than any of the rest of us. Jax, and then Mom and Dad. All at once."

"Jax didn't die," Chiara said. But even as she said it, her throat tightened, and a memory came back to her. Lying awake in her bed and realizing that she would not have known if Jax *had* died. And even though he had broken her heart, she was overcome with grief that she could not even be sure that he was still in the world with her.

Back then a world without Jax had still seemed like the worst thing the universe could throw at her.

It wasn't until months later that she understood how much bigger grief could be. And even so, when her parents died, she remembered that night in the dark and knew that Jax's leaving had trained her for this new, infinitely worse loss.

"No. But he abandoned you. They—they all did. Not that Mom and Dad meant to. But—that's what happened. And you didn't despair. You put one foot in the front of the other and you were there for me. For all of us. So I just want to say —I think you're amazing. Brave."

Chiara discovered that she couldn't speak. There were tears running down her face and her throat was clogged with remembered pain.

"You guys okay in there?" Erin's voice rang out from beyond the curtain.

"We're fine," Chiara said, gathering herself.

"I'm sorry. I didn't mean to make you cry," Auburn said. She was crying, too.

Chiara laughed through her tears and swiped them away. "You called me amazing and brave. Of course I was going to cry."

"I love you." Auburn opened her arms.

"I love you, too."

They clung to each other for a long time. Then they tidied themselves as best they could and brought the dress out front for Erin to ring up.

Willa and Vannah were waiting for them at the register, and they graciously pretended not to see the tear streaks and red eyes, which made Chiara love them even more than she already did. "You guys want to see some photos of what I've got in mind for decorations?" Willa asked.

"Yes!" Chiara and Vannah said at the same time.

Willa pulled out her phone and opened Pinterest. "What do you guys think about this?"

The photos she'd pinned were beautiful—gold and cream, with fall-themed centerpieces. And the decor was simple, too—a lot of impact from just a few touches. "I love it," Chiara said. "I know someone who might be willing to help, too. She's a wedding planner, but I think she'd know how to get some of this stuff for cheap—or she might even have some stuff we could use." She was thinking of Grace Utrecht, who'd done a couple of weddings at Cape House. Admittedly, Grace and Levi hated each other, but Chiara thought she could work out a deal with Grace that didn't put the two of them in each other's paths.

Vannah tilted her head. "So if Jax is in town, does that mean he's coming to reunion?"

Chiara had a moment of sharp panic before reality settled in. "He'll be long gone by then."

Which would make the reunion dance an awful lot like prom—except this time, she wouldn't be heartbroken and crying in a bathroom stall.

"Too bad," Vannah said. "Bad timing."

"No," Chiara said, remembering. Remembering how she'd had to hold handfuls of silk up off the bathroom floor, how her makeup had run, how the night that was going to be the best of her life had turned into the worst. The last thing she needed was Jax, anywhere near another high school dance. "It's great timing."

## 27

He drove Evan from the hospital straight to Meeples.

Evan refused his help getting out of the car, even though he looked, to Jax, exhausted. He walked up the short front path and stopped to admire the new sign.

"I friggin' love it," he said.

"Chiara designed it."

"She's good. But you burned it, right?"

"Sure, but that's the easy part."

Evan rolled his eyes at that.

"What?"

"You never take credit for anything," Evan said.

"I take credit when I deserve credit."

"You do *not*."

"I take credit for what a great kid you've become."

"Well, that's just bullshit," Evan said. "I'm the only one who gets to take credit for that."

"Touché," Jax said, grinning. "Close your eyes." He

stepped in front of Evan and opened the door of the shop. He wanted to see his brother's face when he first looked inside.

Chiara was behind the counter, tapping on her laptop. "Is he here?" she demanded.

"Yup."

Evan stepped in behind him. For a split second his expression didn't change at all, and Jax was terrified that he'd made a mistake.

Then Evan burst into tears.

Chiara ran out from behind the counter and they each got on one side of him and guided him to a seat at one of the tables. They sat next to him and let him cry for a while. Evan managed to form some words—all of gratitude—but mostly he just babbled, emotions too big for speech. And Jax *totally* got it. For one thing, Evan hadn't cried at all, to his knowledge, the whole time he'd been in the hospital, even though he'd lost a sizable chunk of his very valuable small intestine. But for another, Jax felt like he was going to cry himself. Everything in his chest was just way too big for the space he'd allocated for it.

Which was maybe too small, all things considered. Because between Chiara's reaction and Evan's, he felt like his heart had grown several sizes.

"You guys," Evan kept saying through his tears.

When Evan stopped crying, they made him stay in his seat while they gave him a verbal tour of the shop. It was mostly Chiara, really. She explained everything that Jax had built and why he'd done it. She showed him how the table shelves pulled out and told him about the storage behind the front counter. Then she explained about the events she'd planned.

"Holy shit," he said. "You guys—I can't—I can't even."

Apparently, he meant it, because he didn't even try to start another sentence for a few minutes. Then he said, "I feel like I don't deserve this."

Chiara's eyes met Jax's. "You know what, Evan?" she said. "I don't think most of us ever feel like we deserve the good things. But those good things came to you, despite that. They're yours to accept and carry, same as the bad things."

That made Jax's chest feel even less adequate to the size of his feelings. But it seemed to resonate with Evan. He said, "Okay," like what she'd said made perfect sense to him. And then he sighed, like she'd eased something in his heart.

Which in turn eased something in Jax's.

One thing he'd loved about her, back in the day, was that he hadn't felt so much like he was alone in taking care of Evan. She and her family had loved Evan with him, and that had made it easier. Not that Evan was a burden. But—

It helped, having other people care for Evan, too.

And he didn't doubt that Chiara adored Evan. You didn't do all the work she'd been doing as anything other than a labor of love.

Unfortunately, it might not be enough.

What neither of them had said to Evan—but it hung between them in the air, like something slightly rotten—was that it wasn't working. Yesterday's event had brought in sales, but not enough. Today's traffic had been no better than two weeks ago on a Sunday, despite all the publicity Chiara had been trying to generate.

He hadn't wanted to say it to her, but he'd started to wonder if maybe the shop was just in the wrong place. Too secluded, back behind town, too off the beaten track. Walk-ins just weren't seeing it.

Regardless of why business wasn't improving as much as they needed it to, neither of them wanted to break it to Evan right now. It was too much, too soon—and maybe Chiara, like Jax, was hoping that things would still magically turn around. Or that one of them would have a brilliant idea. Labor Day weekend was still two weeks off.

It was suddenly occurring to Jax that maybe he wouldn't be here to see the payoff of all their work.

And shit, that felt all wrong.

Evan looked exhausted. Totally wiped out.

"Want me to take you home?" Jax asked.

Evan looked around the store, then shook his head. "Can I stay here for a little while?" he asked.

Jax couldn't bring himself to say no, not when he knew exactly how Evan felt.

## 28

Monday morning, Chiara and Auburn went and got her car in Aberdeen. On the drive there, Chiara brought Auburn up to date on all the details she hadn't shared with their friends the day before, and Auburn told Chiara how things were with Trey. Short version—good. Long version—Chiara felt a twinge of jealousy as Auburn told her just *how* good.

Auburn had resisted becoming involved with Trey for a long time, but then she'd given in, and look how well things had turned out for her....

Which was *not* a good argument for stupid lust. It was *not*.

Chiara had to repeat it a few more times to herself before she felt convinced.

Twelve hundred dollars, a new head gasket, and a lot of wincing later, the sisters headed back to the beach in separate cars. Chiara listened to Freakonomics podcasts so she wouldn't be tempted to imagine the kiss that hadn't happened.

That afternoon, after they'd both made it safely back to

Tierney Bay, Chiara got a call on her cell from Greg Peppers at Buyathon. He was in a great mood. She had been dragging her ass around all afternoon, thinking about the store's still-flabby sales and the fact that Jax was going to leave. Soon.

"Greg!" she said, trying to sound like a call from him was the high point of her day. Because it should have been.

"Auburn!" he said back.

He'd make a great boss. They'd work together well. Buyathon was supposed to be a fair employer—not perfect, but always trying to improve things for workers.

She was trying to talk herself into something she already theoretically wanted. What the hell?

"So here's the thing. I need you to meet two more people. I literally cannot get them into the same space before Labor Day, and I need to finalize this hiring decision no later than the first week of September because I really need y— whoever we hire—to start work before we get too much further into budgeting season."

He wanted to give her the job. That much was clear.

"Can I convince you to do these last two interviews by teleconference?"

She already knew she was going to advocate for herself to work occasional days or even weeks from Tierney Bay, so this fit her plans. If she was flexible with them about meetings, it was more likely they'd be flexible with her.

"Of course," she said.

"I'll try to get those set up for this week or, at latest, next. Good?"

"Great," she said.

They hung up and she sat, her phone still in her hands.

The door of the shop opened and Jax walked in. His expression was grim.

"You okay?" she asked.

"I'm fine."

She raised her eyebrows. "You sure?"

"I don't want to talk about it."

"Okay." She went into the storeroom and set herself the task of unpacking some of the new shipments. She tried not to feel hurt by the fact that he didn't want to talk to her. Sure, they were friends of a sort now, but it didn't mean it was a good idea for them to start unloading on each other.

After a moment, he came back and said, "Hey. I'm sorry."

She shrugged without looking at him. "It's fine."

"No. It's not fine. I was a dick. I just—I didn't want to tell you, because it doesn't cast me in the greatest light."

She looked over. His shoulders were slumped.

"Does it make you look like more of an asshole than leaving town and ghosting me?" she asked.

A wry smile crept over his features. "Probably not."

"Then why sweat it?"

"Excellent point." He took a deep breath. "I had this idea. I thought I could maybe get a loan. To tide Evan over, to give him more time. Past Labor Day. And, I don't know, I thought if it was big enough, maybe it would help him get the immunotherapy, too. So I went around to the banks here. And then, for completeness' sake, I called all the banks in Bakersfield, including the one I got the loan from to start my own business." He shook his head. "I should have known."

"Known—?"

"I'm borrowed out. I'm on track to repay, but I'm maxed at

the moment. And game stores aren't great bets, even when their owners aren't eighteen," he said.

She took a deep breath. She'd known from his body language where the story was going, but she was still disappointed. A loan hadn't occurred to her, but when he'd mentioned it just now she'd thought it was a good idea. A great one, even. It would give Evan just enough time to pull things together.

"We could try a Bootstrapper," she said. She dropped into the chair next to his.

"A what?"

"When my sister was trying to raise money to save Beachcrest—long story—she did one. Like a Kickstarter, just a different platform. People give you money for whatever—a business idea, a medical procedure."

"I guess? I mean, that feels a little like charity to me."

"It's *not*," she said. "It's people investing in you."

His body language had closed down again, his shoulders curved inward.

"But that's not what this is about, is it?" she asked gently. "Not about the money."

For a moment she wasn't sure he was going to respond. Then he took a deep breath and said, "No. It really busts my hump that I can't take care of Evan the way I want to." He took a deep breath. "I've always believed, you take care of your family. And after all these years, I'm still not in a position to be able to give my family a leg up." He raked a hand, hard, through his hair; it stood more on end than usual and gave him the look of a young, good-looking mad scientist. "It kills me, Kee. That as hard as I've tried to do better than where I came from, I just...can't."

"No," she said. The whole time he'd been talking, conviction had been rising in Chiara. "No, that's just not true. You would *never* walk away from his obligations like your father and your mother both did—"

But she stopped short. Because as the words were coming out of her mouth, she heard them. And apparently he did, too, because he ducked his head as if he were ashamed.

Of course, that was exactly what he had done. Maybe she hadn't officially been his obligation. Maybe she hadn't been family or his, explicitly, to take care of. But they both knew that he had promised her with his words and his body, in every way an eighteen-year-old kid knew how, that he would be there for her. And then he had disappeared.

"Jax," she said, her eyes steady on his. "What the hell *happened*? Why did you leave?"

## 29

The day had worn badly on him. No matter how strong you thought you were, it was hard to ask for money, and even harder to get rejected. And asking for loans had always given him a bad taste in his mouth, even the garden-variety ones he knew were practically an American rite of passage—car, home, business. Over the years, each time he'd taken out a loan, he'd heard Rich's words in his head.

*Build a life for yourself. Figure out how to stand on your own two feet. Take care of the people in your life.*

And then he'd come in here, thinking he'd be able to hide his frustration and bad memories from Chiara—but why the hell should that be true, when he'd never been able to keep anything from her? Except by fleeing town, of course, like the last time.

Still, he hadn't meant to blurt out so much, and he *definitely* hadn't meant to lead them here, to her question: *What the hell happened? Why did you leave?*

His chest hurt, like the secret inside it was battering to get out. And he guessed, after all those years, it probably was.

She was waiting so patiently, too, listening like she'd listened when he was spinning out stories with her, when they were inside each other's heads, bringing what they referred to as the Adventures—SuperJax and SuperKee's story—to life.

He would tell her. Not all of it, but whatever he possibly could without violating his promise to himself.

"My mom started dating that guy. Stan."

She nodded. And her face got the look of someone who smelled something *off,* which was exactly what Stan had been, although they hadn't known it immediately.

Two weeks after the kiss-that-didn't-happen in the Campbell kitchen, Evan had thrown up blood and landed himself in the hospital. And Jax had been the only one home, so he'd been the one to ride with Evan in the ambulance. Because he was eighteen, they'd let him sign the admittance forms, although they gave him such a hard time that he'd spent the entire night terrified that child protective services was going to appear at any moment.

The person who *had* appeared had been Chiara. He'd sent her a text letting her know he was at the hospital with Evan—and that was all it had taken to bring her to his side.

Jax was sitting on the chair next to his brother's bed, watching him sleep, when Chiara walked in. He was so glad to see her that he couldn't find any words except, "Hey."

"Hey." Chiara pulled a chair up next to Jax's.

"You okay?" she whispered.

"Sort of? They're saying he's going to be fine. They think they know what's wrong, now."

"Yeah?"

"They did a million tests, and they're still waiting on some results, but they think it's Crohn's disease. It's a bad thing to have, but it's better to know that that's what it is." He didn't tell her what else he'd found out. That Crohn's patients paid an average of twenty thousand dollars a year for medical treatments.

He was trying not to think about it. It was the only way he could stay sane.

"I'm glad he's okay," she said.

He looked over at her. She was so beautiful. Her hair was pulled back in a messy bun and her eyes were worried, but she was so pretty that it felt better just to look at her. Which felt wrong in its own way. His brother was sick, and maybe he shouldn't be allowed to feel so goddamned happy to see her.

He thought maybe he should tell her it would be okay for her to go. Or that he was glad she was there. But he still couldn't really say anything at all.

She didn't seem to mind. She sat down next to him. Just sat. But it was miraculous how big that felt. Someone there, next to him.

They were silent, listening to the beep and hum of the machines in the room and the bustle of activity in the hallway.

"Where's your mom?"

He shook his head. "I don't know."

He was completely sure that if Chiara or one of her siblings was in the hospital, her parents—both of them—would be right at their side. She had the perfect family. But she didn't say anything. She didn't judge and she didn't pity. She was just *there*. And he was so fucking grateful he couldn't stand the feeling. It was bigger than his chest. Bigger than his whole self.

"She's an alcoholic," he said quietly. He'd told her that a thousand different ways, but never straight out.

"I know," she said. Then, firmly, "She'll show up."

She reached out and took his hand.

Hers was warm and surprisingly strong, and as soon as their fingers touched, a sigh slipped out of him.

"Kee."

"Uh-huh."

"Will you stay a little while?"

"Of course."

He turned to look at her. She was looking back at him with those big, blue eyes, which were trying to tell him something. Or ask him something; he wasn't sure. All he knew was that he wanted to tell her *Yes*. Yes to whatever it was she wanted.

Her gaze dropped to his mouth, and need rushed through him. He needed her. He needed her mouth. It was wide and soft, her lower lip thicker than the upper. Her tongue came out, just for an instant to wet her lips.

He wanted—

He wanted.

He was very aware of the distance between their chairs. It was getting smaller. He was leaning toward her. She was leaning toward him, too.

And then he was kissing her, and even though there were so many more things than he could have guessed that were wrong with the world, everything felt exactly, exactly right.

AFTER THAT NIGHT at the hospital, there was no turning back, of course. And there were so many more kisses that followed that first one, and then after the kisses there were other things. Her hands in his hair, under his shirt, on the bare skin of his back, on the smooth ridged skin of his belly. His hand, when she guided it there, on her breast. His amazement and gratitude.

And many more pleasures in the days and weeks after that. They were together. They were a couple. People at school knew. Maddie and all Chiara's brothers and sisters knew.

Rich knew. And that was the only thing that cast a pall over Jax's outsized happiness. Because although Jax could not point to any behavior on Rich's part that had changed, *something* had. Rich had cooled toward him, ever since that night when he had caught Jax and Chiara almost kissing in the kitchen.

Invitations to dinner came now from Chiara, not Rich. And where once Rich had sought Jax out for almost any job that needed doing, Rich mostly gave those jobs to a new hire these days.

"He doesn't like it," Jax told Chiara, one night, early on.

"Who doesn't like what?" she asked. They were lying together in the bed of Jax's truck in the parking lot of an abandoned mill. They had kissed until Jax's mouth felt bruised and swollen.

"Your dad doesn't like that I'm dating you."

"Why do you think that?"

"It's the way he looks at me."

She shook her head. "If he didn't want me to date you, he

would have told me that. He doesn't pull punches. He's the most honest guy I know."

"You sure?"

"Positive," she said. "You're just feeling guilty because of *this*."

She indicated them, the two of them, alone, in the dark, what they'd been doing.

He shook his head. "Nope. Not feeling guilty. Not at all. You?"

She was quiet for a moment. "No. No. It's funny. I feel—I feel free. I feel more me."

Chiara had said a lot of things to him over the last few weeks. She was generous with words. She told him how much she liked him. How much she liked his hair, his eyes, his hands, the muscles she touched through his flannel shirt and t-shirt and then under his shirts, her hands on his bare skin. She told him she loved being with him.

But of all the things she'd said to him so far, *I feel more me* was the best. Because if there was anything he wanted, it was to give her the same sense of freedom and possibility she gave him.

"Me too," he said. He rolled over and touched his mouth to hers again. And—he forgot to worry about Rich, or anything else.

Sometime during the weeks that followed, Jax's mother started dating Stan, but Jax's attention wasn't on Stan. It was on Evan, who needed more doctor's visits and different kinds of foods and lots of new rules. And on Chiara, who he wanted to be with every second of every day. He wanted to touch her and kiss her and touch her again and in different places, all the places she invited him to—while he marveled at how she touched him back, generously and without fear. When they weren't touching, they were together, working on the Adventures. Or they were planning for prom night and later that same night, when they would be alone together in a hotel room.

He just wanted to be with her, because—and he knew this even though he had no idea *how* he knew it—he was in love with her.

"I was so into you," he said out loud into the quiet of the empty game shop, and saw her whole face go soft and bright.

He wanted to kiss her so bad.

But he also wanted her to know what had happened at his house, while he and Chiara were busy being consumed by their feelings for each other.

He was up and out of his chair then. Pacing. He couldn't sit still, not for this story. It was bigger than him, bigger than his skin could contain. "I had no fucking idea what my mother and Stan were up to, you know? And then the next thing I knew he'd moved in, and he was around all the time. And then—"

He stopped, faced her. "Before I tell you this, I need to say something."

She nodded.

"Evan told me I should tell you this. He wanted you to know."

She shook her head, clearly not getting it, but he needed to get the thought out. It was Evan's story, Evan's suffering, and Jax would never tell anyone without Evan's permission.

"He—Stan—was touching Evan—touching him." He held her gaze. Swallowed. "And getting Evan to touch him."

Her face went gray, bloodless. "Evan," she whispered. "Oh, God, Evan."

"I know," he said, closing his eyes. "He was *eight years old*."

He remembered the look on Evan's face when Evan had finally told him. The guilt. The confusion. He would never forget that look. Never.

"He begged me not to tell anyone. That's why I didn't tell you then."

Jax had been able to convince Evan to let him tell Rich. He'd pushed because he'd known how much his little brother needed an adult ally.

And this was where Jax had to tell his story very carefully.

He opened his eyes.

"I wanted to go to the cops. But I knew—or thought I knew—what would happen. Maybe Stan would get arrested, but maybe he wouldn't. But for sure, child protective services would get called in. And if that happened—it wouldn't take very long before they figured out that my mom was a not-very-functional alcoholic."

"You didn't know where Evan would end up," Chiara said. Very quietly. Very gently.

All he could do was nod.

"I needed to take care of him. I needed to make sure he got into counseling as soon as he could. I had to get him out of there, Chiara. I had to get us out of there."

Her eyes came up and held his. And held and held. "Of course you did," she said quietly. "Of course you did."

## 30

"God, Jax—I—I wish you'd told me."

He was standing, turned slightly away from her, his whole body crooked away from her as if to protect himself. But when she said that, he turned back. He looked, suddenly, much older than twenty-eight. Old, wise, and sad.

"I couldn't tell you," he said. "Evan made me promise not to, and nothing in the world was going to make me break that promise."

It was funny what could turn your world upside down. Someone leaving. Someone telling you why he'd left.

He looked drained, like it had taken everything out of him to tell her. She stood and moved toward him, reaching out a hand and then dropping it at the last moment. She very much wanted to touch him—stroke his arm or his shoulder, pat his back—but she was a little afraid of herself right now. So she sat still, simply sat still, and let everything settle around her.

"It was smart. Leaving. And brave of you. You were eighteen, but you knew what you had to do."

He gave a short, harsh laugh. "Well. I don't know about that. But once it was in my head, the idea of leaving felt like absolutely the only possibility. We had to get far enough away that it wouldn't be likely that Stan would follow us. Since he owned a bar in Seaside, I didn't think he would."

"Does he, still?"

Jax shook his head. "I kept track of him, obviously. He was killed in a drug-related shoot-out three years ago. The bar closed after that. I don't think Evan would have come back here if he were still alive, no matter how nostalgic he was for his year of Campbells."

"You think that's what brought Evan back here? Us?" The thought hadn't even crossed her mind. If it had, she would have invited Evan to a lot more family dinners.

"What else would it be?" Jax asked. "It was just one of many places we lived before Bakersfield. He was reasonably happy in Bakersfield. So why here?"

"Because it's a good place for a comic and game store?"

"Is it?" Jax asked, eyebrow raised. "I can think of about thirty West Coast locations I would have tried before this one."

She had to admit, he was right. But the idea of Evan coming all the way to Tierney Bay because of what he'd experienced in the Campbell household...

On the other hand, she knew what his other "home" had been like, and with the addition of this new piece of info, she could understand why the safety and warmth of her childhood home might have held special appeal.

Tears pricked her eyes. For Evan, at eight. And for Jax, at eighteen.

"You're a really good brother."

He shook his head, hard. "I let him down, Kee. It was the only thing I *could* do."

"*You* didn't let him down. Stan abused him. That's not on you. It's on Stan. You got him out, you got him counseling—"

He didn't try to argue with her, but she could see he wasn't convinced. She wondered how big a piece of the puzzle that was. Was Jax still trying to atone for what he felt like he'd done—or hadn't done sooner?

"So," Jax said quietly. "That's why we left."

"Thank you for telling me," she said. "Now I understand."

Except he hadn't just left. He had disappeared.

Maybe now wasn't the time for this question. She could ask it later. There would be another time to probe what had happened after he'd taken Evan to safety.

But he must have seen it on her face.

"You want to know why I ghosted you. After—what—"

His eyes met hers, and she felt the truth of that long ago night pass between them, so real it made her shiver.

They had agreed to have sex for the first time after prom. She had booked a room at an inn further south along the coast, and he had driven two towns over to buy condoms so rumors wouldn't spread among their family and friends. She'd planned everything exactly—candles, music, new panties and bra.

He'd teased her, as he often did, about her need for planning and order. "Making a list and checking it twice," he said. "Make sure you put 'feel good' on that list, Kee. Wouldn't want you to forget that part."

She swatted him.

And then two weeks and a few days before prom, they'd driven to their favorite parking spot in his truck, and they'd curled up in the back together, drawing, storytelling, and talking. And then kissing. Brief sweet kisses that turned into long, deep, begging kisses. She was pure joy that night, absolute freedom. She didn't think of anything—not the Stanford acceptance on her desk, not what would happen next year, not who she might become some day. Only who she was, right now, fully in her skin. Her joy was hungry. She wanted more of him. They were touching. Hands desperately seeking under clothes. Bodies clinging together, rubbing through clothes, his breath harsh against her ear, against her lips. Her skirt pushed up so she could feel the rough denim of his jeans through just the thin layer of her panties. She unbuttoned him, freed him, and then—it was pure impulse—she said, "Let's do it. Right now. Let's not wait."

"But you have a list."

"Screw it."

He got very quiet. "Kee. I don't want this to be something you regret."

She shook her head. "I won't. I promise. I've spent my whole life making plans and checking items on a list. I don't want to be that girl tonight. I want this to be different. I want this to be just about us. I *love* you, Jax."

It was the first time she said it, but it didn't feel hard to say. It felt like the most elemental and obvious truth. Not saying it would have been a hundred times harder.

He looked at her intently, thought about it, and then nodded, like he knew. Like he knew exactly what it meant to her to throw out the list and the rules. How big she felt right then, too big for her own skin. She needed space inside his, too.

"I love you, too," he said, pulling her close, kissing her like he wanted to stamp the words deep into her, and her whole body felt giddy with it. Then he drew back. "We can leave one thing on the list," he murmured. "*Feel good*."

And then he slid his hand under her panties and got her all wet and ready. He got one of the out-of-town condoms from the truck's glove box, and he rolled it on, showing her so she'd feel safe. They made love right there in the truck in the dark, cool, late spring nighttime air, as close as it was possible to be, all the space they could make for each other, all the joy and freedom and possibility. They kept on most of their clothes, and they groped and fumbled and laughed and tried again. It was absolutely perfect. Way more perfect than any hotel room and all the candles and music in the world.

She felt like her life was starting.

He held her till he had to take her home. When he dropped her off, he said, "You okay?"

"Way better than okay."

"I don't want you to regret it. Or feel bad about it. I know you had a plan."

She shook her head. "No regrets. It felt so good to throw out the plan. It felt so so good."

He leaned over and kissed her. For a long time. No more words.

She touched his face one more time, got out of the truck and walked into her parents' house.

That was the last time she saw him for ten years.

She'd waited a decade to ask this question:

"I understand why you didn't tell me why you were leaving. But what I don't understand is why you ghosted me."

*What I don't understand is how you could ghost me* after what happened between us that night.

She didn't say it aloud. She wasn't ready to make herself that vulnerable, not yet.

At eighteen, she'd formed her own theories: because he hadn't loved her, because he'd gotten what he'd needed from her and moved on, because it hadn't been good for him like it had been for her. Because she wasn't good at it, because she wasn't what he wanted, because she wasn't worth sticking around for.

She didn't want those to be the reasons, but maybe they were.

Later, with the help of friends and family, she'd been able to layer a *fuck you* on top of those fears and worries. Only a dick would have ghosted her after that. He wasn't worth her heartbreak. He didn't get to tell her how to feel about herself.

Now, everything she'd thought she knew dropped away. Waiting for him to answer felt like the longest minutes of her life. For a moment she wasn't sure he *was* going to. Then he said, "I know this sounds like the biggest bullshit answer of all time. But you have to believe me, Chiara. I had my reasons, and they made sense to me at the time. And you have to believe me about this, too." His eyes, the greenest she'd ever seen them, pleaded with her. "I regret it so much, now. You can't possibly know how much I regret it. If I could take back one thing I've ever done, it would be letting you think that night didn't mean anything to me. It meant so, so much."

They were the words she'd always wanted to hear. In a

voice that made it clear that he was speaking the truth from his soul. And she couldn't help it, she took a step toward him. His eyes were searching her face, looking for something he needed from her. And all she wanted was to give it to him. Whatever it was, however much it cost her. He took two big steps, closing the gap between them. His hand came up, sliding into her hair, cupping the back of her head, and then his mouth was on hers, greedy, forceful, perfect.

Her mouth opened to him, right away. Giving him whatever it was. Whatever he was asking for. And he took it, his tongue dipping, tentatively for only a second, then desperately. Silky against hers. He kissed her deep, so they both heard the slick of mouth on mouth, and then he pulled back to nip and lick, which made her knees go weak. He caught her as they buckled and steered her to the solid wall. He pressed her against it so the hard steel of his erection pinned her right where it felt best. And then, still kissing her, he ever-so-gently began working himself against her in a way that was one hundred percent guaranteed to make both of them come—they both knew it from long-ago but well-remembered experience. She remembered, with a thick surge of almost-there lust, how the kiss would drown out both their cries of release.

And she would have let him. She absolutely one hundred percent would have let him, except right then the store phone rang, and they jumped a mile apart. Like when she looked up at him, his back was to one of the new shelves, as far to the other side of the room as it was possible to get.

She laughed.

Half in manic joy, because oh, my *God*, that kiss had felt

good. And the other half because, *What the* hell *did she think she was doing*?

The phone quit ringing, intercepted silently by voicemail.

"Not the best way to drum up potential new business," she said.

He shook his head.

"Jax?"

"Yeah?"

"I mean, we *can't*, right? We can't really—there aren't second chances. Not when it ends like that, with—not even a whimper. Just, nothing. And I understand. I really do. Why you had to leave. But—I'd be crazy, wouldn't I? And you're leaving. And I'm leaving."

He closed his eyes. Opened them again.

"Yes," he said. "All those things are true."

For a long, giddy, brilliant second, she thought he was going to say it.

*But—*

Instead, he turned away, straightened an unruly game on the shelf behind him, and let her have the last word.

She just wasn't sure she wanted it.

## 31

*Just FYI, I'm heading into Portland today.*

Chiara's text woke him out of a fitful sleep Tuesday morning. He'd had to give Evan his bed back—obviously—and he was sleeping on the crappy couch. Which would have been bad enough if his head hadn't been full of that kiss. But given the shitty sleeping surface and a porn-movie-worthy collection of mental images—

He really hadn't slept at all. And he had jerked off twice.

He hadn't felt like this since high school, and he was guessing that was at least in part because no one got him going like Chiara did. He wasn't sure of all the elements in the recipe—one part, sure, was her slim body and supple curves, and one part, sure, was that he had *never* met a woman who could kiss like that, and one part, yeah, absolutely, was whatever it was about their chemistry that lit him on fire and made her wild and alive in his arms.

And then there was the part that felt like coming home. For ten years he hadn't had it and then suddenly it had slid into place and clicked like a key in lock, and you couldn't forget that feeling. That *yes*. That *all is right in the world*.

He wanted more. It was that simple and that complicated.

*Why Portland?*

He didn't mean to be an asshole about it, but what he was really saying was, *I was hoping to spend at least some of the day with you*. Not all of it, of course; he would help Evan with shopping and cooking and whatever else had to be done, play games with him and help keep him from going stir crazy— but he wasn't going to lie. He'd been hoping he'd get to see more of Chiara.

He had no idea how that fit in with the fact that he needed to leave and get the hell back to his real life.

"Hey."

Evan was on his feet, showered and dressed.

"Wow. You look—great," Jax said.

"Thanks. I feel better than I have in months. Asher's coming over and we're going to play Magic."

"You allowed to do that?"

"I'm allowed to do whatever I feel up for, as long as I don't overdo it. The last thing I want is to go back to the hospital."

"Okay. That seems—reasonable." He took another look at his brother. "You're sure?"

His phone buzzed just then, and he couldn't keep himself from checking it out. *I want to scope out other stores. I want to know how the successful ones are bringing customers in.*

"Um, you mind if I—" He looked up from his phone. "Chiara's going to Portland to do some market research and I thought I'd see if she needed me to go with."

"Market research, huh?" Evan asked, smirking. He waved

the back of his hand in his brother's direction. "Go, dude. Research the, ah, market."

"You're not too sick and weak for me to kick the crap out of you, you know," Jax said.

Evan rolled his eyes. "As if you'd *ever* do that."

Jax rolled his eyes right back and texted, *I'll go with you.*

There was a long silence. Then, *I think that might be a bad idea.*

He wasn't buying it. *Two heads are better than one. I might see something you don't see.*

*What about Evan?*

*He's got a friend coming over to play Magic, whatever that is.*

*Magic the Gathering,* she texted back. *It's a card game.* And then, after another long pause. *Okay, but what happened yesterday? Can't happen again.*

She was probably right.

Probably.

*You're the boss. I'll pick you up in twenty.*

*Who says you're driving?*

*You want to drive?*

*No. But I want you to ask, Alpha Man.*

She wasn't flirting, was she? His body definitely thought she was.

*Okay. Which of us is driving?*

Long silence.

Then, *You drive.*

*That's how I like it*, he tapped. Then deleted it. Then tapped it out again and—what the fuck, you only live once —sent it.

He showered in record time, pulled on one of his favorite

t-shirts—"I'm a general contractor, not a magician, but I can see why you might be confused"—and dashed for the truck.

She was standing in front of her beach-cottage-style house when he pulled up. She climbed into the truck, then frowned at him theatrically. "No sexting, either," she said sternly.

"I don't know what you're talking about."

"'That's how I like it?'" she mimicked.

He shrugged one shoulder. "I prefer to drive. Being a passenger makes me antsy."

She rolled her eyes.

She looked amazing. Her hair was in a high ponytail—fucking adorable—and she was wearing a pair of cropped skinny jeans and a white tank top with a green hoodie thrown over it. Both jeans and tank hugged her curves in a way that made his mouth water and any remaining resolve drift away. He wanted to grab the ponytail and drag her into another kiss.

He was going to have a hell of a time keeping his hands off her on the way to Portland and back. Not to mention during a day spent wandering through game stores while she was all buoyant and excited and cute and he had nothing to do except admire the curve of her ass in those jeans.

But he'd done this to himself, and he'd behave himself as long as that was what she wanted.

And not a minute longer.

## 32

"Wow," Jax said, over a very late lunch—or maybe it was an early dinner?—in a Vietnamese cafe downtown. "That was a serious crash-course for me."

They'd been all over Portland, to four different shops in four different neighborhoods. Chiara had to admit, it had been a blast. Chatting in the truck, catching up on life. Stopping for Voodoo donuts. Accepting people's assumptions that they were a couple.

It was an easy assumption to make, because Jax was all flirtation and hands today. And she didn't want him to stop. Once, when he'd put an arm around her after a clerk had assumed they were together, she'd leaned into his body. And loved the wall of muscle supporting her.

It scared her, how simple it would be to slip back into her feelings for him.

"I got an education, too," she said. "I think Evan pictured his store looking like that third one we were in. The one that hosts all those D&D and Magic and Euro board game nights. I think that's what he *wants* it to be."

"With all the dark wood paneling and the big heavy tables, and the bar snacks and beer on tap?"

"Yeah, but I think what you and I are headed toward with Meeples—which is much more like that first one we saw—is the right recipe for the family and tourist traffic."

"You're talking about the place with the kids' toys and all the family and party games."

"Yeah," she said. "And I don't think he disagrees. I've been sending him photos of everything as we go along, and I think he can see the disconnect between his fantasy and the reality. And he's not stubborn about it. He gets it. It doesn't mean he can't do the events he wants to do. It just means that he has to focus on the family-oriented stuff. Even comic-book-wise. There are great comics for kids and ones aimed at feminine audiences now, and he has to put them front and center. But then if someone comes in who's looking for the harder-core stuff, he can have that available, too. And he can hint at both in the window, but he has to do it in a way that doesn't turn anyone off."

"Just that?" Jax asked, laughing. "Okay, sounds easy enough."

"I'm not saying it's easy," Chiara said. "Just that it's possible." She sprinkled her pork meatball with cilantro and basil, drizzled soy mayo on it, and took a bite. "Holy shit, that's good."

"Mine too," he said, hoisting another mouthful of noodle salad.

"The bottom line is, we don't have the formula yet, and we need a bigger, better idea." She finished the meatball and sat in contented silence for a moment. Then she said, "In the meantime, now that we're basically done with research, there's something I've always wanted to do in Portland and never gotten around to." She smirked at him.

"What's that?" He looked—at least by Jax standards—a little nervous, which made her grin.

"It's a surprise," she said. "You drive." On a whim, she added, "I'll tell you *exactly* where I want you to go."

The look on his face informed her that only the fact that they were in a restaurant was keeping him from hauling her over the table.

And she had to admit, she resented that table mightily.

"ROLLER SKATING," Jax said, doubtfully, as Chiara handed her credit card to the fifty-something, silver-haired woman behind the skate-rental counter.

They'd checked in on Evan, again, via text to make sure he was okay with them extending their trip a little. He'd reassured them that he was totally fine. A couple of other friends had dropped by with Crohn's-friendly food, and they were now all playing a very intense game of Scythe. Jax had made him promise not to tire himself out, and Evan had crossed his heart.

"It's the largest roller rink in the U.S.," Chiara said. "And the only one with live organ music."

"It's a D.J. right now. Organ music Saturday night—" The ticket seller looked back and forth between Chiara and Jax. "—if you want to come back then?"

"We're only in town today," Chiara said. "But thank you. We're still very excited to be here."

"She is," Jax amended.

The woman hid a smile.

"Come on! It's pretty cool; you have to admit it." She tugged him over to the seats, shed her shoes, and began lacing up her skates.

"I haven't been on roller skates since I was—" He thought about it. "I think I went to a seventh grade, all-class roller-skating party when we lived in Florida."

"Well, you're in luck. They have a beginner section."

"Screw that," he said. "It's like riding a bicycle, isn't it? You never forget."

He finished lacing his skates, lurched to his feet, and immediately sat back down, hard.

"You never forget, huh?" she teased.

"Okay. Take me to the beginner section."

She led him to where they could use a long bar to guide themselves the length of the first-timers' section. "And look. See—up there? That's the organ. Can you believe the size of that thing?"

"That's what she said," Jax said.

She swatted him. "*Seriously*?"

He shook his head. "No. But her eyes did get very big when she saw it."

And truthfully, having had the full length of Jax pressed to the seam of her jeans yesterday, she could understand that.

"You got very quiet," he said.

Because she was weighing how much she wanted him inside her against how much she wanted to keep her heart safe. Yes, she was going to miss him when he went. No matter what—he'd become a good friend in a few short weeks. But if she didn't let this go any further, maybe she wouldn't end up heartbroken again. Just—sad.

She knew from painful past experience that she didn't do casual sex. Her emotions *always* got involved. And if that kiss yesterday was any indication, she'd fall fast and deep. Just like she had last time.

"Okay. I've got this," Jax said. "I'm ready for big time."

"Need a hand?"

"I'm good," he said, and wobbled out onto the floor behind her. But after a moment, he skated closer to her and took her hand. "I don't need it," he clarified. "But I want it." As he squeezed her hand tight, something in her chest squeezed, too.

The truth was, her emotions were already involved. And maybe she should enjoy the novelty of this moment—organ and all—especially if she was going to get her heart broken anyway.

It only took a few turns around the floor before he was skating like a pro, although he left all the backwards skating to her. Which was fine. Skating with both of her hands in his, while he pushed her gently in front of him, she found herself studying his beautiful face—green eyes, long lashes, strong nose and jaw, full lips. She'd never met anyone she liked to look at as much as Jax. For almost ten years, she'd waited to feel struck by lightning in a relationship the way she had in high school. And these last couple of years, she'd finally decided that maybe it had just been a product of high school. Maybe no one ever felt that way again after age eighteen.

Except she did. Again. Now. Jax, not high school, had always been the magic.

"You're awfully deep in thought for someone who's moving backwards," he said, smirking.

"I'm just—enjoying the view," she said. Because what the hell.

"You and me both." He took a deep breath. "Kee."

Her heart started pounding.

"You asked me what we're doing, and I still don't know. But I know I can't be with you without wanting to be close to you. And I don't just mean I want to kiss you. I mean, I do. God. I fucking want it like nobody's business. And to touch you. Last night I lay awake and I licked every inch of you in my mind, I swear to God."

*Girls Just Wanna Have Fun* hid the sound of her gasp, but he'd seen it in her face; his eyes darkened to match the heat surging up in her.

He shook his head. "But I swear, it's not just that, not that there's any *just* about it. No. It's that I can't be with you without wanting us to be—what we were."

She was breathless. Dizzy. She took his hand and together they skated to the side of the rink. Couples and families spun past, a blur of color; the music could have been anything. All she could see was him; all she could hear was his voice, telling her what she'd long ago stopped letting herself want.

She took a breath. Regrouped. Cautioned herself: *Slow down, Kee.*

"What we were," she repeated carefully.

"I don't even know how to say this. When we were together, even though the rest of my life could be going to shit, I felt like everything was going to be okay. There were a million responsibilities pulling me in every direction, but at the center of it there was this perfect stillness, and it was you. Am I making any sense to you at all?"

He asked this last bit with such desperation—she must have been staring at him with her mouth open. But it wasn't because she didn't understand. It was because she was so shocked to hear him say it. She'd spent so long telling herself that he hadn't ever cared for her that it had become her truth.

But here he was, telling her he'd felt what she'd felt.

A new song came on the speakers. *Can't Help Falling in Love.* She wasn't sure if she wanted to laugh or cry. But she was tired of holding back and being careful. She had spent so much of her life doing the right thing or the safe thing, and when she was with Jax, she just didn't want to anymore. She wanted to let go and fall.

"I know exactly what you're talking about," she said. "I felt like the rest of the world—all the applications, all the expectations, all the demands—fell away. And there was just us. And we were better together than apart. Like the Adventures. Part of why I've never wanted to draw since then is because I've always been afraid it wasn't me. It was us."

He was shaking his head. "No. Don't ever think that, don't. The Adventures were a special thing, and yeah, they were *us*. But you have so much talent. And you have so many things to share and say.

"What you said, about the world falling away—that's how working with you on the shop has been. Just like it used to be. The canvas is different. But it's the same feeling. Like this magic place that's just you and me, and the rest of the world can go fuck itself."

He took both her hands again, even though the two of them were standing perfectly still at the side of the rink. "I don't deserve a second chance, and I know it's hard for there to be unanswered questions, and I know I don't have all the answers about what any of this means, but please, can we—"

He didn't even finish the sentence before she was in his arms, kissing him, and murmuring against his lips, "Yes. Yes, *please*."

## 33

The drive back to Tierney Bay was the longest hour and a half of Jax's life.

"Did you really picture licking me all over last night?" Chiara asked in a tone that was so deceptively casual it took him a second to catch up.

They were only ten minutes outside of Portland, driving straight into the goddamned sunset, because the Sunset Highway was aptly named. Between the sun in his eyes and the heat in his body, he was really hoping he was equipped to get them back to town safely.

"Yes," he said. "When we were in high school, I thought about using my mouth on you *all the time* but there were so few times we were alone and there was never enough time. That was one thing I was going to do on prom night. I was going to make you come with my tongue. There were some days I couldn't think about anything else."

Her head fell back against the headrest. "Oh," she said. "Well. It's never too late."

"Do you think we would get arrested if I pulled over and

went down on you right now on the side of the road?" he asked, trying to match his tone to the one she'd used a few minutes ago.

"Yes," she said. "Yes, I think we probably would, because I would yell that loudly, and also slap my hand on the steamed-up windows just like in that scene in *Titanic*."

"Did you just squirm in your seat?" he asked. "Pretty sure I didn't imagine that. Are you feeling a little—impatient?"

He was. For sure. His cock, which had swelled when she asked him about picturing himself licking her, was now well on its way to hard and tangled uncomfortably in his boxer-briefs.

"More than a little impatient."

"You could get the party started."

"Meaning...?"

"Put your hand between your legs."

She gave him an open-mouthed, outraged look. "Anyone could see."

"They'd have to be up pretty high to see in. So I'll watch, and if I think we're in a position to get passed close by someone in a taller vehicle, I'll warn you."

"You weren't this dirty in high school," she said, but she *really* didn't sound upset about it.

"I *was*," he said. "I just didn't always tell you about it."

"Why not?"

"I didn't want to freak you out."

"You *won't* freak me out."

"Noted." He paused. "You know you can say no to anything you don't like, right? You know you never have to do anything you don't want to with me? You know I will never coerce you? Ever?"

She nodded.

"Good. Now. Put your hand between your legs."

She squeaked and did it. He desperately wanted to cup the bulge in his jeans, but that wasn't going to happen. He had to keep them safe. This was all about her. "How does it feel?" he asked instead.

"Hot. Damp. Really, really good." Her voice was low. A murmur.

He groaned. "Can I feel?"

She guided his palm to her. She hadn't exaggerated. He could feel her wet heat straight through the thickness of her jeans and her panties. Assuming she *was* wearing panties.

It wasn't possible for him to get much harder.

She slid lower in the seat to get more contact with his palm, and he pressed upward to give it to her.

"One rule," he said.

She wriggled against his palm. "Uh-huh."

"You can't actually come. You have to wait for me. I want you to come while I'm buried inside you."

She whimpered.

He took his hand away. "If you rub a finger—just one finger—up and down the seam of your jeans—how does that feel?"

He was ninety percent sure he couldn't come just from talking dirty and watching her stroke herself, but he was shocked at how possible it felt. He could feel the sharp promise of losing control at the outside edge of his senses. He took a deep breath and made himself think about the sad, sad state of his business's books. If Chiara saw them, she'd lose all respect for him. Maybe he should ask her to take a look at them. Other people's math homework was, after all, her specialty.

Okay, *that* had bought him some time. He looked over to find her with her head tilted back against the headrest, mouth slack with pleasure, eyes closed, obediently stroking that single finger up and down—

And he was rock hard again.

They still had probably an hour to go before Tierney Bay.

He reached over and caught her nipple, which was a tight bud under her tank top.

"If you keep doing that I'm going to break the only rule," she whispered, arching her back like she was trying to get more—more of his fingers on her nipple, more of her own finger at her pussy.

"Chiara," he said roughly.

"Uh-huh?"

She was far away, listening to the sensations in her body. His cock was so hard it hurt.

"If I keep doing this *I'm* going to break the only rule."

IN THE END, neither of them broke the rule. He kept teasing her. He told her what to do and when to stop. He brought her right up to the edge and then he made her pull back. He knew *exactly* when she was about to lose control, and he dug deep and found the self-control to make her walk that tightrope. Partly because he wanted to make her feel good. And partly because it was the highest high he could imagine.

It was the hottest hour he'd ever spent in a vehicle. He didn't—couldn't—count the night he'd made love to her.

That had been hot and also something else. Something sacred and complicated that he wouldn't let himself think about right now.

He pulled the truck up in front of her house. He was burning up with urgency, his blood too hot, his pulse too fast, his cock aching. He jumped down from the driver's side, rushed to the passenger side, opened her door, and scooped her into his arms. He kicked the door shut and carried her to her front door.

"Key," he said, breathless.

She extracted a ring of keys from her purse, which she was clutching, and unlocked the door. He kicked that shut behind him, too.

"Which way?"

Now she was laughing. "There's nowhere to go. See that stubby little hall straight ahead? Bedroom's on the right."

He carried her down the hall, pushed her bedroom door open, and deposited her on her unmade bed. He took stock of the situation, which really just meant her. Her cheeks were pink, her eyes were bright, and when he put out a hand to assess, her jeans were wet at the seam she'd teased.

He unbuttoned and unzipped her jeans and yanked them down, taking her panties with them. He knelt between her legs, pulled her towards him, and lowered his face into her damp curls.

Then he paused.

"Are you going to break the rule if I do this?" he asked.

"No," she said. "I can't come from oral."

He raised an eyebrow at her.

"Swear to God," she said, raising a hand.

He bent, parted her lips, and licked her greedily.

"Ohh," she moaned.

Somewhere in the general vicinity of Hillsboro, he'd realized that he could smell her, salty as the ocean but with a sweet tinge that made him desperate for a taste. He'd been dying for her ever since. And she was just as good as he'd fantasized. He alternated between giving her what she needed—first his tongue tight on her clit, then circling the swollen bud, and then flat for more pressure—and giving in to his own impulse to lick straight into the honey-heart of her. And she liked that, too; she fucked against him to get more of his tongue inside her. He gave her a finger, instead, and she cried out when he crooked it up, a tease against her g-spot.

He couldn't take it anymore; he reached down and unbuttoned and unzipped his jeans, freed himself so he was fully upright, though still locked against his own belly by the waistband of his boxer briefs. She saw or sensed it and tried to sit up. "Let me touch," she cried, but he said, "Shh," and pushed her back down again, his mouth and his finger working her together.

He could feel her muscles starting to gather around his finger, and he pulled back. Rocked back on his knees. "You lied to me," he said conversationally. "You can come from oral. If I keep going, you are going to come all over my face."

"Jax," she begged. "Jax, please, *please*."

"What?" he asked. "What?"

"I need you inside me."

"My tongue? My finger?"

"Your cock."

Afterwards he had literally no memory of doing it, but he somehow got his clothes off, and then hers.

"There are condoms in the nightstand," she said.

He had a hell of a time getting the drawer open and she had the nerve to laugh at him. "My hands are shaking," he admitted.

"Let me put it on."

She did, a long, slow unroll that almost made his knees buckle. Then she lay back and spread her legs for him, a gesture that made his chest hurt. There was just something so trusting about it. He'd left her and ghosted her and here she was, still welcoming him. So it took him a moment to recover enough to let himself be welcomed.

She saw the hesitation. "Jax?"

"I just—I didn't think I'd ever be here again. And I'm—I'm so grateful."

Her eyes shone. "Show me how grateful," she said.

A minute ago he'd been in a rush, but now he wanted it to be slow and perfect. He climbed over her and braced himself on his arms, looking down at her. She was so beautiful, with her pale skin and splash of freckles and those mad-blue eyes. He bent his head and kissed her, her mouth soft and yielding. Her arms came up around his neck; her hands plunged into his hair. She kissed him like kisses were another form of begging, wide open and pleading, her tongue showing him what she wanted. He couldn't stop kissing her, not when it was like this, so hot, so honest, so good. He managed to hold himself up on his knees and one arm, found her pussy with his other hand, parted her, so slick, so needy, and lined himself up. Just the tip in her wet heat. Holy *shit*.

"Kee," he groaned. "Oh my God, *Kee*."

She was saying his name, too. Her muscles tightened around the head of his cock as he eased it in. This was what he'd been missing. This was what it felt like to be whole. He took another inch, and she thrust up at him, lifting her hips with a desperate, broken sound. There was a very real chance he wasn't going to make it all the way inside her before one of them started coming. But he wasn't going to rush it, even though the pressure in his balls, the pressure at the root of his cock, at the base of his spine, was killing him. Even though she was starting to contract involuntarily around him. He took another inch, feeling her part to let him in, her hands on his ass now, trying to get him to move faster, trying to get him in deeper.

"More," she gasped, and he obliged, but just a little bit, and a little bit more, until he couldn't get any deeper; he was buried all the way to his base, his balls tight, his cock on the upper side wedged against her sex so that every time he shifted she groaned and hitched her hips. One more and—

He felt her go over; felt the cascade of flutters and tightenings, heard the groan wrenched loose, saw the flush rise up her chest and throat into her face, and there was no way he wasn't going with her, right then and there. It surged up from wherever orgasms came from—the bottom of his spine, the bottom of the fucking world, and he thrust into her, cupping her head, pulling her against him, trying to get as deep as possible as he emptied himself into her.

## 34

O kay, then.

She'd had sex with several boyfriends over the last decade, including the ones Auburn had singled out for disapproval. She'd thought that the sex with those guys was pretty good. Maybe even very good. But she had still compared it to that night in the pickup truck with Jax and found it wanting. She had never, since her first time, felt so connected, so close, to anyone, so transported out of herself. She had wondered if, because that was her first time, she had exaggerated it in her mind. If she'd done it again with Jax, would it have lived up?

Now she had her answer.

"Wow," she said. Because there wasn't any point in lying about it. Her response had made it abundantly clear how much she'd enjoyed herself. Her throat was hoarse from groaning and—more than once—shouting his name.

He'd definitely shouted hers. So if the neighbors were still awake, they knew who'd done the deed.

She didn't actually give a shit.

"Wow indeed," he said. Very slowly, as if it pained him to have to do it, he extricated himself and the condom from her and rolled onto his back. He lay there a minute like he wasn't ever going to move again, then dragged himself upright. "Bathroom—across the hall?"

"Yup."

He disappeared and came back with a warm, wet washcloth. And then proceeded to clean her up.

He didn't do it like it was a chore. He did it like it was foreplay. He was incredibly gentle and incredibly thorough, and by the time he was done, she found herself involuntarily tilting her hips toward him, begging for more warm, wet pressure.

"You like that?" he teased.

"Mmm-hmm."

He replaced the washcloth with his palm and—smirk fading, eyes darkening—brought her to a second—and even more intense—orgasm.

When she regained her head, she found him watching her, intently, his hand on his hard-again cock, a slow, rocking stroke that redoubled her aftershocks.

"Round two?" he asked.

She nodded. She couldn't actually speak.

He sheathed himself in a second condom. This time around, he felt even bigger inside her. And better. She was ultra-sensitive, but the urgency had also gone out of it, so she just luxuriated in each long, thick stroke, not needing anything from it, just loving the feel of him. She could watch him, too, the muscles straining in his arms, the swell of his pecs from bracing himself, the quiver of abs. The expression on his face, so intent on something she couldn't see, but also the moments when he came back to her and looked right into her eyes, making sure she was with him.

She was. At some point, their eyes locked, and she couldn't look away. And then it was like she was following him up, the steady increase in pace, the tension winding tight in his body and face. She felt like he was guiding them both home; all she had to do was open herself to him, which she did willingly, and he would make sure she got there.

"Shit," he said suddenly, his face contorting. And then he yelled, "God! Kee!" his whole body rigid. And her emotions felt wound so tight, her feelings for him, that even though she didn't come again, something unfurled itself like release in her chest, unlocked by the abandon on his face.

He was very quiet for a long time. Then he said, "I have literally never done that. Had sex again after, what, like, five minutes?"

"Maybe it was ten?" she hazarded.

"Well. It's a first for me."

"Me too. But I guess I'm wired for multiple rounds so maybe it's not so surprising. You aren't."

"I thought I wasn't. You may have rewired me."

She smiled, pleased with herself.

He got up and disposed of the condom, came back again with a washcloth.

"Now we can do it again," she teased.

"No." He sounded so alarmed that she laughed.

He returned the washcloth to the bathroom and returned to her bedroom. In the meantime, she'd found some pajamas —Math Inspires Me, with a pi sign instead of the "p" and "i"—and climbed under the covers. He looked down at her, and for the first time, doubt crept over his features.

She saw it, and it made her stomach clench. Her first instinct was to push him away, any way she could. Make some glib comment about letting himself out. Or—she didn't know what, but *something*. Anything, so she didn't have to find out what the doubt on his face meant.

But then she made herself put on her big girl pants. He'd been more than clear about his feelings earlier. "You look a little freaked out," she said, sounding steadier than she felt.

"I don't want to assume," he said. "That you, um, want me to—stay."

He sounded so uncertain. Nothing like the man who for weeks had always seemed to know exactly what came next.

And just like that, the vise around her lungs loosened and her stomach unclenched, and everything was okay.

"I want you to stay," she said. "Climb in."

He still looked unsure. "I don't have pajamas."

She grinned. "Pajamas are optional. Would you feel better if I took mine off?"

He shook his head and reached for his boxer briefs, stepping into them. They were a good look on him, snug around his thick thighs and perfect ass. She wanted to reach out and cup the bulge—but she figured he could use a break. He climbed under the covers and wrapped an arm over her, big spoon to her little. She could feel his breath in her hair. The heat of his body warmed and comforted and soothed her, and even though she was very tired, she made herself stay awake a while, just to feel him next to her. He was there, and hers, for now at least.

## 35

He climbed out of a deep sleep to an urgent case of morning wood. And it wasn't helping anything that his erection was sandwiched firmly between his own body and the curvy one next to his. Chiara's amazing ass was wedged very thoroughly against him, and somehow his hand—his arm was looped over her—had wrapped itself around her breast, and he could feel her nipple hard against his palm.

Rationally, he knew that nipple didn't necessarily mean she was turned on, but his hard dick didn't believe it. And he tried to behave himself; he *really, really* did, but somehow he found himself very gently teasing the nipple. And then—and there was really no excuse at all for this—teasing the other one, too.

He felt the moment when her breathing changed and she woke up, and he froze.

"Don't stop," she whispered. She was kicking her way out of her pajama bottoms as she spoke, and with one clever hand behind her, she worked his waistband down and freed him. She edged a leg up over his.

"Condom," he said.

"Oh, shit, yeah," she said. That made him smile; he rolled very unwillingly away from her, found one, glided it on, and eased himself back against her soft, warm curves. The leg—smooth as silk—teased its way back over his, and this time he took advantage of what she was offering. He nudged himself up against her warm, wet sex, and she hissed out a breath and backed up to meet him. The position made her tight. He reached around to tease her clit until she softened and opened for him. Even then, he took her slowly again—partly out of respect for her but mostly because last night he'd loved every one of those slow, snug inches. He loved the way she let him in.

He made her come with his fingers on her clit, and then he sped up his pace, thrusting hard and deep until he came with a groan.

He got up and tossed the condom, then returned and threw himself face down beside her with a groan of contentment that made her laugh. She snuggled close, and he slung an arm over her and let himself breathe in her apple-pie scent all the way to the center of his soul. How was it possible that she smelled exactly the same? That she could still, all these years later, make him feel like everything was going to be all right?

"Will you draw for me?"

She stiffened.

"It doesn't have to be the Adventures. Just, anything."

He expected resistance, but instead she exhaled, deeply, and rolled away and out of bed. She left the room and came back with the sketchbook and pencils, lay down beside him and opened it.

"Someone discovered SuperJax's true identity," Chiara said. "He had to leave the country."

"Or the planet," Jax said.

"Yeah."

She sketched it—the spacecraft, with SuperJax inside. SuperKee on the ground, watching, as he went. His heart flared, wild and soft. The expression on her face. Wrecked. He never wanted to hurt her like that again.

Which meant that he could never tell her the deal he'd made.

Which meant that there would be a secret at the center of what was between them.

And everyone knew that a secret like that would find its way out somehow. Like a splinter rising to the surface of skin.

Tell? Don't tell?

"He had to stay there for ten years," Chiara said. "So everyone could forget. People have short memories."

"But one person didn't forget," Jax said.

"Even though he did the magic thing-a-majig on her."

"The magic *thing-a-majig*?" He gave her a disbelieving look.

"You know. Like in *Men in Black*." She drew it. SuperJax holding up the wand with the weird blue flash that matched the color of SuperKee's eyes. SuperKee's eyes going spiral and blank.

Jax laughed. "Right. The magic thing-a-majig. How could I forget. He thought it would work on her, but she wasn't like other people. She was a superhero. So she forgot a little bit. The superhero part of her brain held onto the knowledge."

Chiara started a new frame. "And then, just as his ten years in exile was up, SuperJax had to come back to planet Earth."

"Why? Why did he have to come back?"

"Unbeknownst to SuperKee, she was in danger." She pitched her voice low. Ominous. "From E-CommerceMan."

Jax screwed up his face at her. "There is no such superhero as E-CommerceMan."

"Of course there fucking is. He has a dollar sign on his shirt and a cape made out of money. Or maybe Buyathon gift certificates."

Apparently she couldn't resist that image, because she was already drawing it. Jax watched her face, aglow. Her eyes were fixed on the page, her hand moving so fast it was like one of those sped-up Instagram artists.

"When SuperJax made SuperKee forget him, he inadvertently also made her forget who *she* was," Jax said. "She forgot she was a superhero who could do anything. Which put her totally at E-CommerceMan's mercy. She didn't realize that all she had to do was use her superpowers to defeat him."

"And," Chiara said, "when SuperJax tried to convince SuperKee of her superpowers, she was like, what the hell kind of mushrooms were those?"

"But SuperJax is forbidden by the superhero council rules to practice his powers in front of anyone who doesn't already know about them. So he can't show her."

"Oh, but then E-CommerceMan kidnaps SuperKee and takes her—"

"—to Seattle—" Jax supplied.

"—where he forces her to work long hours—" Chiara was breathless.

"—doing other people's math homework—"

She glared at him. But she was trying to hide a smile. While drawing as fast as she could. Just sketching, really, but her strokes were gaining confidence, and she still had it, the ability to bring a whole scene to life with very few lines. The ability to get a whole emotional palette across in the hunch of a character's shoulders or the quirk of her mouth.

His own heart was going a million miles a minute. And for all the things he'd done in the last ten years, he was pretty sure the last time he'd loved something this hard and with this much of himself was the last time he'd watched her draw. "But SuperJax swoops in and rescues her."

"Nope," Chiara said. "He tries to, but he's just a couple of minutes too late."

"That's dark."

"No, you *idiot*, she saves herself," she said, and drew it for him.

Just before SuperJax could get himself on the scene, SuperKee cleverly figured out how to use the edge of her bracelet to cut the ropes binding her. Then she overpowered E-CommerceMan and bound him in his own cape.

"Which is good symbolism, right there. Tied up in your own greed," Jax said.

"As she was doing it, she felt this rush of power. Her power. Her superpowers."

"Just then, SuperJax shows up."

"And just like that, SuperKee remembers. Everything."

On the page, SuperKee's head split open like Zeus birthing Athena. It loosed a memory. SuperJax, touching her hair. Looking tenderly down at her.

Also, this grown-up SuperJax was incredibly ripped.

Which made Jax feel like his muscles were too big for his skin, in the best possible way.

"I am not that buff," he said.

"You feel that buff when you're on top of me."

Other things were going to be too big for his skin too, any moment now.

She was writing. Filling in SuperKee's speech bubble.

It read, "I missed you, SuperJax."

He pushed sketchbook and pencil to the side, cupped her head and both hands, and kissed her, mouth parted and wet, hot and giving. She opened to him and took his tongue, and his whole body felt like it was forged out of steel.

"I missed you, too," he whispered.

## 36

They took a long shower. It was Chiara's fault. She soaped a hand and grabbed Jax. He leaned against the wall and watched with a breathless, grateful look as her fist moved over him. When it was done, he said, "You're still the best hand job I've ever had." Then he returned the favor, supplementing fingers with the handheld shower nozzle and his mouth, supporting her weight when her orgasm knocked her legs out from under her.

Afterwards, they walked into town together and got themselves a booth at the back of the Tierney Bay Diner.

They'd barely settled themselves when Chiara said, "Oh, *shit*. Don't look now, but Levi, Mason, and Trey are about to walk in."

A minute later the Campbell brothers—and their honorary third musketeer—were standing over Chiara and Jax's table.

"Breakfast, huh?" Levi said, darkly. "I thought we talked about this, Walker."

Across from her, Jax stiffened. "Not your lane, Levi." His

voice was level, and if she hadn't spent the last night with him, much of it in a state of boneless relaxation, she might not have seen the subtle tension in his shoulders and jaw.

"Oh, but I think it is. Because the last time you traveled this highway, you fucked it up royally and hurt at least two people I love."

"Levi," Chiara warned.

But her brother was on a roll. "You think you can just come back here and pick up where you left off? Reclaim her like something you left behind?"

Jax was out of his seat in a flash and up in Levi's face. He was shorter than Levi, but buffer, and it occurred to Chiara—suddenly and alarmingly—that she didn't know which of them she'd pick in a fight.

"You don't know anything about this, Campbell," Jax growled.

"I know you don't deserve her."

Her brother was all bristling alpha male, looking about as scary as it was possible for tall, dark, and six-plus-feet to look, which was pretty damn scary. Plus he was flanked by Mason and Trey, who were physically intimidating—although they both looked a tad dazed by how fast things had escalated.

Luckily, Chiara had nearly three decades of experience with her brother. "Shut up, Levi."

He had the grace to looked affronted. "I'm watching out for you."

She rolled her eyes. "I can take care of myself."

"You heard her," Jax said, his voice still pitched to growl.

"Don't taunt him," Chiara said, exasperated. "What is it with you guys? If you get into a fistfight in Lily's diner, she's going to kill you both. Or Kincaid will." She gestured to Lily's truly scary-looking tattooed ex-con husband, sitting in the back of the diner.

Okay, maybe he didn't look that scary, after all, cutting up his daughter's pancakes and showing her how to dip them into maple syrup.

Whether it was Kincaid's wolf-in-bunny-rabbit-clothes performance or Chiara's warning, the two men both eased off, Levi taking a few steps back and raising his hands in the universal sign of *okay, okay*, and Jax sliding back into his seat, looking slightly sheepish. And Mason and Trey? They both looked incredibly relieved. She was pretty sure neither of them had ever thrown a punch, although she wouldn't want to bet against either of them in a fistfight, either.

"Chiara, can I talk to you a second?" Levi demanded.

"I'm having breakfast here," she said.

"It'll just take a minute."

She followed him outside the diner.

"Are you *out of your mind*?"

He was really pissed.

So was she. "First of all, you leapt to the assumption—"

"That you're sleeping with him. Yes. That's usually true when men and women have breakfast together. So shoot me." He raised his eyebrows. "Or just tell me I'm wrong."

"You're not wrong," she said on a long exhalation.

"Right. So—you were saying?"

"It's none of your business and you know nothing about it."

"This family is *always* my business," Levi said.

She shook her head. "Hannah is your business. But I'm a grown woman, and I've proven I can take care of myself—and everyone else who needs it, too. I'm not your business anymore, as much as I love you. And as much as I know you love me."

He deflated further, but he didn't give up. He wouldn't have been Levi if he had. "I don't want you to get hurt again. That guy will rip your heart out and trample on it."

She shook her head. "I don't think he will, Levi."

But she wasn't nearly as confident as she sounded. They still hadn't talked about what they were doing, what it meant, or whether or how it might continue after they were both no longer in Tierney Bay. And now that she was standing here, talking to Levi, that omission felt huge.

As long as she'd known Levi, and as well as she knew how to handle him, he knew her just as well. "Please, sis. Please, just be careful. I know how to bail you guys out of financial trouble. I know how to beat up people who put you in danger. But I have no fucking idea how to fix you when you break."

"I won't break," Chiara said.

She was sure of that, at least, and he must have seen it, because he nodded. "Okay," he said. "Okay."

They walked back inside together. Trey and Mason were sitting a few booths away. Chiara shot Lily a grateful smile, and Lily gave her a nod back, then an incline of the head. *Everything okay?*

Chiara nodded and slid back in across from Jax. He reached out and took her hand, and there it was again, the sense that everything really *was* okay. What had he said? *There were a million responsibilities pulling me in every direction but at the center of it there was this perfect stillness, and it was you.*

Maybe it wouldn't last. Maybe they'd go their separate ways and it would turn out to be just one amazing night.

But she'd been with guys who were stable and certain, who wanted to promise her money and family and security.

And she wouldn't trade last night for all the certainty in the world.

AFTER BREAKFAST they agreed it was time to look in on Evan, so they strolled back through town, hands linked, towards Evan's apartment. They were on the main street, parallel to Park Street where the game store lay. Stores here had their doors thrown open in the summer heat. They had gorgeous window displays. Chiara found herself feeling wildly jealous of their access to the tourist traffic.

She and Jax drew even with the alleyway that crossed between Main Street and Park. And Chiara stopped, staring at it.

"God, I'm an *idiot*," she said.

"I don't think so," Jax said. "You're the smartest person I know. Also the most beautiful. And you are fucking fantastic in be—"

"No, I mean, I can't believe I didn't think of this sooner. We need a sign here. Not just a sign. A treasure trail kind of thing. For kids to follow. Like a scavenger hunt. A big sign right here —" She indicated where there were a few other assorted directional signs luring people into the shops that lined the alley. "Bright colors. Waist or chest height for adults. Geared to get kids' attention. And showing some scavenger hunt elements, like, I don't know, animal footprints, that you can find in the alley. And then we put signs with those elements. Footprints, or game pieces, or—it doesn't even matter. Clues, basically. And customers have to hunt for the next clues. And then at the end, there's the game store, and the last clue is inside.

"And we'll have prizes for everyone who shows up. And then we'll have demo games out on the tables—"

"And food," Jax said.

"What?"

She'd been in a reverie, and he snapped her out of it.

"Food," he said. "I've been thinking about it a lot. And the one place I want to go back to, of the ones we saw in Portland? Was the dark one with the paneling and the beers. And I don't even *like* the strategy games that much. Except Terraforming Mars," he said quickly, seeing the expression on her face. "I make an exception for that. But I'd go back to that place. Because, beer."

"Food," she repeated. "You're totally right. I bet I could get Lily interested in doing Tierney Bay Diner desserts in the store, at least for Labor Day weekend. And we could do Italian sodas. On hot days, people would totally go for that. They'd come in after the park for them. Oh my God. It's genius."

"We *are* superheroes," he said, shrugging.

She gave him an affectionate little shove.

"Seriously," she said. "Thank you, Jax."

"For what?"

"For ... all the hard work. And believing in the vision."

"Don't thank me," he said. "We haven't saved the store yet."

"*We*," she said. "Does that mean you want to help me and Evan get it ready for Labor Day?"

She held her breath. It would have been braver, she knew, to ask the real question: How long are you staying?

Except it wasn't *fair* for her to ask that question when she didn't know the answer to it herself. So she stuck with the other version. The cheap, cheater version.

And right now?

He was nodding at her.

"Yeah," he said. "It does. I'm going to make those signs. And I'll help you however I can with the food part. I don't know shit about catering or serving food or any of that. But I am pretty good with hustling my way into permits and things. Something about looking pretty to bored bureaucrats..."

She threw her arms around him. "Thank you. Thank you!"

"Well," he said, into her hair, next to her ear. "It's not totally selfless. I'm going to get something out of it, too."

The feel of his breath ruffling her hair made her instantly breathless.

"After we check on Evan," she said. "Are you, um, busy?"

"Very busy," he said. "Very, very—" He nuzzled his way along her ear and down her neck. "Very busy."

## 37

A few days later, Chiara convinced Jax that it would be safe to show up with her at one of Auburn's famous Beachcrest campfires. Even though those campfires did, from time to time, attract multiple Campbells, at least one of whom Jax didn't trust not to corner him and yell.

That said, he could take care of himself. He wasn't scared of Levi. And he did love him some fire-roasted hot dogs.

Still, he hadn't quite anticipated the current moment. Somehow, Chiara and Auburn and their women friends—some of whom Jax knew as former classmates—had drifted away from the fire, leaving him mainly in the company of Levi, Trey, and Mason.

Right now, it was safe, because they were all talking about what constituted the perfect marshmallow. And, as always at a campfire, there were representatives from all camps. Levi liked his charred. Trey had infinite patience and would gently toast on all sides to a perfect, even golden tan. And Mason did that thing that Jax had never understood where he pulled off each layer as he toasted it, ate it, and re-toasted the rest.

Eventually, Jax had to admit he hated marshmallows.

"But if you pass me the graham crackers, I'll be a happy man," he said.

They all looked at him like he was crazy. "Does Chiara know?" Levi demanded.

He figured that meant they were making some progress towards acceptance of whatever was happening between him and Chiara.

"Yes," he said. "Back in high school we were at a marsh-mallow roast once together and I had to fess up."

"S'mores are one of Chiara's favorite foods." That, believe it or not, was Mason, whose voice was low and rough, prob-ably from disuse. Jax could count on both hands the number of times Mason had spoken to him.

He nodded. He did love how the Campbells did sibling protectiveness. They were worried he'd break her heart. Or keep her from her marshmallows. They covered all the bases.

"Hand me a marshmallow," he said.

They all watched as he toasted it. He went with Trey's approach. One, he felt like it was above reproach—you had to respect someone who could patiently toast like that. And two, he knew that was how Chiara liked it. He fucking remem-bered, like he remembered everything he'd ever known about her. How much parmesan cheese she'd put on her spaghetti with sauce. How sharp she liked her pencils. How much fric-tion and in exactly what spot it took to make her come.

Chiara had not pressured him to show up at the campfire. "If it's too much, you don't have to be there," she said, almost shyly. And he understood what she was saying. If he didn't want to be her boyfriend *publicly*, she wasn't going to guilt him into it.

But he did, that was the thing.

He'd started thinking about the future, which he never let himself do. Because the last time he'd let himself imagine a future—a future *with* someone—was ten years ago. And look how well *that* had ended up.

Not so well.

But now he was thinking about whether Bakersfield was the only place for him. True, his business was there, and rebuilding would be a royal pain in the ass. The kind of pain in the ass you would only undertake for someone you cared deeply about. Two someones. And a place you loved.

But Chiara wasn't planning on staying in Tierney Bay. And if Buyathon was what she really wanted, then that was what he wanted for her, no matter how mysterious it seemed.

So—he didn't know. He just fucking didn't know.

"Hey."

He looked up to find her standing over him, expectantly holding out a hand and smiling.

Levi handed him a graham cracker, pre-loaded with chocolate, and a second one for the top. Jax slid Chiara's marshmallow between the two crackers and handed it to her.

She looked at it like he'd hung the moon.

He shrugged. "Your brothers reminded me how much you like them."

Mouth full of marshmallow, she seemed to finally take in the implications of his seating arrangement. "Sorry! I didn't mean to abandon you to these maniacs."

"We've been behaving ourselves," Levi said with a shrug. "We haven't hazed him yet."

"You haven't hazed *me* yet," Trey pointed out.

"There's always time," Levi said darkly.

"Want to take a walk?" Chiara asked.

"Sure," he said, getting to his feet.

Levi pointed two fingers at his own eyes and then at Jax.

"I'm watching you, Wazowski, always watching," Jax intoned, in his best Roz voice, which—he'd been told—was pretty damn good.

Levi cracked up, then sighed. "All right, Walker. Here's the deal. We need a fourth for two-on-two hoops tomorrow because my friend James is out of town. So. If you subject yourself to that, I'll quit giving you a hard time."

Jax hesitated. Not because he didn't want to. But because he remembered that, too. Shooting hoops with Rich and, often, Mason. And once, when Levi had been home from school on break, him, too. He remembered the affection among the males of the Campbell family and how for that one afternoon, he'd been folded into it, seamlessly.

Still, it hadn't counted in the end.

But he couldn't hold Rich Campbell's actions against his sons.

Jax nodded. "It's a deal," he said.

He took Chiara's hand, and they wandered down onto the beach. The tide was low, and dark was just falling, the sunset still shades of deep pink, purple, and orange low on the horizon. They moved out of the circle of the firelight until they were alone in the dark.

And then everything stood still, and it was just them, like it had always been.

"Hey," he said to her, squeezing her hand as they wandered down the beach. The ocean was a soft roar beside them, but that didn't change the stillness.

"Hey," she said, and squeezed back.

## 38

"We're gonna do this," Chiara said to Jax as they lay in her bed. It was Thursday night, the night before Labor Day weekend. "We're gonna save the store."

"Hell, yeah," he said. "And we're not just saying that because we're both steeped in happy sex hormones." He stroked her hair, his breath moving the strands and sending thrills to every nerve ending.

She laughed. "Seriously. I'm feeling really optimistic right now."

"Me, too," he said quietly.

She and Jax and Evan had done everything in their collective power to make the shop ready for Labor Day weekend. And it was ready. Jax's gorgeous signs would draw kids from Main Street to Park Street. Her own demo tables and fun in-store experiences would guarantee they stayed long enough for Evan to sweet talk them into buying. Food and drink would bring people across the street from the park. And on top of that, she'd handed out a second scavenger hunt to every shop in town—one that ended up with another set of prizes at Meeples.

For the first time, she felt confident they'd win this battle for Evan.

She'd been thinking about his other battle, too. He'd been healthy since coming home from the hospital, but she hadn't forgotten what Jax had said. She'd read up on the procedure Jax had mentioned, and even found a few minutes to talk to Evan about it.

More and more, she wanted to help, and her last round of research had given her an idea of how she could. She had a few more things she wanted to look into, and then she'd bring up what she'd learned with Jax.

Getting the shop ready had taken a lot of energy. She hadn't gotten much sleep—between working on the shop, staying on top of her own work, and making love to Jax—but it had been one of the best weeks of her life.

She saw what Jax meant when he said that working on the shop was like the experience of drawing the Adventures together. They fed each other—every idea she had excited him and drew more out of him.

Like the two of them in bed.

But it was all coming to an end.

Earlier that day, Chiara had fielded her third interview with Buyathon. She did her damnedest to wow the last two interviewers, and she thought she'd succeeded. But her heart wasn't in it. Because she wasn't sure it was what she wanted.

More and more she was asking herself if Jax's needling was true. Maybe she didn't want to do other people's math homework anymore. Maybe she wanted to do exactly what she was doing now. Making small businesses more successful. Not necessarily only by ironing out their books. But also by being creative about how to fix what wasn't working.

She could stay in Tierney Bay and do that.

But ... did she want to stay in Tierney Bay given that Jax was probably—almost certainly—leaving?

She wasn't sure.

And, there was a voice in the back of her head, long familiar. Her father's. He wasn't having any of her doubts.

*Make a plan and stick to it. That's the best way not to get derailed by your own fear and hesitation.*

It was natural to get cold feet when you were committing yourself to something new. It happened even when people were marrying people they loved. Moving to Seattle and taking a high-level corporate job was a big decision. It was natural she should have some second thoughts.

She needed to stick to the plan.

Yet, for better or for worse, the question she was about to ask Jax was not a stick-to-the-plan question. It was the exact opposite.

She pulled away so she could see his face. "Do you think—?"

He was waiting patiently, watching her, and she could see the affection in his eyes.

"Is there any chance—?"

"Spit it out, Campbell."

"You didn't take me to prom," she blurted out.

She saw his eyes widen, but that was the only sign that she might have surprised him. "I didn't," he agreed.

"I want a do-over."

A smile edged up the corners of his mouth. "Do you."

"Reunion is September 14."

Now he was grinning. "You think I owe you a dinner dance, huh?"

"You kind of do."

"I kind of do." He took a deep breath. "Actually. I called my apprentice today and gave him the go-ahead to start the project without me. He was just about ready to supervise a project anyway. He'll do great. So that gives me a breather. I could extend my stay through September 14." He tilted his head a little. "But are you sure you'll still be here then?"

"I told them I'd start September 17," she said.

She'd shocked him; his face froze. For a second she thought she'd hurt him—but then his features straightened out, and she realized he was confused because she'd implied she already had the job. "I mean," she amended, "I don't have the job *yet*. But I said I could start September 17. You know. If they offer it to me. And if I, you know, take it."

Her heart had stopped. It was waiting—waiting for him to say something about her not leaving Tierney Bay. About not taking the job.

He blinked, then smiled. "You're going to get it. Of course you are."

"Well. We'll see."

"You're totally going to get it. How could they resist you? I can't."

He reached a hand out, slid it behind her head, and tugged her toward him. "I can't resist you at all," he murmured, and lowered his mouth onto hers.

## 39

H e kissed her to make her stop talking and also so he wouldn't say what was on the tip of his tongue. *Don't take it! Don't go!*

Rich had said to Jax: *She'll go to college and she'll meet amazing people. And she'll do amazing things. She'll have the opportunity to become anyone she wants to be. But I know her, too. She loves hard, and she'll try to hold back part of herself so she can stay the person you're in love with now.*

*I don't want that for her, and I don't think you do, either.*

He'd shaken his head. No. And he'd meant it.

Ever since he and Chiara had gotten back together, he'd felt like he was flying—in the best and worst possible ways. All the elation. All the terror.

This was what he imagined skydiving would be like. So much exhilaration, edged with fear. He couldn't stop, and he didn't want to, even though they were only one small mistake —one long-held secret—away from crashing.

He kissed her now and felt it. The soaring. The falling. The blood surging in his veins—a few choice ones in particular. And the chaos in his brain. The way his heart felt like it was going to beat right out of his chest.

Her lips were so soft. Her tongue was quick, silky, pure pleasure against his. When she was especially turned on, as she was now, she bit. Not hard. Little nips. And her hands clenched and unclenched—in his hair, on his shoulders, on his ass. She never stopped moving. It made him insane with lust. It made him want to pin her down and hold her still and fuck her into the bed. *Mine. Stay there. Don't go.*

He wedged a thigh between hers, and she squeezed her legs tight around it. Bit him again. He groaned and kissed her longer. Harder. He showed her, with his tongue, what he was going to do to her, and underneath him, she went soft and yielding. Holy fuck, that was hot. He reached down and tucked a hand under the elastic waistband of her pajamas. Into the insubstantial lace of her panties. Found her slick and hot. He teased a fingertip around the swollen nub of her clit, sweetly taunting her with questions as he did: "Like that? Just like that? What do you want, pretty girl? What do you want me to do to you?"

"Let me—"

"What—?"

"Let me suck you."

That was *not* what he'd expected to come out of her mouth. But he wasn't complaining. He rolled over and she tugged his boxer briefs off, slid down his body, and took him in her mouth. It was the first time she'd done it since high school, and when she'd done it back then, it had always been way too quick and furtive, stolen moments in his truck or on the beach. Half the time she'd finished him in her fist; the other half, he'd done it himself after he'd taken her home, in the dark and quiet of his bedroom, thinking about a someday when they'd have a house together and they could do—

*This.*

She had taken him deep, so deep he could feel the back of her throat, and she'd wrapped her hand around the base of his cock so he was completely surrounded by pressure and heat. Her hair was everywhere. He collected it into an impromptu ponytail, which he held in one hand. He promised himself he would not pull it. Only assholes pulled women's hair while they were giving them blowjobs.

And holy *shit* what was she doing with her tongue? She had *not* done that, or *that*, or—

She was going to make him come. *No* one made him come with a blow job; he'd thought he just wasn't wired that way. But she was going to.

"Kee," he whispered.

She bobbed off him, her lips slick, her cheeks pink, her eyes bright. He wanted to kiss her so fucking bad, he could taste it.

"I want to come inside you. I want to kiss you while I'm fucking you. I want to hold you while I come."

Jesus. By nature he wasn't a talker, but she pulled it out of him. He rolled towards the nightstand, grabbed a condom, and sheathed himself.

She held her arms and legs open, that welcome of hers, and he went into them and slid deep, deep and so fucking easy. Just the right amount of resistance, slick but slightly sticky, tugging over the head where she'd teased him right to the edge a minute ago. She was gasping and pulling on him, wanting him to ride harder over her pubic bone, he knew what would get her off, so he did it, just the way she was asking, ignoring the pressure building in his body, listening to her body tell him how to make her come.

It was a long slow build; she was panting and arching and clenching her muscles tight to hold onto the sensation, but he didn't give up, he just held the rhythm, watching her pupils blow wide, watching the flush flow over her face like a wash of pink, watching her mouth open with surprise and pleasure. She was still coming when she reached for his head and pulled him down, kissing him, licking his mouth, yanking the orgasm out of him by its root. And it wasn't just the sheer physical pleasure of it, it was feeling so goddamn plugged into her, so he couldn't tell where her mouth started and his ended, who was inside whom.

It was like flying, and falling.

The problem with skydiving was, once you were in free fall, it was too late to turn back.

## 40

The shop opened at nine on Friday morning, the start of Labor Day weekend, and at ten forty-five, she, Jax, and Evan stood behind the counter, looking at one another with dread in their hearts.

No one had come in.

Of course it was still early, and of course it was only Friday, and of course it took some time for word to spread and things to build, but *still*.

"It's okay," Evan said. "I mean, whatever happens, it's going to be okay."

She smiled at that. No doubt, it was true for him. Whatever happened, even if he had to close the shop, Jax cared about him and would support him. If you had Jax in your corner, *really* in your corner, nothing bad would ever happen to you. He just wouldn't let it. He'd do everything in his power to make it okay. And Evan had grown up with that knowledge as part of his worldview. It was pretty impressive that he had managed not to lose his faith, with his barely-there parents, his run-ins with Stan, and his health challenges. But here he was, proof of his own resilience—and Jax's love.

She'd grown up believing her parents would always protect her. But then she'd had a look at real life. People disappointed you. They left when you'd thought they were in it for the long haul. They ghosted you when you thought you mattered. You'd thought you had them in your corner, but it turned out you were wrong.

Or they died. That happened, too.

Just like Auburn had said in the Bay Boutique dressing room.

The new bells that she'd installed over the door rang their charming little chime, and two elementary-age children bounced through the door, parents in tow.

"We did it!" the younger of the two announced. "We found all the clues! Is there a prize?"

"There *is*," she said. She came out from behind the counter with her treasure chest in her arms. "You can pick one thing out of here."

She'd remembered the dentist's office and how much she'd loved that moment when the toy chest was opened and she was told she could pick one. Even though she'd known, from age eight or so on, that the toys would always prove to be a total disappointment. It wasn't the toys. It was the choice.

The kids were just as delighted as she'd thought they'd be.

She could tell the parents were antsy, though. They looked like people with *plans*.

"I have an in-shop scavenger hunt," she offered, quietly, to them. She didn't want to sandbag them. Parents got super hostile when you did that; she knew that from working restaurant jobs in college. You'd get more dessert orders from asking the parents quietly than from announcing dessert out loud to the kids and forcing the parents' hands.

They exchanged looks. "Uh, sure," the mom said, shrugging. "That's fine."

She handed the scavenger hunt to the kids, and they began racing around the store. "What's this?" one called.

It was a game she'd set out on one of the tables, called Leaps and Ledges.

Evan was there in an instant. "Let me show you this one. It's super fun." He sat down with the kid, and a few minutes later, had her fully engaged in the game.

There was another chime, and another, and within a few minutes, they were all so busy they didn't sit down again for the rest of the day.

## 41

Jax woke Tuesday morning with his arm looped over Chiara and her warm, bare ass nestled up against his morning wood.

They'd left the shop Monday night tired but satisfied. It had been a long but incredibly successful weekend. Mid-day Sunday, Evan and Jax's mom had arrived in a rental car, fresh from the Portland airport and her flight from Bakersfield. Jax didn't try to argue with her about why she'd been able to fly now and not two weeks ago when Evan had most needed her. He'd learned a long time ago that to expect his mother to follow the normal rules of parenting was a recipe for disappointment.

To her credit, she'd worked like a fiend all weekend, flying back and forth from customer to customer and shelf to shelf like she'd been born to retail. She had singlehandedly sold more games on Monday than he and Evan combined. Of course, the three of them—Jax, Chiara, and Janice—had done everything they could to make sure Evan didn't tire himself out. He didn't seem tired, though. He was jazzed up about the store's success, already planning for next summer.

Next summer was still a long time away, especially in beach retail terms, but the fact that it was even a possibility felt like a huge success. The shop had made enough that if Evan had a good fall and kept building on their progress so far, Meeples would make it through the barren winter months without having to close.

Evan had hugged and thanked Jax and Chiara so many times that they'd had to ask him to stop.

"You take care of yourself, stay healthy, and don't blow my investment," Jax said, ruffling his brother's hair. "That's the kind of thanks I want. Besides, it was fun."

Evan cast a sidelong glance in Chiara's direction—she was chatting with Janice in a corner of the store—and then a questioning one at his brother. "How fun, exactly?"

"That's none of your business."

"I just—I like her for you. You smile a lot around her. And you know what else? She was really serious before you came. She's been a lot happier since you showed up. I think you should think about staying."

"You know she's leaving, don't you?"

"Well, yeah, I knew she was looking at a job in Seattle," Evan said. "I just—did she get it?"

Jax shook his head. "Not yet. But she will." He examined his brother's expression more closely. "You don't think she will?"

"Oh, I think she will. I don't think she'll take it."

"Why not?"

"Because she's in love with Tierney Bay."

For a brief, luminous second, Jax had thought he was going to say, *Because she's in love with you.*

He frowned.

"Well," Evan said. "We'll find out soon enough, right?" He didn't sound bent out of shape about it. "But either way, I think *you* should stay. Selfishly, it would be nice to have some help around here."

Jax didn't say that he'd thought about it. Or that he'd had a long chat with Trey after the two-on-two game last week, talking to him about the state of the development and contracting situation on the Oregon coast. He just said, "Keep dreaming, bro." And gave his brother a one-armed man-hug.

When he and Chiara had gotten back to her place last night, they'd been so bone tired that when she'd rolled toward him in bed, he'd made a *Help!* face, and they'd both started giggling. Then they'd wrapped their arms around each other and fallen asleep without even having sex.

Which he was planning to remedy now. He was supposed to have brunch with Evan and his mom today before she flew back to Bakersfield, but there was still an hour until he was scheduled to meet them. Chiara, lying beside him, had lost her covers, and she'd gone to bed wearing a shorty nightgown that had ridden up to her waist, baring a pair of all-lace pink panties. The visual was killing him—and he'd had a night of dreams that had featured him licking, sucking, and fucking pretty much every available part of her. He decided it was time for her to wake up, and that the best possible way to accomplish that would be to kiss her awake. Starting with the pink panties.

He had her moaning and thrashing inside of a minute, her hand in his hair.

"Wow," she said, when he lifted his face to smile at her. "That is a *good* way to wake up."

He gently rested his chin on her pubic bone and grinned up at her. He was just catching his breath before he climbed up her body to give her another reason to celebrate this morning when he became aware of a chorus of vibrations in the room. It took him a second to understand.

"Our phones are both going nuts."

Blame the success of the weekend or the high of getting Chiara off before she was even fully conscious, or maybe the amount of blood flow that had been diverted from his brain, but his first thought wasn't worry. Instead, he thought maybe something good had happened with the store. Someone wanted to interview them. Or partner with them.

Her phone was closer and she reached it first. Her expression went blank, then alert. He felt the stupid grin slide off his face. His belly knotted.

"We'll be right there."

She ended the call. Her mouth was set in a grim line.

"It's Evan," she said.

---

## 42

J ax had not looked up from his hands for an eternity. He was in the waiting room, which was decorated in shades of brown that Chiara couldn't imagine had ever cheered a sad person up. Or healed a hurting one. Or otherwise served any purpose other than the make a grim situation grimmer.

Evan was in emergency surgery; he'd spiked a fever which had turned out to be the result of an abscess, one of the most common side effects of his surgery. Sometimes you could drain an abscess without surgery, but this wasn't one of those cases, so he was under general anesthesia again.

Janice had disappeared. She'd been pacing every bit of linoleum she could find, sometimes going back outside to pace in front of the emergency entrance.

"I don't sit still," she told Chiara. "Text me when there's news."

Jax, for his part, was sitting so still that Chiara was worried about him. He was like a statue—frozen.

"Hey," she said, sitting beside him and putting an arm around his shoulder.

He didn't pull away, but neither did he lean into her touch —or show any emotion.

"Mr. Walker?" The voice had a Caribbean lilt; Chiara guessed Jamaican. She and Jax looked up to see Evan's surgeon, Dr. Henry, standing in the doorway, her mask down, one stray box braid escaping from her cap. Jax shot to his feet, but the expression on his face was flat. Chiara knew him well enough to spot the tight lines of fear etched at his mouth and eyes. Her stomach clenched.

"Your brother's going to be fine. It's good your mother made him come in. He'll be awake soon and you can see him."

Chiara watched the terror drain out of Jax's face. His shoulders softened, but he didn't loosen his fists.

"He'll have another few days of recovery, but he should be home again soon. And it's nothing he did. It's just that this sometimes happens. Bacteria from the gut gets out during the surgery. We do everything we can to prevent it, but intestinal surgeries always carry this risk." Her soft, dark brown eyes took in the slump of Jax's shoulders, the defeated expression on his face.

"Crohn's is tough," she said quietly. "My daughter has it. She's twenty-four. I was a cardiologist, but I switched specialties to be able to help patients with inflammatory bowel diseases. Has anyone talked to you about any of the immunotherapies for Crohn's?"

Jax nodded.

"I think they could help him. They changed my daughter's life."

"His insurance won't cover them," Jax said.

Dr. Henry closed her eyes, took a deep breath, opened them again. "I'm sorry," she said, simply. "We hear that all the time. I'm going to give you an email address. There are some clinical trials that open up here from time to time."

"Yeah?" Jax said. It was the first time he'd looked hopeful since before they'd seen his mother's text message three hours ago.

"But if he does one of those, he won't be guaranteed to get the treatment. He might get the control."

And just like that, the hope was gone from Jax's face, and Chiara felt a surge of anger and frustration so fierce it almost bowled her over. She *had* to do something to help. She *had to*.

Dr. Henry shook Jax's hand and went out again. Jax came back and sat down next to Chiara. He didn't look at her. She felt like he was a million miles away.

"I'm so glad he's going to be okay," she said, feeling like it was completely inadequate.

"He's *never* going to be okay," Jax said.

She wanted to argue with him, but she knew that wasn't what he needed right now. He needed this fixed.

She wanted, desperately, to fix it. She wanted to take care of him, the way he did for everyone else. To make it so he didn't have to bear this alone.

He sat heavily in the waiting room chair. "I'm going back to Bakersfield," he said. "I'm selling my condo, I'm going to rent something dirt cheap, and I'm going to use the money to pay for Evan's procedure."

His shoulders were slumped and his posture utterly defeated. She couldn't stand to see it.

She thought of what he'd said the day he'd told her what Stan had done to Evan: You take care of your family.

She wanted him to be her family. It was that simple.

"Don't do that," she said. "You don't have to do that. I can help pay for it."

He turned on her. "What?"

"I want to help pay for the immunotherapy."

"What the fuck are you talking about? You can't afford to do that."

"Yeah, I can. I've got a little saved. I was going to help Auburn with a problem she was having, but then she came up with her own fix, and I have money saved for the move to Seattle, and—" She hesitated. "I know you weren't able to get a loan, but I'm pretty sure I could—either against my business or my house—"

He flinched. She saw it. But she didn't understand. Not then. Not yet.

He was shaking his head. "No. No way. You're not using your Seattle move money on us."

"No, I mean, I've been thinking about the move, and I'm not sure it's the right thing for me. I've been thinking, what if I stayed—?"

"Stop," he said. "Just stop. You're not staying. You have the chance to take your dream job."

"You've said it yourself. Maybe it's not my dream job."

It felt so good to say it out loud. Just like it felt so good to finally admit to herself how strongly she felt about Jax.

"No. You're not going to give up the perfect job because I can't do my own job." His jaw was set, his mouth grim.

"It's not because you can't do it," she said. "It's because

you shouldn't have to do it alone. It's like you said. *You take care of your family*."

He looked at her like she was stark raving mad.

"Evan and I are *not* your family."

The tone registered first. So much scorn that she shriveled.

And then the words, which served as an absolute, complete rejection of her.

She felt like she'd been punched in the stomach. She must have flinched, because he looked away, frowning. "I'm sorry," he said. "That was—harsh." He wouldn't meet her eyes again.

"I know I'm not your family," she said. "But I guess I thought—"

Suddenly it felt absurd, what she'd thought. That after two weeks of mad, nostalgia-fueled sex, he might want them to make a life together, when everything he'd ever done had pointed to the opposite of that fact.

Everything that had happened between them, all the intimacy and intensity, that had been in her head and her heart. She'd done again what she'd done the first time: projected her own neediness onto him.

"No," she said. "I'm sorry. I thought this time was going to be different. But it's not, is it?"

He hung his head for a long minute. And then he looked up at her. All the green had gone out of his eyes. They were dull and flat.

He shook his head, took a deep breath, and said, "This was always how it was going to to end."

## 43

She got out of bed the next morning only because the shop needed her. She took a shower (but didn't wash her hair because she didn't have the energy to blow it dry) and pulled on a pair of jeans and a t-shirt. She picked up her phone and saw a text from Auburn: *How's Evan doing? How are* you?

She started to reply: *Evan's fine. I'm good.* But her fingers wouldn't cooperate. It was like they knew it was a lie and didn't want to participate. She put the phone in her purse. She'd reply soon. As soon as she got to the store.

She walked into town—it seemed to take forever, because her limbs responded slowly, like she was moving underwater. But eventually she made it to Meeples, opened up, and flipped the hours sign to *Open*.

She tried not to look around, but it didn't really matter because even the smell of the game store made her want to cry. The mildew and dust and old book smells had gradually been replaced with a new and welcoming set of smells, of fresh cardboard and cut lumber and new paint, and all those smells had somehow, in her head, gotten tangled up with Jax. There was no getting away from him.

She didn't have to look at the demo tables, though. Or the shelf that held Terraforming Mars. Or the blank wall behind her where he'd urged her to paint a mural.

No way *that* was going to happen now. She'd taken one look at her sketchbook this morning, still out on her nightstand, and almost been sick to her stomach. She'd closed it and shoved it in a drawer, along with the pencils. Where it all belonged. Where it should have stayed.

Where her feelings for him should have stayed.

Her phone buzzed.

*I'm headed back to Bakersfield first thing tomorrow. Mom is going to stay with Evan a few days.*

What did it say that her strongest feeling was relief because she wouldn't have to see him in the store, pass him on the street, run into him in the diner? He was leaving and she was glad.

Her phone rang, and her heart took off like a jackrabbit —*maybe? maybe?*

But it wasn't Jax at all. It was Greg Peppers from Buyathon.

"Hello?"

"Chiara?"

"This is she."

"This is Greg Peppers at Buyathon, and I'm calling to offer you a job!" He was obviously delighted with himself. "HR wanted to make the call but I insisted."

"Oh, wow." She could tell he was waiting for her to say more. "Thank you so much, Greg." She tried to put a little oomph in her voice. To convey the enthusiasm she knew he expected. The enthusiasm she'd expected to have. After all, it wasn't his fault that she'd just gotten slammed in the gut.

It was her own fault. She'd lined up her belly like a soccer ball for a free kick. *Hurt me again.*

Chiara yanked herself back to the moment. "I'm thrilled to hear that. Obviously I'll have to see the offer in writing before I can give you an answer, but I can tell you that I'm very excited about what Buyathon and I can offer each other."

The business-speak struck her, suddenly, as painful. And pathetic. Why couldn't people just say what they meant? Why did they have to play games? *Greg, I'm going to take the job as long as you guys offer me the salary you know I'm worth. Because I don't have a good reason to refuse it.*

They chatted for a few minutes longer, and by the time she got off the phone, there was an emailed offer letter in her inbox. At $10K more salary than she'd been hoping for.

*That's my girl!* Her father's voice said.

But there was something ragged in her chest, something it hurt to draw breath around.

Of course she was going to take it. Because getting out of Tierney Bay suddenly felt like the only way she'd be able to breathe.

Everything here reminded her of Jax.

THAT NIGHT she had to go to family dinner. "Had to" was not a phrase she'd ever applied to family dinner, but tonight it felt like the worst kind of chore. Even getting dressed seemed impossible. But she made herself put on a clean pair of a jeans and a pretty top. She brushed her hair and applied a little bit of mascara and lipstick. She needed to do at least a passable job of convincing her family that she wasn't falling apart, or Levi would murder Jax and go to prison for the rest of his life.

As soon as she showed up in the dining room at Beachcrest, they all looked up at her from the table. Auburn, with her emotional X-ray powers, said, "Oh, Kee, shit, Evan—?"

"He's fine," Chiara said quickly. "He's going to be okay. It was just—scary. For him, for all of us."

"You look—?"

"I'm fine," Chiara said. "Really. Just hungry and tired."

Auburn's eyes narrowed.

"How's Jax doing?" Hannah asked.

"He—"

Auburn's eyes tracked her.

"He's—"

If she were even a tiny bit better liar, she would say, "He's doing okay now that Evan's doing okay," and she tried, she really did.

But she couldn't do it.

Instead, she burst into tears.

And then the fun really started. Auburn popped up to get a box of tissues. She was back a second later, parceling out the tissues one by one. Hannah asked, over and over again, "What happened?" Mason sat and resumed eating his dinner —because tears were really not his thing. Trey hung back, looking sympathetic and a little awkward. She sort of wished they could all take their cue from him, but that wasn't how her family worked, and when Hannah and Auburn sandwiched her into a hug, she was honestly kind of glad it wasn't. She cried and cried until she couldn't cry anymore and then she sat down and dug into her chicken noodle soup.

When she hit the bottom of the first bowl, Auburn replaced it with a fresh one and said, "Talk."

"Well," Chiara said. "I got the Buyathon job, and I'm going to take it."

"Oh!" Auburn said, and then, "Congratulations!" Her forced tone and happy-for-you smile made Chiara's heart hurt more.

Hannah started to cry, and Auburn put her arms around both sisters, drawing them all together into a huddle. Levi told her he was going to miss the shit out of her, and even Mason said, "Things won't be the same without you."

And then Hannah asked, "But what about Jax?"

Everyone stopped crying and hugging and congratulating, and stared at Chiara. And she could see from the expression on Auburn's face, soft and sympathetic, that her sister had already guessed.

"We broke up."

"Oh, Kee," Auburn said. "Are you *sure* that's what you want? I'd be the last person to tell you not to take your dream job for a man, but I'd also be the first one to tell you that if it's making you this miserable..."

"It wasn't me," Chiara whispered. "He told me to take it. He doesn't want a serious relationship."

Mason froze, Auburn and Hannah exchanged stricken glances, and Levi's hand came down too hard on the table.

"Maybe he's just upset about Evan," Hannah said, big-eyed and hopeful.

Chiara felt her whole self lean eagerly towards Hannah's suggestion. Maybe...maybe...

But then she thought of the flat, cold look in his eyes. His words. *This was always how it was going to to end.*

"I just feel so stupid," she whispered. "I mean, what kind of idiot sets herself up like that twice?! He dumped me! He broke my heart. He ghosted me."

They were all quiet, so quiet you could hear the hum of the big industrial refrigerator in the kitchen, the roar of the ocean outside.

"Dad told him to."

At the sound of Mason's voice, Chiara's blood stopped in her veins. Her heart stalled, too. Everyone turned to look at Mason, and he looked back at all of them, like a deer suddenly caught in headlights. For a moment, Chiara thought he was going to bolt, but he held still.

"What. The. Hell. Are. You. Talking. About?" Auburn demanded.

Mason tugged on his bangs, a sign he was agitated. "Dad paid him not to contact you."

"He *what?*"

Auburn had a voice, even if Chiara did not. She felt frozen from the inside out, unable to move or speak. Only her heart soldiered on, sluggish and painful. It could not be true. Mason had to be lying.

Levi recovered first. "Mason, that's a huge accusation," he said. "You better not be making it up."

"Why would I make something like that up?" Mason looked genuinely puzzled.

And Chiara knew, with all the force of a tsunami: Mason

wasn't lying. He simply *didn't*. He didn't have a deceptive bone in his body.

"How do you know?" Auburn whispered. "How do you know he did that?" She looked like she was going to be sick. Chiara totally understood, because she was pretty sure that if she moved or spoke or breathed, she was going to throw up.

Mason looked like he would do anything to walk away from this conversation, but he took a deep breath.

Chiara held hers.

Mason tugged his hair again, closed his eyes, and said, unwillingly, "I heard Dad say it."

"Dad said that—to you?"

Chiara was grateful that Auburn and Levi could still speak, and voice her own questions, because she sure as hell wasn't able to get a word out.

Mason shook his head. "No. He said it to Jax. I was standing outside his office. I overheard."

There was a hand on Chiara's arm. Auburn's. Then another; Auburn had come around behind her chair and was holding her. Hugging her. Anchoring her.

"Do you—" Chiara choked out. She felt wild. Untethered. "I have to—"

"Go," Auburn whispered, and Chiara threw one glance back at her siblings with their identical blue eyes and worried expressions, and then took off, running.

## 44

Jax wished that drinking himself into oblivion was an option, but his mother's history had made him cautious on that front. So instead he was flipping channels on Evan's TV and trying as hard as he could not to think about the look on Chiara's face when he'd told her to take the Buyathon job.

He'd done the right thing. He knew he had.

Rich would agree with him.

*In five years or ten years, Jax, you'll have built a life for yourself. Figured out how to stand on your own two feet and how to take care of the people in your life. And maybe you and Chiara will get a second chance then.*

But it had been ten years, hadn't it? And he still wasn't the man that Rich had challenged him to be.

It was the surging sense of helplessness that got to him. That helplessness was familiar. He'd felt it once before, when he'd realized that Stan wasn't being generous to Evan by playing catch and one-on-one with him. Stan wasn't being fatherly when he worked with Evan on his homework. And he wasn't being helpful when he took Evan's rides off Jax's hands. He was being a predator.

But Jax had said yes to it all—to all the games and the offers—because he wanted the time for himself.

Because he wanted the time alone with Chiara.

Jax had let Evan down, and then he'd lost Chiara anyway, because there had never been room in his life to juggle all those pieces. He'd never had any right to think he could take care of her the way she deserved, without taking that care away from someone else in his life who mattered.

The sound of pounding on Evan's apartment door broke through the haze of bad TV and his own dark thoughts. He got up and went to peer through the peephole. When he saw who it was, his heart started throwing itself against the walls of his chest.

He cautiously opened the door to let Chiara push past him and into the apartment.

"Why didn't you *tell* me?"

"Tell you what?"

"My dad. Paid. You. To. Break. Up. With. Me."

He had a split second to pretend he had no idea what she was talking about. And it seemed so far-fetched that she could have found out … but at the same time, if she knew, then he wasn't the only one, which was a painful kind of relief. She knew, and it wasn't because he'd told her. He hadn't betrayed Rich or himself—or Chiara.

"How did you find out?" he asked quietly.

"You answer me first! Why didn't you tell me?"

"I couldn't."

"What kind of bullshit is that?"

"If I had told you he'd given me money to leave you alone, he would have known. You wouldn't have been able to look him in the eye—and you know it."

That shut her up.

"How did you find out?" he asked. He felt both weary and alert.

"Mason overheard your conversation with my dad."

He closed his eyes. Of course. Mason had been there. It had just never occurred to Jax that Mason would have stayed and listened. Because Mason was so quiet, you could almost forget about him.

He opened his eyes to find her staring at him. He could see the anger, but there was something else too. A stillness. Curiosity.

"Tell me what happened," she said. "Tell me everything."

HE WAS FLOATING through the day after their lovemaking in the haze of his feelings for Chiara. He wanted to be with her again, right that second. He wanted to run his fingers through her thick hair and touch her soft breasts and kiss her full mouth. He wanted to bury himself in her and to know everything that was in her head.

And then Evan had asked him, all innocence, "Jax?"

"Mmm-hmm?"

"Why do men have hair on their penises?"

It had taken a long time to get the whole story out of him. And a lot of tears. Stan had done a good job of convincing

Evan that if anyone ever knew "their" secret, he'd be in really, really big trouble.

Jax assured and reassured Evan that he was not in trouble. Doing his best not to create more shame than Evan was already feeling, he had explained to Evan that no one could or should make him do what Stan had been making him do. Then he gently, gently extracted from Evan permission to talk to Rich.

If he'd thought their mother would have been remotely useful, he would have talked to her, but he wasn't hopeful on that front.

And then, even though he wanted to drive to Stan's house and kill him with his bare hands, he went to his shift at Cape House. He was forty-two minutes late, and when he showed up—Evan in tow, because there was no fucking way he was leaving his brother with their mother, who was already a couple of drinks in—Mason said, "My dad wants to see you in his office."

Jax set up Evan in the lobby, with his DS gaming console, while Mason watched. Then Mason shadowed Jax all the way to his father's office. He disappeared when Jax went in—or so Jax had thought.

Rich looked him over with sharp eyes. "What's going on?"

Even though he had Evan's permission to tell Rich, it still felt like a betrayal to tell the story. He kept seeing Evan's face, so puzzled and fearful. So ashamed.

But he had no choice but to tell. He needed help, and Jax knew that if there was anyone in the world who could help him, it was Rich.

So he told him everything.

Rich listened quietly, giving away the intensity of his

emotion only with flinches and winces and a clenching of teeth that looked like it must hurt.

"That *bastard*," he said. "Jesus. Evan." He closed his eyes, tight. Then opened them and assured him, "You did the right thing, coming to me with this. Thank you for trusting me."

Tears filled Jax's eyes. It was going to be okay. Rich was going to make it okay.

This. *This* was what it felt like to have a father.

"You aren't going to try to confront him," Rich said. It wasn't a question.

"God. I want to."

"No," Rich said definitely. "That ends badly. That ends with you getting the cops called on you. That ends with Stan looking like a victim. We have to call the cops."

Jax was already shaking his head.

He could see that Rich was a little puzzled. Of course, because as sympathetic and understanding as Rich was, he hadn't walked a mile in Jax's shoes. He hadn't thought through it all.

"They'll take Evan away."

"Of course they won't."

"They *will*," Jax said. "Mom's never lasted more than two days sober. They'll put her in rehab and they'll take Evan away."

Rich took a deep breath. "I don't think that'll happen."

Much later, Jax understood that what Rich meant was that it *shouldn't* happen. By then he also understood how many people couldn't count on the system to protect them.

"Can you promise me? Absolutely promise me? That it won't?"

He spotted the very moment that Rich knew he couldn't

promise. He shook his head. Then he rested it in his hands for a long time, and Jax felt the beginnings of despair bloom in his stomach. The smartest and best man he knew had no idea what to do next.

But then Rich sat up. Nodded. "I know how to fix this."

Rich reached out to a general contractor friend in Bakersfield. Called in a few favors, found Jax and his brother and mom an apartment. Found Jax a really damn good job, apprenticing with the friend. Jax heard him on the phone. "He's a good kid. Hard worker, good with his hands. Loyal. Lots of integrity."

Not enough loyalty or integrity to have taken care of his brother, though. Jax's stomach was knotted so tight he couldn't imagine ever wanting to eat again. But even through his anger at himself, Rich's words felt good. Rich thought he was a good kid, a hard worker. Thought he was good with his hands. Loyal. Had lots of integrity. The words warmed him up and slowly unknotted him. So did what Rich did next. He came around the desk and hugged Jax, which he'd never done before. "This isn't your fault," he said. "None of this is your fault. And we're going to get Evan help. Counseling. I'm going to make sure he's okay."

A surge of relief swept Jax. A terrible thing had happened to Evan, but Rich was going to help, and with counseling, Evan would be able to move on from this.

Rich's warmth made it feel possible to imagine going to Bakersfield. To imagine life going on. Evan would be safe. He'd get help. Jax would have a steady job. Meanwhile, Chiara would go to Stanford and they could still be together. Jax could get his brother and mother settled and then maybe move to be nearer to Chiara.

He said those things out loud. He wasn't really looking at Rich when he said them. He was deep inside his own head, thinking about how this wasn't the end of things, it was the beginning, and how Rich was more like a father to him than any of the other men who'd lived in his house, including the one who'd actually fathered him.

He was thinking that, and picturing the future with Chiara, when Rich said, softly, "Jax."

Jax looked up, and Rich was looking at him with a peculiar expression on his face. Later, Jax knew it for what it was.

*Guilt.*

He offered Jax enough money to pay first, last, and security on the apartment and to get him and his mom and Evan through the first month until he'd have a paycheck at his new job.

It was too much, but there was no way Jax could turn it down, so he swallowed his pride. "I'll pay you back."

"It's a gift," Rich said. "And I want to pay for counseling for Evan. Once you know how much that's going to be, you can let me know and I'll send you checks as needed."

Jax's mouth fell open, his whole body flooded with gratitude. "You can't do that—"

"I need something in return."

"Of course. Anything."

Rich took a deep breath. Blew it out again. "I need you not to contact Chiara again."

At first Jax couldn't actually believe he'd said that. Yes, he'd suspected that Rich had mixed feelings about Jax dating his daughter. But Rich cared about him.

Didn't he?

A terrible, dark feeling was settling in the pit of Jax's

stomach. And as he watched Rich scrabble together some random papers on the desk, he recognized the feeling. Anger. "What are you *talking* about?"

"Jax," Rich said gently. So gently. "I wouldn't be a good father to her if I let her get tangled up in a situation like this one."

"She won't be tangled up in anything. We're leaving the situation behind."

"You're leaving Stan behind. But that's not the situation I'm talking about. I'm talking about the fact that you're effectively the sole caretaker of an eight-year-old boy and a forty-something woman. I'm talking about the fact that you're not in the position to take care of anyone else." Rich took a deep breath. Now the expression on his face was something else.

Apology.

"I know you love her. I can see it all over your face. And I know you don't want to hold her back. And sometimes, when you love someone, you have to get out of their way. So you don't drag them down." Rich took a breath. "Chiara's going to go to college and she'll meet amazing people. And she'll do amazing things. She'll have the opportunity to become anyone she wants to be. But I know her, too. She loves hard, and she'll try to hold back part of herself so she can stay the person you're in love with now.

"I don't want that for her, and I don't think you do, either."

It wasn't out of *love* that Rich was trying to help Jax and Evan. It was to get him the hell out of Tierney Bay. Out of Chiara's life.

All the warmth that had settled in his chest turned into a big block of ice. Shame. He'd always thought of shame as hot, but this was cold.

"You don't think I'm good enough for her."

He waited for Rich to protest. Even just a little. A bluster of explanations that didn't come.

"Jax," Rich said.

He hated the way Rich said his name. Fucking *hated* it.

## 45

"**N**o," she said.

She was going to be sick. Literally.

"Where's the bathroom—"

He pointed and she ran. Pushed the door open and knelt in front of the toilet and hung there until the nausea edged back a notch.

When she came back outside, he was standing in the hallway outside the bathroom.

"Are you o—"

He stopped, obviously because any idiot could see that she wasn't okay. She wasn't sure if she was ever going to be okay again.

Like when she'd lost her parents.

Like when she'd lost Jax, the first time.

"Did you—did you think about telling me?"

"I did. Once you'd accepted Stanford and were there, once Evan was doing well in counseling, I thought maybe I'd tell you. But then—"

His voice broke.

"But then my dad died," she said, filling in for him. "And *of course* you couldn't tell me. You didn't want that to be the last thing I knew about him."

He shook his head.

He'd held onto this secret all these years. Ten years, and he'd never told her the one thing that would make it all make sense. And she didn't know whether to punch him or kiss him for it.

Not that it mattered. He was looking at her now with utter blankness and indifference. "You had a boyfriend at Stanford. I saw on your Facebook. And it looked pretty serious, and the idea of going to you and telling you what your dad had said to me just felt like—messing with your head for no reason. I mean, you'd lost him, and I couldn't take *more* of him away from you. All I could think about was how much you loved your dad. More than anyone else."

"How are you not angry?" she demanded. "How are you not filled with rage and shaking your fist at the sky?" Her eyes raked his face. "Jax. Don't tell me you *still* think he was —right?"

"His methods were wrong," Jax said.

"But you think he was right to—use you to manipulate me? Some Machiavellian bullshit about how the ends justify the means?"

"No. He was wrong about that, too."

"God! I am so angry! At both of you!" She closed her eyes.

Jax shook his head. "This is why—" he said. "This is why I didn't want you to know. Because—God. I didn't want you to hate him. He loved you so much." He raked a hand through his hair. "He tried to break us up because he didn't want you to make a mistake that would ruin your life. He really believed what he said. I was angry at him, yeah, but—I knew he loved you as much as I did."

"Well, he had a really shitty way of showing it," she said, and now she was crying in earnest.

He didn't step forward to hold her or comfort her. He just stood there, eyes on his shoes, until she was able to take longer, deeper breaths. Then she looked up, and found him watching her. His eyes were sad.

"The thing is—" His gaze skittered around the apartment, and she saw it for the first time. Evan's apartment—cruddy couch, two different board games strewn out on the coffee table, dishes piled in the sink and dirty on the end table. It was just an eighteen-year-old boy's bachelor pad—there was nothing unusual about it—but right now it felt like an omen. "He was right. That I would drag you down. Maybe you would have come to visit me on weekends instead of staying at college and doing your homework. Maybe you would have spent too much time with me when you should have been doing the Young Business Leaders of America or whatever club. Maybe you would have married me instead of going to business school."

"No! None of those things would have happened," she said. "I would have been able to figure out how to love you *and* be who I wanted to be."

She wasn't sure why she was arguing. She was so tired. She wanted to go home and sleep for hours. Mourn the things she was losing all over again. But some stubborn bit of her wouldn't let go.

He frowned. "But eventually my life would have worn you down. All the times my mother tried to get sober and didn't. All the times Evan was in and out of the hospital. All the times I couldn't pay a bill and had to work a second or a third job. I mean, just look at what's happening now. You want to take the money that was supposed to fund your move to a new city and spend it on my brother. Because I can't. This is exactly what your father was talking about. This is why he didn't want you with me. And—" Jax raked a hand through his hair, until it was all standing on end. "I can't blame him. Because he was *right*."

"No," she said. "He wasn't. If he thought you weren't good enough for me, he was wrong. You're the best man I know, Jax. You take care of everyone in your life. Look at what you did for your brother in the shop. You saved that shop for him."

But as she was saying it, he wasn't looking at her, and she realized something. Jax's life had required him to harden himself against everything and everyone. Every relationship required two things of a person—loving, and letting himself be loved. And Jax would never be able to give her that second thing, even if he had done a better job of the first one than anyone else ever had.

It was even possible her father had known that. Had foreseen it. Maybe he had guessed it would come down to something like this. It didn't make him any less of a horror show for having engineered their breakup behind her back, but it turned her anger down to a dull roar.

"I got the Buyathon job," she said.

He smiled a little bit. "I knew you would."

That made her smile, too, even though every part of her hurt.

"So, you're going to go back to Bakersfield," she said.

He nodded. "I'll try to sell my place and get a smaller one. I'll use the money to pay for Evan's treatment."

"And you—don't want—you don't want me to be part of that. Part of—what happens next."

For the first time since they'd been in the hospital waiting room together, his gaze came back to hers. And there was something so full of longing in his eyes that, for a moment, she thought maybe she'd been wrong. Maybe this time really was different, maybe he would remember what it had been like these last couple of weeks, the joy of the work, the sweetness of the connection, the long, hot, nights. He would say, *Your father was wrong. And I know that because* this *is right.*

Instead he gave a short, tight nod. She'd seen that gesture before. It was the way he reached a decision. A conclusion.

She felt a wild flare of hope.

And then his gaze flattened and he said, "No. I don't."

## 46

A week had passed since he left Tierney Bay, and he kept expecting to feel a sense of relief—or at least a sense that he'd made the right decision—but instead he mostly felt like he was wearing a too-tight tie.

He had contacted a realtor about selling his condo and put it on the market, and he was in the process of getting some help from a good friend who knew all about staging properties for sale.

He'd found a studio apartment in a rundown building not too far from his mother's place, and had a date tomorrow to sign the lease and put down first, last, and security. It was about an eighth the size of his condo, but he could live with that. The thing that really bothered him was the sense that he was moving backwards, losing ground.

He was packing up a box of books in his bedroom when he heard the doorbell ring. He went to the front door and found his mother there.

"When were you going to tell me?" she asked, and pushed past him, into the foyer.

"What are you talking about?"

"You're moving to Tierney Bay, and you weren't going to tell your own mother?"

For a brief moment, he saw the fantasy his mother had conjured for herself: Jax in a U-Haul, driving into Tierney Bay. Pulling up in front of Chiara's house with all his possessions on board.

Then a curtain came down on the absurd vision, along with a wave of pain. "What are you *talking* about?"

"Linda Barnes told me that her daughter is staging your condo for sale."

Ah. The rumor mill.

"I'm selling it. But I'm not moving to Tierney Bay," he said. "I'm moving to an apartment a couple of blocks away from you."

He wasn't sure what to make of the expression that moved over her face. It couldn't be—disappointment—could it? Relief, maybe. He'd mistaken it.

"What about Chiara?"

"What about her?"

"You two looked awfully cozy in the shop last weekend."

He had a vivid, tempting flashback to the way it had felt to move around Chiara as they helped customers in the shop. Each pass had been its own chemical reaction. And all through, he'd known that at the end they'd go home together, and he'd be able to—

Not anymore. He cut the thought short, brushed away the memories, the teasing images.

"Things didn't work out with Chiara."

"Why not?"

He hunched his shoulders. "Mom, this is none of your business."

Now he knew the expression on her face for sure: hurt.

He wanted to apologize—but he couldn't bring himself to do it. What he really wanted was for her to leave. Right now. Take her curiosity and her questions and her hurt away.

Instead, she took a step toward him, and he reflexively took one back. "Jax," she said.

"You know what? This isn't a good time. I'm packing."

"You broke it off with her, didn't you?"

No. Not this, not right now. He couldn't do this, couldn't have some kind of mother-son moment. "Since when do we have heart-to-hearts?" he demanded, wanting her out. Out of his head space, out of his condo, out of his life.

But this time, even though he saw the flicker of hurt, she straightened her shoulders and kept coming. "I know we've never been close. And I understand why."

"I don't want to talk about this right now." His throat was tight enough that it was hard work to speak around the lump in it.

"You've had to push everyone away. Me included. And that's the truth. Your father left and I wasn't there for you. I wasn't there for you the whole time you were a teenager and trying so hard to take care of Evan. And I know that's why you're afraid to take chances emotionally. I know that's why you're afraid to let people take care of you."

God, she was so full of it, with her new age advice and the tender look in her eyes. "I don't need a therapist, Mom," he said. "I don't want your psychobabble. Chiara and I weren't a couple. We hooked up because we were both in Tierney Bay. For old time's sakes. And we ended it because she's moving to

Seattle and I live in Bakersfield. Period. And I've never pushed you away."

They both knew what he wasn't saying. *And I could have.* But he had always given her what she'd needed. Even though, yeah, she was right: She hadn't been there for him when it counted. But what could you do? You couldn't hold that against a person forever. That was just bad karma.

"I'm just trying to help, Jax," she said quietly.

"You want to help?" he asked, and he couldn't help it; his voice was sharp. "Stop living in a perpetual state of denial and own up to the fact that if we don't do something, Evan's going to have a colostomy bag."

And there—the look on her face—shock and dismay— told him he'd gotten her off his back, at least for the time being.

## 47

E very day this week, Chiara had been in the shop, and it still wasn't any easier. She kept thinking that she'd stop remembering conversations she'd had with Jax. Or the feel of his hands on her body. Or the way he'd looked at her, as if she were the only thing that mattered.

But if anything, she'd felt worse as the week had worn on.

Evan was home, recuperating. Safe, and, for the time being, reasonably healthy. He'd be in this afternoon for a short workday, and tomorrow, if things went well, he'd try a longer day. And then he was going to begin training her replacement, Asher's friend Tamara.

The door opened, the bells rang. Auburn stood there.

"You can't hide from me forever."

"I'm not hiding from you."

"Come on, Chiara. You didn't come to family dinner last night. You *never* miss family dinner."

"I was—busy."

Auburn raised her eyebrows. She came over to where Chiara stood and put her arms around her sister. A big, chocolate-chip cookie-scented hug. And Chiara released a breath that she hadn't realized she'd been holding. Her shoulders sank. And her belly, which had been full of knots —well, it was still full of knots. But it did make her optimistic, for one tiny second, that she might survive.

"I take it what Mason said about Dad was true?"

Chiara nodded.

"You going to tell me that story?"

She closed her eyes. She was very, very tired.

"You have to tell me something that will make me hate Dad a tiny bit less than I do right now," Auburn said. "Because I don't know about you, but it's eating me up."

Tears filled Chiara's eyes. Auburn drew back, took a close look at her sister, and gently led her towards the tables where she pulled out a chair for each of them.

"Talk."

So Chiara did, telling Auburn exactly what Jax had told her.

"God. That—" Auburn stopped. "That *fucker*. It makes me wish I'd done a hell of a lot more to push back on him and the way he treated you and Levi."

"What do you mean?" Chiara asked.

"He was so exacting with the two of you. Levi because he was the oldest, and you because you were the first girl. By the time he got around to me and Mason, he didn't have time to kick my ass and guilt me into overachieving. I'm hella sorry now I spent so much time being grateful his radar wasn't trained on me. I should have been fighting to get him off you and Levi."

"He never guilted me," Chiara said.

Auburn raised an eyebrow. "Sure he did. What do you

·think all that, *I know you won't disappoint me, Kee* stuff was about?"

She'd forgotten about that phrase, until Auburn mimicked her father's sternest tones. Then it came flooding back, along with the expression her father had worn on those few awful occasions when she *had* disappointed him. Like when she'd gotten a D on a test in calculus.

"He drove you guys hard," Auburn said. "He was kind of a tyrant, whether you realized it or not."

It took Chiara a minute to reframe some of her memories, but she could see the faintest outlines of what Auburn was describing.

"He made me design a multi-step improvement plan for myself when I got that D on that test in calc."

"Exactly."

"And what about that college application spreadsheet? That was intense."

"Very," Auburn said. "He was exacting. He had a vision for what he wanted you and Levi to be, and he wasn't interested in compromising. And I think—" Her eyes searched Chiara's face for something. "It's not super surprising to me that Jax didn't fit into that vision."

Chiara shook her head; sighed. "That's not the part I hate so much. I mean I wish he hadn't felt that way. And I wish he'd *told* me that he did. But the fact that he was willing to use Jax's love for Evan to keep him away from me—? What kind of a person does that?" The anger flared up again, hot and choking; it felt like it was going to drown her if she didn't do something—run out of the store flailing her arms, maybe.

"Kee?" Auburn asked.

She started to cry. Because she was so hurt and angry and

because she would *never, ever, ever* get to tell him. She would never get to ask her father why he'd done such a stupid, idiotic thing, and she'd never get to yell at him and tell him that she hated him. She'd never get to explain to him about how paternalistic and alphaholic he was, or how she was never going to talk to him again—

Because she couldn't talk to him ever again.

"Oh, Kee," Auburn said, and wrapped her sister in her arms.

"I feel like I'm losing him all over again," Chiara whispered. "I'm losing the man I thought he was. Who wasn't the man he really was."

"Hush," Auburn said. "You know what? I'll tell you what's really happening. You're letting go of the hero-worship. He died right when you were in the middle of it and you never got to grow up and learn that he was a human being, just like all of us, and that he was going to make awful mistakes and be a shitty, classist bastard and piss you off. We all got deprived of that—maybe except for Levi. We'll have to ask him sometime. I know I always think Mom would know exactly what to do. Even now, I find myself thinking, If Mom were here, she'd know what to say to Chiara! But the truth is, if they were alive? We'd be angry at them for shit *all the time*. Because they were just people."

Chiara cried harder then, and Auburn held her while searching out a small pack of tissues in her purse. She passed them over, one by one, until they were all soggy.

"And now you have to stop crying because there are no more tissues," Auburn said, making Chiara laugh, just a little bit. "And I am so, so sorry but I have to go because I have to be at a staff meeting five minutes ago. Are you going to be okay? I can come back afterwards—"

"I'm going to be *fine*," Chiara said. After all, she'd survived this all before. She would survive it again.

Auburn scanned her sister's face, then nodded, seeming satisfied with what she saw there. She gave her one last hug and hurried out, and Chiara watched her jog up the street.

Then she broke down in tears again. For her father. For Jax. For her high school self.

And her right-now self, too, because even though she *knew* her heartbreak couldn't really be worse this time around than the last time, right now, it felt like it was going to turn her inside out.

## 48

"So, yeah, there's not much more to show you."

"Sylvia did a great job," Patty Labine, the real estate agent, told him. "I like the dish towels."

"Yeah. Those are hers. So are pretty much all the towels in the whole place."

"It makes a difference."

"So you guys say."

"Realtor open house tomorrow, market open house Sunday. You ready? I need you to put the break-and-bake cookies in the oven, pull 'em out, and leave the house, by 12:45."

He nodded. "Got it."

She was letting herself out the front door when she pulled up short. "You have a visitor," she said.

"Yeah?"

She stepped back to let him see.

His brother was coming up the path.

His *brother*. What the fuck was Evan doing here?

"I'll talk to you soon," Patty said, and disappeared down the path with her adorable gray bun.

"What are you doing here?" Jax demanded.

"How about, 'Great to see you, brother mine! Thank you for flying down from Oregon to stop in and say hello!'"

"How about, 'I'm thinking of flying down to California, mind if I stop by?'" Jax raised his eyebrows.

Evan had the decency to look ashamed. "I tried to call, but you didn't answer."

"Smashed the hell out of my phone on the work site today. I have a new one on order. Should be here by Monday at the latest." He gave his brother a stern look. "You could have called Mom and figured that out. You shouldn't be traveling."

"Doctor didn't say anything about that," Evan pointed out. "She said take it easy."

"Flying is easy," Evan said. "I wasn't the pilot or anything." But he looked a little gray, and Jax pulled the door wide open and ushered him inside. He settled him on the couch and offered him a big glass of water and some grapes. Evan took both gratefully.

"Seriously, man, what are you doing here?"

"I'm here in case you want to talk about anything." Evan shrugged.

"What would I want to talk about?"

Evan raised both eyebrows. He'd let his moth-eaten beard go full gamer-nerd scruffy, which Jax hated, but you couldn't argue with an eighteen-year-old about bad hair choices.

For a moment, the brothers stared at each other over Evan's snack. Jax was the first to look away. When he looked back, Evan was watching him with curiosity but no judgment.

"Who's watching the shop?" Jax asked.

Evan smiled. "Asher's friend Tamara."

"Is Chiara still in Tierney Bay?"

Evan's smile got bigger. "That shouldn't matter to you, should it? Since you're in Bakersfield?"

Jax closed his eyes.

"I remember when we used to have dinner at the Campbells," Evan said.

Part of Jax wanted to stop the conversation dead in its tracks. But most of him wanted to know what Evan was going to say. If the only little bit of Chiara he could have was Evan's memories of her, then he'd take it.

Evan took his silence for permission to continue. "I really liked going over there."

"Me, too," Jax said.

"I liked playing with Hannah. Even though she was a baby."

"She was six."

"I know, but I was older. And I loved Mrs. Campbell's food. That woman could *cook*. Rumor has it Auburn is the one who inherited that gene. But you know why I liked going over there most?"

"Why?" Jax asked.

"Because of how you were when we were there. All the worry lines went out of your forehead. I didn't really understand it at the time, but I think I understand it now. I liked being there because when we were there, there were grownups taking care of us. There were grownups taking care of *you*. You didn't have to be the grownup."

Jax felt so much pressure behind his eyes. If he breathed

too hard, it would burst right out of him, so he held his breath.

Evan sighed. "I just want you to know. I don't take any of it for granted. Not then. Not now. You were the best big brother anyone could have. You *are*. And I just want you to be happy. That's why I came down here."

Jax seized the opportunity to lighten the moment. "I thought it was so I could talk to you if I needed someone to talk to?" he teased.

"Oh, right," Evan said. "That, too." He sized up his brother with a long glance. "What do you love most about her?"

Startled, Jax said, "What?"

"Chiara. What do you love most about her?"

"Who says—?"

"Jax," Evan said sternly. "You're not fooling anyone."

He couldn't look at his brother, but the words spilled out, against his will, anyway. "She makes the world hold still. For just a second."

Evan nodded like that made perfect sense to him. "Asher does that to me," he said. "He, um, doesn't know it, though."

Jax felt a moment of surprise, followed by the shock of realizing how un-surprised he was. The brothers' eyes met, recognition of the size of the revelation.

"Thank you. For telling me."

"You're the first person I've told."

"You should think about telling him."

Evan gave him a long, hard look.

Jax sighed. "I know. I should take my own damn advice."

"I didn't say anything," Evan said, with a smirk.

"No," Jax agreed. "You didn't really have to."

"She's still in Tierney Bay," Evan said, quietly. "She's going to stay there through reunion, and then she's going to Seattle. And she's—she's unhappy. No. She's miserable. I think that's fair to say. I'm not telling you that for any particular reason. I just thought even though you are in Bakersfield, it might matter to you."

"It matters to me," Jax whispered.

Evan grinned. "Yeah, dumbass. I know."

## 49

"Hey," Evan said, coming in through the front door of Meeples. "I thought Tamara was minding the store today."

"Tamara got the stomach flu," Chiara said. "We figured if we infected all our weekend customers that wouldn't be good for business."

It was Friday. The reunion dinner-dance was tomorrow night. Sunday, Chiara would drive a U-Haul to Seattle with all her belongings on board, and by Wednesday, she would have started her new job at Buyathon.

Everything was falling into place.

Well, almost everything. And she was getting better at not thinking about the thing that wasn't in place.

Who was she kidding? She thought of him a hundred times a day. She'd been thinking of him when she'd seen Evan get out of his car across the street. In fact, for a split, insane second, she'd thought she'd *seen* him, and her heart had taken wing. And then she'd looked up again and it had only been Evan.

A broken heart was an awful lot like a bad flu, hallucinations and all.

Evan set his overnight bag down.

"Where'd you go?" she asked.

"Nowhere in particular," he said. "Just needed to get away for a day. Prove to myself that I'm not fragile. And I had to save someone's ass. All in a day's work."

She smiled at that. "You don't seem very fragile to me. And whose ass?"

"Long story," Evan said, waving a hand. He started breaking down a box with a penknife. "Everything go okay while I was gone?"

She nodded. "Good sales. We're still getting people coming in and asking if they can do the scavenger hunt, so clear word-of-mouth carryover."

He grinned. "You're a marketing genius, you know."

"Hardly. It was basic stuff." She leaned over her laptop and tried again to get the email to Buyathon HR to go through with her W-9 information. "Crap," she said.

"What's wrong?"

"I've been trying to get this email to go to Buyathon all morning. And I keep getting error messages. The WiFi's fine, no other Internet traffic is affected. I've made the file smaller, I've checked the address a million times. I just keep getting error messages and bounces." She sighed. "Okay. One last thing to try. I'm going to paste the PDF in the email instead of doing it as an attachment."

"It still goes out as an attachment, I'm pretty sure," Evan said.

"Well. Nothing else is working. I'm going to try it."

She sent the message again, and again heard the frustrating ping of the same stupid error message she'd been getting for hours. "Fuuuuck," she said. "It's like the universe doesn't want me to take this fucking job."

She exited the email app, closed the PDF reader, and reopened everything yet again. She was going to give it one more try and then she was going to—

Well, she'd go find someone with a fax machine. They still had to exist somewhere, right? Maybe Cape House still had one buried in a back office.

Evan was looking at her, a peculiar expression on his face. "What?" she said, swiping at her mouth with the back of her hand, then checking her teeth with her tongue for food. Not that she'd had anything to eat since she'd brushed her teeth.

"Do you want to take that—" he hesitated. "—*fucking job*?"

"Yes," she said, not looking up from what she was doing. And then, suddenly, really hearing the question, "No."

Evan looked a little, but not very, surprised.

"No," she repeated.

She surveyed the shop. Looked at Evan, who had the world's worst beard; she wished Jax were here to talk him out of it. Looked at all the work they'd done together to make the shop what it was. At the blank space where there was still no mural, at the counter—just the right height—the shelves, the racks. At the two teenagers playing Magic at one of the demo tables, deep in their world.

Her father would probably accuse her of a lack of ambition. He might even guilt her, intentionally or not: *I know you won't disappoint me, Kee.* He'd had another thing he said sometimes. *I know you'll make the right choice.* Which had always terrified her a little bit, honestly, because obviously he knew what the right choice was, but she always had to guess, and what if she got it wrong? She'd almost never gotten it wrong because she'd learned to read him so well, because she'd known what kinds of things he expected from her and how to make him proud.

The truth was, if he'd told her in high school that he wanted her to break up with Jax, it would have been one of the hardest moments of her whole life. She would have had to weigh a lifetime of pleasing her father against the strongest and best connection of her life. This new, perfect thing.

And maybe Jax would have won out.

And maybe her father had known that, and he'd set it up so he never had to be the bad guy or the loser.

The truth was—just as Auburn had said—that even her father didn't know what the right choice was sometimes. He'd certainly fucked it all to hell with her and Jax.

"My dad wanted me to take this, um, *fucking job*," she said. "My dad wanted me to go to Stanford and go to business school and work in finance and become the CFO of something, someday."

Evan raised an eyebrow. It was a very thick eyebrow, and with the beard, it gave him the look of a wise gnome. "And what do *you* want?" he asked.

She shut her laptop. Gently but firmly.

"I want to stay in Tierney Bay. I want to finish raising my baby sister. I want to help small businesses thrive. I want to work in your game shop. If you still need my help."

Evan pumped a fist. "Absofuckinglutely."

*Also, I want to marry Jax Walker and have his babies*, she thought.

Four out of five wasn't bad.

Except that it was the fifth thing that Chiara wanted so badly that it made her stomach hurt.

*I know this wasn't what you wanted for me, Dad. But you gave up the right to have an opinion when you took away my right to have one. Even if it took me ten years and a few weeks to figure that out.*

She had figured it out, though. And now she was going to find out whether she'd figured it out in time.

## 50

"What are you doing?"

Chiara dragged her eyelids open and found Auburn standing over her.

"I'm resting," she said.

"Don't you have a reunion to go to?"

Chiara rolled over and buried her face in the pillow.

"Uh, no you don't." Auburn grabbed her sister's shoulder and tried to roll her back over, but Chiara made herself a dead weight. "Kee. You're not going to let him ruin reunion for you. Willa said you guys worked for hours last night and all morning on setup and decorations, and that it looks ahhhhmazing. You have to go enjoy the fruits of your labors."

Chiara shook her head. And pointed to her phone, lying face down on her nightstand. Auburn picked it up, flipped it over, held it out for Chiara's fingerprint, and said, "Oh."

"Yeah."

Auburn was quiet, reading through the string of texts Chiara had sent Jax since last night.

*Can we talk?*

*Jax?*

*Please?*

*I've been thinking a lot, and I know what happened with Evan messed with your head. And you weren't yourself. I should have seen that and given you more space. And then afterwards at Evan's apartment, I was a mess. I'd like to talk now that we're both calmer.*

*My father made a dumb mistake. And he almost ruined things for us. Twice. I don't want him to ruin things for us now. I don't think he has to. Let me tell you why.*

*Please, answer. Or call.*

Auburn closed her eyes.

"Pretty bad, right?"

"Maybe his phone was turned off."

"Maybe," Chiara said.

"Or he lost it."

"Maybe."

"That stuff does happen."

"It does."

They had had a very similar conversation, ten years ago. Awake, in the dark, late one night, tears streaming down Chiara's face. *The worst part is, he won't talk about it. He won't tell me why. He won't tell me anything.*

Auburn lay down next to her sister. "Kee?"

"Mmm-hmm."

"I think you should still go."

"That's what you said in high school. And you were wrong."

"Was I?"

"I cried in the bathroom."

"What happened after that?"

Chiara had forgotten that there was an "after," because when she thought about prom night, she always remembered crying in the bathroom.

"My friends came in. And made me go back out on the dance floor."

"And then?"

"We danced. We shut the floor down."

It hadn't repaired her broken heart or made her forget Jax. But it had been a good reminder that life would, slowly and lurchingly, go on.

She thought of what Auburn had said to her in the dressing room at Bay Boutique, about how many people had left her in such a short time. She had mourned for Jax, and she had mourned for her parents—but she had never really, truly mourned for the girl she had been. Someone who'd been on the verge of discovering her freedom and bravery and capacity for love—before she'd gotten smacked down.

She'd never quite gotten up again.

"You know how you said you'd like to see me date guys I actually like?"

"Mmm-hmm," Auburn said.

"Do you think I date guys I don't like because it won't break my heart if they abandon me?"

Auburn's smile was tinged with sadness. "That sounds about right."

Chiara bit her lip. "I don't want to do that anymore." She took a deep breath and crossed her arms. "I want to figure out what I want to do and who I want to be with and where I want to be. I want to make sure I'm choosing things and not just accepting them because wanting more is too threatening.

I want to throw out the plan and just—do. It's scarier. But it's a hell of a lot more fun, too."

She rolled over and reached for her phone.

"What are you doing?" Auburn asked, clearly worried that she was about to text Jax again.

She held up the phone to show her sister. The chat on the screen was the one named *Badass Reunion Bitches*. Willa had named it.

"I'm calling in reinforcements."

Fifteen minutes later, the doorbell rang, and Auburn let Willa and Vannah in.

"Up," Willa said, hooking a finger.

Willa was wearing a gorgeous deep maroon gown and her twists were fixed in a structured updo. Her makeup was smoky and dark. She looked like she belonged on a Hollywood red carpet, not standing in Chiara's bedroom. Vannah wore a glittery pale-blue dress that swirled around her ankles, and her red hair loose. Her makeup was fresh and natural. Just looking at them revived Chiara.

"We don't have much time," Willa said. "Into the shower."

Ten minutes later, Vannah was blow-drying Chiara's hair and Auburn was pouring the bottle of white wine that Willa had brought along. A few minutes after that, Willa, holding her makeup case, frowned disconcertingly into Chiara's face. "Like Van's," Chiara said. "The natural look."

But when Willa was done and Chiara looked in the mirror, she saw that her friend had done something much more dramatic. Deep shimmery shades, tipped-up eye liner, and ruby red lips. Chiara barely recognized herself—in the best possible way.

She looked beautiful. And strong.

She looked like someone who wouldn't take a job she didn't want, or miss a reunion she cared about because a guy had dumped her, or cry in a bathroom—if only because that would totally and completely wreck her eye makeup.

"No crying in the bathroom tonight," she said, sitting up straighter.

"That's right," Willa said. "No crying in the bathroom."

Then they very carefully slipped her dress on, making sure not to muss her hair or ruin her makeup, and she looked at herself for a long time in the mirror.

"Let's go dance," she said.

They clinked glasses, and then they all went out to Willa's car together.

## 51

She was having a good time.

Like, she wasn't over the moon, but there were a *lot* of people here that she wanted to see. Her friend Lucy, who'd been the only reason she'd survived two semesters of PE. Her friends Devon and J.C. who'd introduced her to Magic the Gathering, which she had secretly played with them after school, every other Thursday, without fail (they'd promised to visit the shop tomorrow). Her high school English teacher, who'd worn cardigan sweaters and had dubious personal hygiene but had introduced her to Toni Morrison.

She danced with Devon until he got a little drunkenly handsy, and then she danced with Willa and Vannah, whose unselfconsciousness made Chiara feel like she, too, could dance like no one was watching.

And then she had one too many glasses of champagne and found herself sitting at the table by herself, watching Vannah dance with Bryce Avers. Bryce had undergone a complete physical transformation, and was borderline *suave*.

Vannah looked up from Bryce's shoulder with huge "what the hell happened" eyes, and Chiara gave her a big thumbs up and tried to ignore the sinking sensation in her belly.

Maybe this hadn't been such a good idea after all. Grief had a way of coming and going at the most inconvenient moments—

She would just go to the bathroom, not to cry—

Well, she didn't think so—

And then there was a little stir at the front of the Cape House lobby. Someone had come in. Someone wearing a tuxedo, which was total overkill for the dress code, but holy *shit*—

He was tall and broad and filled out that tuxedo like he'd been made for it. He was wearing a bowtie and a cummerbund that *exactly* matched her dress. His eyes were vivid green and fixed on her, and he was crossing the room with purpose, like, oh, God, like he was coming for her.

Bruno Mars' *Just the Way You Are* came on.

Startled, she tilted her head, asking, *You?*

Because she'd *loved* that music video so hard. It had appealed to the cartoonist in her. And of course, he'd known that.

Jax grinned and nodded. "Will you dance with me?"

Her heart was pounding and her eyes had filled up with tears that right now were in the process of totally ruining all of Vannah's amazing makeup work, but she didn't care. She didn't care at all, because here they were, and he hadn't ghosted her, and he hadn't left her—or if he had, he'd come back for her.

There were a million things to say, but she didn't really want to say any of them right now. She just wanted to follow him out on the dance floor—which she did—and let him take her in his arms—which he did.

He was warm straight through all the layers of their clothes. His arms held her tight, but not too tight, and she felt the muscles in them flex. And the muscles of his abs, too, against the soft curve of her belly. That flex of hard muscle had always caused an instant and fierce melting, and now was no exception. She rested her head on the strong curve of his pec and *ached*.

She didn't know what it meant—whether he was here just for reunion or whether he was here for reunion and her or whether he was here for her and forever, but right now it didn't matter at all, because he was here.

When the song ended, he said, "You want to take a walk and talk?"

As soon as they were outside in the fresh air, tangy with salt and heavy with the fog moving off the ocean, she demanded, "Why didn't you reply to my texts?" It wasn't at *all* the thing she wanted to ask but it was the only thing that came out of her mouth when she opened it.

"You *texted* me? But I was such a *dick* to you in the hospital and at my brother's apartment—"

"You were a dick," she said. "But your little brother was sick and you were scared, and if I'd had any idea that my father had made you feel like you weren't good enough for me, I never in a million years would have tried to give you money. So—yeah, you were a dick, but I also get it. And I freaked out, too."

They climbed over the seawall and onto the beach—he lifted her down, making sure no part of her dress snagged on the concrete. She held her skirts up with one hand and he took the other one and held it tight.

"He should never have done that," Chiara said. "He was so wrong. But—I still wish you'd told me. You're right, though. He would have known if you had. And you needed that money."

Jax nodded. "In my heart, I don't believe he would have taken the money away from us. Not Evan's therapy money. I should have stood up to him and told him that if he believed in me enough to give me all that money, he should also know I'd do what it took to be a good partner to you. But instead, I bought his version of us, and I regret that more than anything else I've ever done. Kee, you have to believe me. Knowing I'd hurt you ripped me apart."

She let him pull her back into his arms, and she lifted her face to his for a kiss. And she felt it all in that kiss—all the fear and the pain and, especially, how much he'd missed her.

"I thought he was right, too, you know?" Jax said. "I thought that if I stayed away for five years or ten years, I could do what he said. Build a life for myself, figure out how to stand on my own two feet. Take care of the people in my life. Earn a second chance with you."

"He—he *said* that?"

He nodded. "It was the last thing he said to me before I left."

She'd moved past the capacity to be shocked by her father's cruelty. She understood, a little better now, that he'd held himself and everyone around him to impossible standards, and that for him, challenging Jax to meet those standards had been an imperative. A sick one, but a real one.

She also understood exactly how devastating it must have felt to Jax.

"You know that you've already done that, don't you? I can't imagine a man I would admire more, Jax. It's true now and it was true then. You were working a job, supporting them, taking care of your mother and your brother, which isn't something every man would do. Your dad didn't. Evan's dad didn't. But *you did*. You *always have*. I never, ever, not for a second, doubted that you would take care of me the same way you took care of them. I never doubted that your love would make me safe."

"And I didn't trust that," he said. He said it like it hurt him, like the words were knives and he was trying not to cut himself.

"Well, of course you didn't. No one had ever given you any reason to feel like you were safe or loved or taken care of, except maybe my father. And then, when it mattered, he found a way to tell you you were good, but not good enough to be his family." Saying it out loud, so baldly, made her stomach hurt.

She took a deep breath, held his beautiful green gaze. "But you're good enough to be my family. I have always wanted to be your family."

He pulled away from her then. And stared back at her, and she saw it there, finally, laid completely bare for her. All the hurt. All the fear. All the vulnerability.

And all the love.

## 52

"You—" he said.

The wind had whipped tears up in his eyes.

No, he was actually crying.

"You're—"

She stepped up and wiped the tears away. Put her arms around him again and held him. She was smaller than he was, but it felt like he could fold himself into the comfort she offered. The promise.

"Of course you're my family," he said.

Her eyes were big and shiny, watching him, and when he said that, her mouth quivered and one tear slid down her cheek.

"And I'm so, so sorry I ever made you feel like you weren't. You and Evan. And my mom, on good days, when I don't want to kill her."

He kissed her hair. Then lifted her chin so she was looking up at him. Tears shimmered in her eyes, too. He pressed a kiss to her forehead, and then to her mouth, and she reached up and wrapped both arms around his neck and kissed him like the world depended on it.

"I won't leave again," he said. "I won't walk away from this. I'll stay and I'll fight for it, and I'll talk about it, and we'll figure it out. I promise."

She tilted her face up and let him take her mouth, let him sweep his tongue in and show her how he claimed her and would not, ever, let her go.

When they pulled apart this time, she said, "Auburn says if my dad hadn't died I would have had to rebel eventually. I spent way too long seeing things through his eyes. Signing up for extracurriculars to get into college instead of going after the things that really mattered to me. And believing that I was better off without you instead of going after you. He told me that, after you left. That I was better off without you."

Once, the words would have made him flinch, but Rich had lost his power over them. Jax nodded. "I figured he probably had."

"It makes me mad that he's gone, and I can't ask him why he did it. Or whether he regrets it, now. I can't stand up to him and tell him off."

"But we can have a lot of sex, live together, get married, and have babies, which would be good revenge," Jax said. He hadn't exactly meant to say all that, but it felt like the truest thing either of them had said yet.

Her eyes were huge. "Yeah?"

"Absolutely. I mean, not right this second—except the sex part—but when we're ready."

"Are you—staying in Bakersfield?"

He shook his head. "I was thinking I'd come back up here and shack up with Evan for a while."

"Or me," she whispered.

That made him smile. A lot. He bent and kissed her, taking a nip of her soft lower lip. Then a lick. Then he was kissing her again, until her tongue started stroking over his in a way that was causing a serious tuxedo-pants tent problem.

"We could go back to my place now—"

"We *could*," he agreed. "Or we could go back inside and dance some more."

So they did. They danced to every song, until they closed down the dance floor. Then they said goodnight to their classmates and went back to Chiara's house.

In the truck on the way home, she said, "You know, you don't have to let me help with Evan's treatment. I get why that struck a bad nerve. But if you want my help, it's yours. And family does help each other out," she said, raising her eyebrows. "I'm sure if you told Levi you needed help—"

"Don't do that," Jax said, alarmed.

She laughed. "I won't. Unless you want me to."

The thought of all the Campbells mobilized on his behalf terrified and thrilled him. Because he knew: They would help if he asked.

He had to hold his breath for a second then. Otherwise he might have been crying again, and twice in one day was too much for him.

"What?" she asked.

"If you're my family, does that mean they're my family, too?"

"Of course," she said, in a "no duh" voice. "Have you *met* us?"

"IT'S NOT AN INN," Chiara said, as he unzipped her dress, his lips warm against her neck, one hand already reaching for the clasp of her bra, the other dipping into her barely-there lace panties, finding her wet and ready.

"And you're not a virgin," he said.

The dress fell to the floor. He picked her up and deposited her on the bed. "No," she agreed, giving him a coy smile.

"Which is good. Because I'm really, really impatient."

He showed her. She was impatient, too, even after he'd rolled on the condom and was buried all the way to the hilt in her softness. She wanted more, and she grabbed his ass and worked her body up against his to show him. "It's been way too long," she grumbled, when he pulled back, teasing.

So he didn't hold back. He gave her what she wanted, long and slick and full and deep and more forceful than he'd ever been with her, until she was moaning his name and begging for more, and then he pushed them both over the edge.

Afterwards they lay side by side on the bed, holding hands. He was smiling ridiculously.

"Stay right there," he said, rolling over. "I have something for you." He crossed the hall to toss the condom, then tugged on his tux pants—commando—and ran out to the truck. He came back with the project he'd been working on the last three days. A balsa wood storage tray that would fit perfectly in her Terraforming Mars box.

"Oh, my God, Jax, it's *perfect*." Her eyes filled up with tears. "I love it." Then she grinned and swiped at her eyes. "I have something for you," she said.

"You do?"

"Mmm-hmm," she said. She rolled over and dug her sketchbook out of the nightstand and handed it to him.

"When did you draw this?"

"Yesterday afternoon," she said.

"Before you knew I was coming back?"

"Around the time I realized I was going to have to come get you if you didn't come back."

His heart, which he'd been pretty sure couldn't be any fuller, grew another size or two.

In the first frame of Chiara's cartoon, SuperKee and SuperJax meet up again at a superhero reunion.

"As one does," Jax said, smiling.

It's been years. And they miss each other. But they've been kept apart because superheroes can't be together. The Cosmic SuperHero Organization forbids it. So for years, ever since they got caught messing around in high school, SuperKee and SuperJax have been denying their feelings for each other.

It's the last night of the reunion, and SuperKee and SuperJax are on guard duty—someone has to stand guard because obviously if anyone disrupted the superhero reunion, the world would be very vulnerable. It's like the G8 summit in that regard.

So they're alone in the dark, standing out on the edge of the hotel roof. The sky is vivid with stars. Below them, the rest of the superheroes are dancing and partying.

Jax turned the page.

"Wait, what?" he demanded. "You *stopped*?"

"Well, of course I stopped," she said. "You have to help me write it."

Her cheeks were pink, from the orgasm and the

excitement.

"Well," he said. "I want SuperKee and SuperJax to realize that there's a loophole in the rules. It says that if you are willing to give up your superhero powers, you can live an ordinary human life. And you can love."

She was very quiet for a minute, gently brushing her fingers over the stars she'd scattered in the sky. "What happens if you give up your superhero powers?" she asked, finally. She turned her head and looked at him—full on, for the first time. And he looked right back, steady and sure.

"What do you think?" he asked.

"I think," she said. Her eyes were wet again. "I think they realize that all the powers they thought they had because they were superheroes, they actually had because they loved each other. And they don't have to give up those powers at all. They're just as brave and just as smart and just as able to do scary or difficult things as they were before. They just have to go ahead and *do* them."

"That's what I think, too. And I think when you give up your superhero powers, then you just get to be exactly who you are. With no pretending or hiding."

"No pretending," she repeated. "No hiding. And no—no running away."

He shook his head. "No running away."

Very slowly, because she wanted the moment to last a long time so she could remember it and savor it later, she moved into his arms.

"I love you," he said.

"I love you, too," she said.

His mouth came down on hers, a long, sweet, deep hello-again.

## EPILOGUE

The door of the shop chimed. Evan and Asher jumped, Jax looked up, and Chiara—snapped out of her own trance—set down her drawing tablet.

"Dinner's here!" Auburn announced. She came into the store holding several brown bags full of food, trailed by Trey, Levi, Mason, and Hannah.

"Welcome to the first ever Campbell family game night," Chiara said, grinning.

Asher got to his feet, looking uncomfortable. "I'd, uh, better go—"

"No way," Auburn said. "I got you lasagna. That's what Evan said you liked."

Asher looked around, blushed, and sat.

Auburn began passing out food.

"It looks ahhhhmazing," Auburn told Chiara, gesturing at the mural behind the registers.

It was a montage of SuperEvan scenes. In one, he was building Gizmos as big as his own body. In another he was using an asteroid storm to raise the temperature on Mars.

Building a small development at the juncture of three hexes of Catan. Riding railroads across the Ticket to Ride U.S. Map, hand out the window, waving.

"You put me in the games," Evan had said, with so much delight that she had felt like she'd done magic instead of just drawing. She said as much to Jax, and he said, kissing her nose and her chin and then her mouth (with a lot of tongue): "Your drawings are kind of magic."

When she'd finished the mural, she'd been alone in the shop. She added the last brushstroke, set the brush down on the can of blue paint, stood back a long time, and looked at her handiwork. Then she said, out loud, "Dad, look what I did."

And since all she had now was the father she gave herself, and since she had faith that people could change to become more like the people they wanted to be, she imagined that if her father had lived, he would have seen the error of his ways and grown to understand that she was perfectly capable of finding her own way in life. So she let him say back to her, in his warmest voice, "That's my girl."

She'd been drawing a lot more recently. She wasn't sure where it was all going, but maybe there would be a book someday. She was taking cartoon and illustration classes online, and even though she still couldn't draw a human hand that actually looked like a human hand or a nose that actually looked like a nose, it didn't matter because she could tell a story with pictures. Which, it turned out, was all she'd been trying to do in the first place.

She'd kept her business going, but she'd scaled it back so she had a lot more time to work on her newest project, which was making posters for events. She did a lot of them gratis for the businesses in town—but she was starting to make money doing high-end posters for other organizations, too. She was starting to earn a word-of-mouth reputation that in recent weeks had brought in phone calls from Portland companies and nonprofits, including Powell's Books, her second favorite store in the entire world, after Meeples. And, she, Asher, Tamara, and Evan were designing a game together. It was a game about saving a small business from bankruptcy.

Meanwhile, Jax had moved his contracting business to the Oregon coast—which mostly meant starting from scratch. But he was cheerful about it, and his work, too, spoke for itself. Last week, he'd gotten a job building a ten-thousand square foot oceanfront home for one of Trey's rich friends.

"No one needs a ten thousand square foot house," Jax had confided to Chiara.

"Don't tell him that. Promise you won't," she'd whispered back.

"It'll be our secret."

Evan and Jax's mom was contemplating a move to Tierney Bay. Jax's relationship with her had softened considerably recently, especially after she chipped in a thousand dollars to the cost of Evan's treatments.

"Where did that come from?" he asked.

"My skirt business has really taken off. I'm doing kilts now. Are you interested?"

"No, Mom," he'd said. "Not in the slightest."

"A lot of men like the breezy feeling—"

"*Mom.*"

"Sorry. No kilts. I'll make a skirt for Kee, instead."

He guessed that if she moved to Tierney Bay they'd probably invite her to family dinners and family game nights, and he could live with that. She wasn't perfect, but she was his mom.

Evan's treatments were going well. When Levi heard about the bribe his father had used to separate Jax and Chiara, he'd said he wanted no part of the money. He'd insisted on paying Jax back the repaid "loan," and when Jax had resisted, Levi had redirected the money to Evan's care. Evan and Jax had hooked up with the organization Chiara researched, and it had helped them apply for the drugs Evan needed at reduced cost, based on his income—which, as a small business owner, would probably never be very high. He was doing great—no pain, no other symptoms, and no serious side effects—although he had to be a little careful about germs. It just meant that the game store had an above-average number of hand sanitizer stations, which, given the amount of traffic it was getting these days, was not a bad thing. Not only had Meeples thrived right through the middle of an Oregon coast winter, but it was doing better this spring than anything Chiara had predicted.

Trey had moved in with Auburn at Beachcrest. They were ridiculously happy and over-the-top in love. And Beachcrest was doing the best business of its existence, to the point where sometimes they could refer visitors to Cape House. Once upon a time it had always been the other way around.

Not that Levi begrudged it.

He saved all his begrudging for Grace Utrecht, the wedding planner.

And Mason—

Mason was his usual self, which was to say no one knew anything about what was going on with him. If Chiara asked how he was doing, he shrugged and said, "Pretty how, thanks." And if she probed more?

He shut down.

The Campbells—and Evan and Asher—had finished up eating and were organizing themselves into games. Evan and Asher were going to host a table of Terraforming Mars and Auburn wanted a Pandemic table.

"You want to save the world or start a new one?" Jax asked.

Two clusters were forming around the two tables.

"Mmm," Chiara said. "I want to sneak out and go walk on the beach. And then I want to have a lot of sex. And then I want to have breakfast at the Tierney Bay diner."

"What if they put the pieces away all wrong?" he murmured.

"I don't care."

The biggest grin ever crossed Jax's face. He grabbed her hand and they bolted towards the door.

"Chiara. Jax. Get your asses over here," Auburn ordered.

But it was too late. The chimes over the door were already signaling their escape.

# ACKNOWLEDGMENTS

This book is dedicated to Bell Boy, my gamer dude.

I am so grateful to my readers, who make this job possible —your support of me and love for my characters keeps me going. So many hugs.

To Emily Sylvan Kim and Tina Shen of Prospect Agency: You're so good at what you do, in all the ways, and I deeply appreciate your work on my behalf.

To Sarah Murphy, who gave amazing feedback on a first draft of *So True*, and to Sarah Sarai who edited the next draft, thank you for all the ways you have made this a better book. I couldn't do the hard work of revision without your editorial and moral support.

And because every author needs at least three Sarahs in her life, thank you to Sarah Conerty Jordan, my terrific virtual author assistant.

Most of *So True* was written during the Covid-19 crisis of 2020, while my family was under stay-at-home orders. So I have been especially grateful to the friends, colleagues, and family who have given me love and support (often via Zoom) during these difficult, unsettling, and painful times.

Bell Girl, Bell Boy (x2), and Mr. Bell: You are the best. There are no other three people on earth I can imagine having survived quarantine with, and I love you, if possible, even more than I did on the day that we adopted our new not-at-all-normal. Also, a shout-out to Mr. Bell for tech support, because there's an extra helping of it these days.

I don't often enough thank my parents for always encouraging my love of writing, and for reading all my books. There aren't many nice things that can be said about Covid-19, but I am grateful to it for kick-starting our once-a-day-ish conversations. My sister, too, is a devoted reader, which is only one of about a bajillion things I love about her.

In addition, I have so much love and so many thanks for the local saviors of my sanity, Darya, Molly, Ellen, Cheryl, Aimee, and Soomie; and the more geographically (but not ever emotionally) distant ones, Lauren and Tracey.

So much love and so many thanks to (in no particular order) the improv class, especially Michelle; the members of my centering prayer group; the Nerdy Girl Gamers; the Effing Awesome Writer Chicks (we WILL retreat again); Rachel and Kate for endless moral support and advice; the authors on The Corner of Smart and Sexy; my fellow Romance Mastermind cohort, especially Dylann and Christina for epic amounts of beta reading; the Jingle Ballers; and my other author friends, especially Christine, Mauri, and Amber. Thank you all for making at least the first half of 2020 manageable. Every little way you support me helps me put words on the page and get them "out there" into the world.

# ALSO BY SERENA BELL

## Returning Home

Hold On Tight

Can't Hold Back

To Have and to Hold

Holding Out

## Tierney Bay

So Close

So True

So Good (2021)

So Right (2021)

## Sexy Single Dads

Do Over

Head Over Heels

Sleepover

## New York Glitz

Still So Hot!

Hot & Bothered

## Standalone

Turn Up the Heat

# ABOUT THE AUTHOR

*USA Today* bestselling author Serena Bell writes richly emotional stories about big-hearted characters with real troubles and the people who are strong and generous enough to love them. A former journalist, Serena has always believed that everyone has an amazing story to tell if you listen carefully, and she adores scribbling in her tiny garret office, mainlining chocolate and bringing to life the tales in her head.

Serena's books have earned many honors, including an RT Reviewers' Choice Award, Apple Books Best Book of the Month, and Amazon Best Book of the Year for Romance.

When not writing, Serena loves to spend time with her college-sweetheart husband and two hilarious kiddos—all of whom are incredibly tolerant not just of Serena's imaginary friends but also her enormous collection of constantly changing and passionately embraced hobbies, ranging from needlepoint to board games to meditation.